"I don't know what I would have done without you today,"

he said as he covered her hand with his.

Something in his voice—and maybe the way he was looking at her, with warmth in his eyes— ignited a spark in her. A spark she fully intended to douse before it blazed out of control.

It wasn't hard to figure out what was going on here. Nathan was feeling overwhelmed. And Caitlin was the one person who was on his side. They had to be careful about mistaking gratitude and desperation for something more…personal. She did not need a messy relationship with her business partner. Especially now, when his emotions were so precarious, his life so complicated.

"There's no need to thank me again," she said lightly, trying to pull her hand away.

His fingers tightened on hers. His hand was as warm as his gaze, and she felt the spark inside her flare dangerously.

She had worked out the reasoning behind *his* behavior, but how was she supposed to explain her own?

Dear Reader,

Make way for spring—as well as some room on your reading table for six new Special Edition novels! Our selection for this month's READERS' RING—Special Edition's very own book club—is *Playing by the Rules* by Beverly Bird. In this innovative, edgy romance, a single mom who is sick and tired of the singles scene makes a deal with a handsome divorced hero—that their relationship will not lead to commitment. But both hero and heroine soon find themselves breaking all those pesky rules and falling head over heels for each other!

Gina Wilkins delights her readers with *The Family Plan*, in which two ambitious lawyers find unexpected love—and a newfound family—with the help of a young orphaned girl. Reader favorite Nikki Benjamin delivers a poignant reunion romance, *Loving Leah*, about a compassionate nanny who restores hope to an embittered single dad and his fragile young daughter.

In *Call of the West*, the last in Myrna Temte's HEARTS OF WYOMING miniseries, a celebrity writer goes to Wyoming and finds the ranch—and the man—with whom she'd like to spend her life. Now she has to convince the cowboy to give up his ranch—and his heart! In her new cross-line miniseries, THE MOM SQUAD, Marie Ferrarella debuts with *A Billionaire and a Baby*. Here, a scoop-hungry—and pregnant—reporter goes after a reclusive corporate raider, only to go into labor just as she's about to get the dirt! Ann Roth tickles our fancy with *Reforming Cole*, a sexy and emotional tale about a willful heroine who starts a "men's etiquette" school so that the macho opposite sex can learn how best to treat a lady. Against her better judgment, the teacher falls for the gorgeous bad boy of the class!

I hope you enjoy this month's lineup and come back for another month of moving stories about life, love and family!

Best,

Karen Taylor Richman
Senior Editor

Please address questions and book requests to:
Silhouette Reader Service
U.S.: 3010 Walden Ave., P.O. Box 1325, Buffalo, NY 14269
Canadian: P.O. Box 609, Fort Erie, Ont. L2A 5X3

The Family Plan

GINA WILKINS

Silhouette®

SPECIAL EDITION™

Published by Silhouette Books

America's Publisher of Contemporary Romance

For my parents, Vernon and Beth Vaughan,
in recognition of your golden wedding anniversary on
April 29, 2003.
I love you both.

 SILHOUETTE BOOKS

ISBN 0-373-24525-4

THE FAMILY PLAN

Visit Silhouette at www.eHarlequin.com

Printed in U.S.A.

Books by Gina Wilkins

Silhouette Special Edition

The Father Next Door #1082
It Could Happen To You #1119
Valentine Baby #1153
†*Her Very Own Family* #1243
†*That First Special Kiss* #1269
Surprise Partners #1318
**The Stranger in Room 205* #1399
**Bachelor Cop Finally
   Caught?* #1413
**Dateline Matrimony* #1424
The Groom's Stand-In #1460
The Best Man's Plan #1479
The Family Plan #1525

†Family Found: Sons & Daughters
**Hot Off the Press
§Family Found
‡The Family Way
*The McClouds of Mississippi

**Previously published
as Gina Ferris**

Silhouette Special Edition

Healing Sympathy #496
Lady Beware #549
In from the Rain #677
Prodigal Father #711
§*Full of Grace* #793
§*Hardworking Man* #806
§*Fair and Wise* #819
§*Far To Go* #862
§*Loving and Giving* #879
Babies on Board #913

**Previously published
as Gina Ferris Wilkins**

Silhouette Special Edition

‡ *A Man for Mom* #955
‡*A Match for Celia* #967
‡*A Home for Adam* #980
‡*Cody's Fiancée* #1006

Silhouette Books

Mother's Day Collection 1995
Three Mothers and a Cradle
   "Beginnings"

GINA WILKINS

is a bestselling and award-winning author who has written more than fifty books for Harlequin and Silhouette. She credits her successful career in romance to her long, happy marriage and her three "extraordinary" children.

A lifelong resident of central Arkansas, Ms. Wilkins sold her first book to Harlequin in 1987 and has been writing full-time ever since. She has appeared on the Waldenbooks, B. Dalton and *USA TODAY* bestseller lists. She is a three-time recipient of the Maggie Award for Excellence, sponsored by Georgia Romance Writers, and has won several awards from the reviewers of *Romantic Times*.

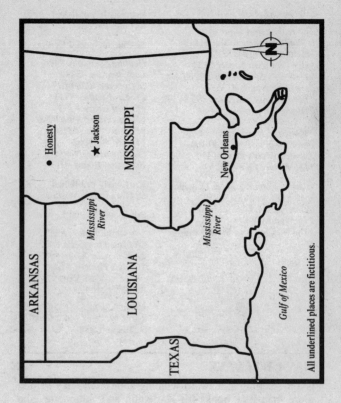

ARKANSAS

MISSISSIPPI

• Honesty

★ Jackson

*Mississippi
River*

LOUISIANA

*Mississippi
River*

New Orleans

TEXAS

Gulf of Mexico

All underlined places are fictitious.

Chapter One

Nathan McCloud tried to be discreet about checking his watch for the third time in fifteen minutes. It was almost 2:45 p.m. and his tee time was 3:30. If he got away within the next five minutes, he would still just barely have time to change, grab his clubs, and...

A loud sigh of exasperation cut into his mental calculations. "Nathan, would you *please* pay attention? We need to make this decision today."

He gave his partner his most engaging smile. Caitlin Briley was always a pleasure to look at, and he usually enjoyed teasing her and spending time with her. But he was impatient to escape on this perfect autumn afternoon. "That last one sounded good. Why don't we give her a call?"

He knew he'd said the wrong thing when Caitlin's heart-shaped face darkened with a frown. "You haven't been listening."

He cleared his throat. "Of course I was listening. Uh, what was wrong with the last one?"

Tapping a red-nailed finger on one of the job applications spread on the desk in front of her, Caitlin replied curtly, "This woman said she would like to work for our firm because it would be nice to be on the *right* side of the law for a change. She also wanted to know if her compensation could include free legal representation on occasion."

Nathan winced. "Maybe I wasn't listening closely enough. I'm not sure she's what we're looking for—though she might prove entertaining," he added thoughtfully.

Rolling her eyes, Caitlin let out what might have been a strangled growl. "We aren't looking for entertainment. We're trying to find an efficient, professional, reliable office manager."

"Couldn't you just pick someone? You're good at that sort of thing. I trust your judgment."

"You aren't 'trusting' me with this responsibility, you're trying to dump it on me."

Caitlin always had a knack for cutting right through his BS. Nathan sighed in resignation. "Okay, you're right. I don't really care who you hire as long as she's pleasant to work with and doesn't interfere with my schedule."

"Your schedule?" His partner looked at him in disbelief. "You barely *have* a schedule."

"Exactly. And I like it that way."

"We need a good office manager to bring some order to the chaos in this place. And you should have some input into choosing the person we hire."

"If I promise not to criticize your choice, will you take care of this?" he wheedled. "I'd stay and help you, but I have an appointment this afternoon."

"With a client or a fishing rod?" she asked suspiciously.

"A client," he assured her. And then, because he considered himself a fairly honest guy—for a lawyer—he added, "And a set of golf clubs."

She had looked momentarily mollified, if still skeptical, but now she was frowning again. "Darn it, Nathan."

He considered reminding her that *he* was the senior partner here. He had run this firm by himself for two years before he'd impulsively taken on a fresh-out-of-law-school partner just over nine months ago because his workload had gotten heavy enough to interfere with his leisure time.

Caitlin had been the first lawyer he'd interviewed, and he had hired her because she had the most beautiful smoky-gray eyes he'd ever seen—in addition to a thick, shoulder-length curtain of glossy brown hair, an intriguingly dimpled chin, and a petite yet nicely curved figure. Add those attributes to a more than respectable résumé, and he could find no reason at all to send her on her way after that first meeting.

He didn't know then that he had hired the Attila the Hun of ambitious young lawyers.

She had swept into his lazy little practice with a gung-ho, conquer-the-legal-world attitude that exhausted him. Apparently, she had added him to her list of things about this office that needed to be changed.

But he still thought she had beautiful eyes, he mused, losing himself in their depths for a moment.

She drummed her fingers on his desk. "You really aren't paying attention to any of this, are you?"

"Did you know you get little sparks in your eyes when you're annoyed? They just sort of glitter, all silvery in the gray."

"They must be glittering like crazy right now, then."

He propped his chin on his fist and gazed at her. "Actually, yes. And a very enticing sight they are, too."

Her invariable reaction when he flirted with her was to

speak gruffly and busy her hands. She did so again this time, shuffling noisily through the applications she was suddenly studying with renewed interest. "I suppose I could narrow these down to two or three and call them in for interviews. I would, of course, expect you to sit in on those interviews with me and help me make the final decision."

"Why? You know what you're looking for in an office manager. Hire whoever you like. I have no doubt that whoever you choose will be perfect for the job."

She was the one who pointed out, "You're the senior partner. You should have the final say in major decisions like this."

He shrugged. "My decision is that you should make the decision."

"A lot of help you are," she muttered.

He grinned. "Glad to be of assistance. Can I go now?"

She leaned back in her chair with an expression of surrender. "Go. Enjoy your golf game. And if you really are playing with a client, try to talk a little business while you're out there."

"If he beats me, I'll bill him for my time," Nathan promised, already out of his chair and headed for the door before she could change her mind.

There had been plenty of times during the past nine months when Caitlin had wondered if she'd done the right thing joining Nathan McCloud's firm in Honesty, a city of 30,000 people in southern Mississippi. At the beginning the offer had seemed almost too good to be true. A partnership right out of law school? In a one-man office that was already making money and was doing so well that Nathan had been turning down cases?

After looking over the books and the day-to-day operations—Nathan had given her unrestricted access to his business records—she had seen the potential for turning this small office into a thriving law firm. At the very least, a few years of practice here would be a great springboard to the partnership track in an established, big-city firm.

Caitlin had lofty career ambitions. Unfortunately, her partner was what she termed "motivationally challenged."

A month after their confrontation, on the first Thursday afternoon in October, Caitlin was sitting in her office leafing through a thick file and admiring the practical color-coding system the new office manager had instituted when Nathan burst into the room without knocking. "You have to do something about that woman."

She took a moment to study the frown that creased his attractive face and darkened his blue eyes to near navy. "Which woman is that?"

"That...that dictator you hired as an office manager. She's out of control."

"I hired her because you were conveniently unavailable the day of the interviews," she reminded him. "And you promised not to criticize my choice."

"How could I have known you were going to hire Irene the Terrible?"

"You might want to shut the door to continue this conversation," she suggested mildly. Waiting only until he'd kicked the door closed, she added, "Irene is a very nice woman and an extremely efficient office manager. I don't know what you have against her."

"She's a tyrant. She has my files so organized I can't find anything. When I mess them up, she gives me a look over those little glasses of hers that makes chills go down my spine. I feel like she's taking mental notes of all my shortcomings and she's going to bring them up when she gives me my annual employer evaluation."

"She works for *you.*"

"Right. Has anyone mentioned that to *her?*"

Shaking her head, Caitlin closed the file and watched as Nathan plopped into a chair, lanky limbs sprawled, sandy hair tousled. He looked like a sulky teenager, she thought ruefully. An extremely attractive teenager, but a handful, none the less. She was almost five years younger than Nathan, so why did she feel like the older one at that moment?

"Irene has only worked for us for three weeks and already she has our office running like clockwork," she said. "She's gotten the clerical staff—all three of them—into shape, so that stacks of overdue filing have been cleared away. Our bills have all been paid. On time, I might add. She's switched to a new phone service that's saving us 20 percent a month. Our appointment process has been streamlined so that we've significantly cut down on the number of clients sitting impatiently in the waiting room."

"Exactly." Nathan nodded forcefully. "She's scary. It isn't normal to get that much accomplished in such a short time."

Caitlin couldn't help laughing. "You're being ridiculous."

A sharp tap on the door interrupted their conversation. It was followed almost immediately by the entrance of the woman they had been discussing. The brown and beige jacket Irene Mitchell wore over a straight brown dress did little to enhance her tall, angular figure. Plastic-framed reading glasses dangled from a gold chain around her neck, neat pearl stud earrings completely hid her almost nonexistent earlobes, and a functional watch was strapped around her bony left wrist. Her long, narrow feet were encased in sensible brown pumps. The only signs of frivolity in the woman's appearance were the color of her heavily sprayed, meticulously curled, red hair and the crimson lipstick that coated her thin lips.

Caitlin noted that Nathan automatically straightened in his chair when Irene entered. He reminded her of a student who had been goofing off while the teacher was out of the room and hoped to hide that fact upon her return. Smothering a smile, she turned her attention back to the office manager. "What can I do for you, Irene?"

The older woman set a stack of correspondence in front of her. "I need your signature on these. The mail runs in an hour, so you'll need to sign them promptly. Mr. Mc-Cloud, your letters are on your desk awaiting your attention. Would you prefer that I bring them in here?"

"No, that's okay. I'll get to them in a few minutes."

Irene glanced at her watch. "Your next appointment should be arriving in fifteen minutes. You'll want to sign your letters before then, of course."

Nathan cleared his throat. "Of course."

Irene continued to look at him.

"I'll sign them," he repeated, holding up his right hand as a pledge. "As soon as Caitlin and I are finished here."

Seemingly appeased, Irene nodded and moved toward the door. "I'll buzz you when your appointment arrives, Mr. McCloud. And, Ms. Briley, don't forget about your meeting at two this afternoon."

"I won't forget. Thank you, Irene." Caitlin had invited the office manager to drop the formality of surnames, but she persisted in using them, even though she preferred being addressed by her first name. Caitlin had figured out it was a waste of breath to argue with the woman's eccentricities.

"I'll be back to collect the signed correspondence—from *both* of you—shortly," Irene added as she let herself out of Caitlin's office.

Nathan released a gusty breath as soon as the door closed

behind Irene. "See what I mean? She's impossible. You've got to fire her."

Caitlin reached for the stack of correspondence and a pen. "I'm not going to fire her. She's much too good. And she's actually very nice—as you would find out for yourself if you would give her half a chance."

"I've given her plenty of chances. I smile every time I speak to her."

"Ah, yes, the patented Nathan McCloud grin," she murmured without looking up from her signatures, not surprised that Irene hadn't fallen for such a practiced tactic.

Ignoring her, Nathan continued, "I've tried complimenting her appearance."

"Plan B—fulsome flattery. That didn't work, either, I'm sure."

"I even brought her flowers on her first day of work. She thanked me, then put them in my office because she said they made her sneeze."

"So none of your usual tricks worked. Have you tried just talking to her? One professional to another?"

"You think that would work?" Nathan asked doubtfully.

"It's certainly worth a shot."

"I still think you should fire her."

Caitlin folded her hands on top of the now-signed correspondence and shook her head. "I hired her—on my own—because you didn't want to be involved. If you aren't happy with her performance, it's up to you to fire her."

She would have sworn his face paled at the very suggestion. "Me? No way."

"That's what I thought. So I suppose you'd better find a way to get along with her," Caitlin advised sweetly.

He glared at her in return.

The speaker on Caitlin's desk suddenly buzzed. "Mr. McCloud?"

Nathan jumped out of his chair as if the woman could see through walls. "I'm on my way to sign those letters right now."

"Actually, you have a call on line two. It's Mr. Alan Curtis from San Diego, California."

Nathan looked surprised. "The attorney who handled my father's estate," he murmured. He motioned toward Caitlin's phone. "Mind if I take the call in here?"

"Of course not." She gathered her letters. "I'll take these out to Irene."

"Kiss-up," Nathan murmured, reaching for the receiver.

She only smiled at him as she left him to his call.

Nathan watched Caitlin leave her office, wondering if he'd ever mentioned to her that he liked the way she walked. Smooth strides, soft sway of hips, head up and shoulders squared—very appealing. Of course, if he did tell her, she would get all gruff and flustered the way she always did when he complimented her, which was actually something else he found intriguing about her.

Did she react that way when any man flirted with her or just with him? And what would she do if he cranked it up a notch and suggested they actually go out sometime? It was a suggestion he'd been contemplating for several weeks, waiting until the time seemed right to approach her about it.

Only mildly curious about the call from his late father's attorney, he lifted the telephone receiver to his ear. "Nathan McCloud."

"Mr. McCloud, it's Alan Curtis. I'm glad you were available to take my call."

Nathan's eyebrows rose. "You make it sound important. Is something wrong?"

Nathan's father, along with his much younger wife, had

died six months earlier in a tourist helicopter accident in Mexico, leaving a three-year-old daughter behind. The estate had been settled weeks ago, and Nathan couldn't imagine any problems that might have arisen since. The child had been left in the custody of her maternal great-aunt in California and had inherited all her parent's assets, since Nathan and his two adult siblings had refused any claim.

For reasons Nathan still didn't fully understand, his father's will had named him executor of the child's inheritance. He'd retained Mr. Curtis's services for the monitoring of those details. He had expected to be contacted only in cases of emergency. What sort of crisis could have arisen already?

"I'm afraid something *is* wrong, Mr. McCloud. Barbara Houston has been diagnosed with colon cancer."

Barbara Houston was the woman who had taken in Nathan's orphaned half sister. He'd met her only once, at the joint funeral service for Stuart and Kimberly McCloud in California six months ago, but she'd made a very good impression on him. He'd felt comfortable that little Isabelle would be raised in a loving, supportive home. "I'm sorry to hear that. Is it bad?"

"Very bad, I'm afraid. Her chances of survival are slim."

Nathan sank into Caitlin's desk chair. "Damn."

"Exactly. You see why it was imperative that I contact you immediately."

His head was starting to hurt. He raised his free hand to massage his temples. "What's going to happen to Isabelle?"

"Mrs. Houston and I spoke at length this morning. She sees only two options. Her preference would be for you to come get the child and have yourself named guardian."

Nathan spoke without hesitation. "That isn't possible."

"There's really no one else to take her, Mr. McCloud. Your stepmother's parents are both dead and her only sibling is an unmarried brother who is on active military duty, stationed overseas. Mrs. Houston is widowed and has only one daughter, who is divorced and raising four young children of her own. There simply is no one else. Unless one of your other siblings…?"

"Mr. Curtis, I'm not sure how much you know about my father's history here."

When Nathan paused, the other man spoke with audible caution. "I'm aware that your father was a prominent business leader there in Mississippi and had considered a run for the governor's office."

"He was a gubernatorial candidate," Nathan clarified. "The campaign was in full swing, he was backed by some very influential people in his party, and he had a solid standing in the polls. He could very well have won the office. He was quite a hero here in his hometown, the first native son to run for such a high position in our state. And then, six months before the election, he announced that he was dropping out to marry one of his campaign volunteers—Barbara Houston's niece, Kimberly Leighton."

"Um—"

Nathan continued in a deliberately nonemotional tone. "It was a bit messy at the time because Kimberly was thirty years his junior, and pregnant. Oh, and my father was still married then—to my mother."

Nathan could almost hear the other man wince. "Mr. McCloud, I—"

"I'm trying to explain why it wouldn't be a good idea for me to bring my father's child here. My father tore his family apart four years ago. He humiliated my mother and broke my younger sister's heart. My brother hasn't been quite the same since Dad bailed out on us. We're still trying to rebuild our relationships with each other. Even if I were prepared to raise a toddler, which, believe me, I'm not, my family would never be able to accept her.''

"I'm sorry. I—well, I wasn't aware that you were so estranged from your father. He told me you visited him here in California a few times, and he named you your sister's executor.''

"I was the only one to maintain a relationship with my father,'' Nathan admitted, ''much to my family's dissatisfaction. I didn't approve of his actions, but I didn't want to completely sever all ties with him. I hoped my brother and sister would be able to make some sort of peace with him, but his death put an end to that. I hold nothing against little Isabelle, so I didn't mind agreeing to be available in the event of an emergency, but bringing her here, trying to raise her—well, I'm afraid that's simply out of the question.''

The older man sighed heavily. "Mrs. Houston suspected that would be your answer. It seems we have no choice but to resort to the only other option.''

Nathan didn't like the sound of that, nor the tone in which the attorney had spoken. "What's the other option?''

"The child will have to be put up for adoption.''

Grimacing, Nathan cleared his throat. "That seems rather…drastic.''

"The circumstances *are* drastic, Mr. McCloud. Mrs. Houston is very ill. She isn't able to care for an active toddler any longer.''

"I could help with the expense of a full-time nanny.''

"I'm afraid that would only be a short-term solution. I'm not sure you understand the gravity of Mrs. Houston's condition. Her cancer was already at an advanced stage when she was diagnosed, and this particular type of cancer is very aggressive. She's only expected to live for another few months. The child must be placed soon. Mrs. Houston is ready to relinquish her to the California Department of Child Services. She's very fond of Isabelle, but she's simply too ill to concentrate on anyone's well-being except her own.''

The headache was rapidly intensifying. Nathan rubbed harder at his temples, which had absolutely no effect against the pounding. ''I need time to think about this.''

''I understand. But our time is limited, I'm afraid.''

Picturing the pleasant-faced, kind-eyed woman he'd met at his father's funeral, Nathan was aware of a wave of sadness on her behalf. Barbara Houston had seemed like a very nice woman, only in her mid-fifties. He hated to think of her suffering so terribly. ''Can you give me a few hours to process this, Mr. Curtis? Isabelle's okay for now, isn't she?''

''Mrs. Houston was hospitalized several days ago, but the child is fine for now. She's staying with Mrs. Houston's pastor and his wife. Mrs. Houston called me from the hospital, and I visited her there. Frankly, she looks terrible. Worrying about her great-niece isn't making her any more comfortable.''

Nathan got the message. Time was running out, fast. ''Give me until tomorrow morning. I'll call you first thing,'' he promised, glancing up as Caitlin reentered her office. ''Don't do anything until I talk to you, okay?''

''I'll be expecting your call.''

Nathan hung up the phone, then buried his face in his hands and groaned.

''Nathan?'' He heard Caitlin's footsteps as she moved closer. ''Are you okay?''

Slowly lowering his hands, he looked up at her, taking some comfort from the genuine concern reflected in her warm gray eyes. "How do you think I'd stack up as a father?"

She lifted both her eyebrows. "This is a rhetorical question, I hope."

"Not exactly. I have to decide whether to take my father's three-and-a-half-year-old daughter and try to raise her myself or to let her disappear into the California child services system and hope she's quickly adopted by a decent family."

Caitlin knew a little of his family history. Of course, no one could live for long in this town without hearing the details of the juiciest scandal to rock this area in decades. She had already joined his firm when his father died, and she'd run the office during the few days Nathan was in California for the funeral. So she wasn't surprised by his reference to his half sister, but she certainly appeared flabbergasted by everything else he'd said. "There's no one else to take her?"

"Not a soul. The great-aunt who's been raising her is very ill. I have to make a decision very quickly—by tomorrow morning."

"I'm sorry. No wonder you look so upset."

"Yeah. Hell of a choice I've got here. Take in a three-year-old and completely alienate my already-screwed-up family or farm the kid out to strangers and give up the right to ever see her again." The final words were gruff as he forced them through his suddenly tight throat.

Caitlin only looked at him.

On an impulse he pulled his wallet out of his back pocket. He didn't carry many photographs, only two. An old family photo of his parents, himself and his two younger siblings taken when Nathan was sixteen. And a snapshot of a little blond princess with enormous blue eyes and several deep dimples. He held that one out to Caitlin.

She studied it with her lower lip caught between her teeth. And then she looked up at him again, her smoky gray eyes almost black now. "Oh, Nathan."

He swallowed, nodded and slipped the photo back into its place opposite the old family portrait.

The desk speaker buzzed. "Ms. Briley? Is Mr. McCloud still in there?"

"I'm here, Irene."

"Your appointment has arrived, Mr. McCloud. She seems quite nervous. You probably shouldn't keep her waiting long."

"Right. Give me five minutes, then show her to my office."

"Yes, sir."

Stuffing his wallet back into his pocket, Nathan pushed a hand through his tumbled hair. "I'd better go to my office and get ready for Mrs. Danoff."

"Nathan?"

Caitlin's voice made him pause in the doorway. "Yes?"

"What are you going to do?"

He pushed his hand through his hair again. How could he even consider taking in a three-year-old? He had never even committed to a pet. He did pretty well just taking care of himself. It would shatter his mother's already-broken heart, and his siblings would probably never speak to him again—not that they said much to him these days, anyway.

But could he sign her away? Turn her over to strangers with no guarantees that she would be treated well, never to see her again or know what had happened to her? She was his sister, damn it.

Realizing that Caitlin was still waiting for an answer, he sighed. "Beats the hell out of me."

Chapter Two

Caitlin had little chance to talk with Nathan again that afternoon. Both of them were busy with back-to-back appointments, and then she had to leave early for a dental appointment.

Tired from a long, busy week, she wasn't really in the mood to socialize that evening, but she had little choice. Once a year, the Honesty Chamber of Commerce held a reception to recognize the community's prominent volunteers, and all the local business and society leaders attended. There was no way Caitlin would miss such a chance to mingle with influential neighbors. It was simply too good an opportunity to increase the visibility of the McCloud and Briley Law Firm.

She knew Nathan would be in attendance, though this was hardly his preferred choice of entertainment. His mother was one of the five volunteers being honored that evening for her active role in local children's charities. Nathan wouldn't dare skip the event.

As she dressed in a suitably conservative yet sophisticated black cocktail sheath, she wondered if he had made a decision about his little sister's future. Surely he would come to the conclusion that adoption was the only alternative. She couldn't imagine Nathan trying to raise a three-year-old on his own. Heck, she couldn't picture *herself* raising a toddler, and she was a hundred times more organized than Nathan!

And then the image of the golden-haired little girl in the photograph popped into her mind. She knew Nathan had met the child on several occasions during the past three years. During those visits with his father's new family, he had accumulated several amusing stories about his cute-as-a-button, incredibly bright-for-her-age little sister—stories he had shared with Caitlin during the months they'd worked together because no one in his family had wanted to hear them.

She could see both sides of his family's conflict. While she admired Nathan for maintaining some ties with his father, his mother and siblings still bitterly resented Stuart McCloud for publicly abandoning his family in favor of a woman half his age.

Caitlin hadn't lived here four years ago, and hadn't yet met Nathan, but she had certainly heard plenty about the scandal. The gossip columns and TV newscasts had been filled with talk of the gubernatorial candidate's affair with a young campaign volunteer and the subsequent pregnancy that ended his thirty-year marriage…and his political career. The press had been vicious, camping outside the homes of the betrayed wife and adult offspring, hoping for juicy quotes and photos. She remembered how sorry she had felt for the McCloud family then, and how much she had admired the poise and restraint Stuart's wronged wife, Lenore, had shown in the wake of the debacle.

She had met Lenore several times during the past nine months. Nathan's mother dropped in frequently at the law offices and had been unfailingly gracious to Caitlin. She knew the woman was much admired in Honesty—hence, the recognition from the Chamber of Commerce later this evening. Yet Caitlin also knew that Lenore had never forgiven her ex-husband for his betrayal. And while Lenore and Nathan maintained a good relationship, she had resented his refusal to sever communication with his father.

If Nathan *were* to bring his father's late-life child into his family's midst, his mother and siblings would consider the gesture a slap in the face. A betrayal almost as cutting as his father's. Knowing how much his family meant to him and how hard he had worked to repair the rifts that had developed between them during the past few years, she understood how reluctant he would be to further widen the chasms. And yet, because family *was* so important to him, and because Nathan had loved his father despite his flaws, she knew how hard it would be for Nathan to turn his back on his baby sister.

She certainly didn't envy him the decision he faced during the next few hours.

Nathan was beginning to worry that his head was in danger of exploding. So many thoughts were ricocheting through his mind that he wouldn't be surprised if he developed dents in his skull.

He knew he hadn't been his usual charming, personable self during the chamber of commerce event. He'd been aware of the puzzled and concerned looks he'd received all evening as he'd responded to conversational gambits with absentminded and sometimes monosyllabic replies. People were used to his brother, Gideon, sitting in a corner and glowering during social events, since Gideon would rather sacrifice nonessential body parts than to attend functions like this. But Nathan enjoyed social gatherings, usually staying right in the middle of the activities and generally being the life of the party.

"Nathan, are you sure there's nothing wrong?" his mother asked as the evening drew to a close. "You've been so distracted all evening."

He managed a smile for her. "Sorry, Mom. I hope I haven't spoiled your big party."

"Of course not." She raised a hand to touch the rose corsage she had been given earlier to designate her as one of the special honorees of the event. "I've had a lovely evening. I'm simply concerned about you."

"I, um, have a lot on my mind," he said, stalling.

This was definitely not the time to bring up his father's name, nor to remind his mother of little Isabelle's existence. As much as he would have liked to discuss his dilemma with his mother, he was convinced that he already knew what her response would be. Lenore McCloud would not wish harm on any child, but she couldn't be objective where this little girl was concerned. She would expect him to give the child up for adoption without a second thought. She would even try to convince him that he would be doing Isabelle a disservice if he were to prevent her from being placed in a two-parent home.

And maybe she would be right, Nathan mused. He was all too aware of his own shortcomings as parental material. Who was to say there wasn't a perfectly wonderful couple waiting to give Isabelle a loving, supportive home?

A tall, somber, dark-haired man approached the relatively quiet corner where Nathan had sought refuge and where his mother had found him. "Just wanted to let you know I'm out of here,'' the newcomer said to Lenore. "Congratulations on your award, Mom.''

Though her younger son had arrived barely twenty minutes earlier, Lenore didn't protest the brevity of his appearance. Nathan knew Lenore was pleased that Gideon had shown up at all. She smiled at her younger son. "Thank you for coming, Gideon. I know this isn't your sort of thing.''

Gideon's firm mouth twisted in a wry half smile. "You got that right. But I knew you would be hurt if I didn't make an appearance at this wingding in your honor.''

Though she couldn't resist preening a bit, Lenore reminded him that there had been four other honorees that evening. Gideon shrugged off the others as unimportant.

"Hold on a minute, bro. I'll walk you out,'' Nathan said on an impulse.

His brother lifted an eyebrow. "I'm sure I can find my truck.''

"Yeah, but I want to talk to you about something.'' Nathan moved aside as two of his mother's friends approached her. "See you later, Mom.''

"Don't leave without letting me know,'' she admonished before turning to her friends.

Suspecting that she would try again to find out what had been on his mind all evening, Nathan nodded and vowed to take his leave of her when there were others around to prevent any personal conversation. Walking toward the exit, he spotted Caitlin working the crowd on the other side of the country club ballroom. He couldn't help smiling at her earnest and eager expression. She certainly wasn't missing the opportunity to promote the law firm.

It wasn't the first time he'd thought that she should have gone into politics. She must have shaken the hand of everyone in attendance this evening; if there had been any babies in the room she would probably have kissed them.

Caitlin was most definitely destined for professional success. Whether she would find what she craved here in Honesty with him as her partner—well, that remained to be seen.

He and Gideon had just reached the door when their sister, Deborah, caught up with them. "You aren't both leaving, are you?" she protested, blocking their way. "I have to stay until Mom's ready to leave, since I drove her here."

Deborah didn't live in Honesty, but she had come to attend the reception for her mother. Like Gideon, she'd known it was important to Lenore for all her children to show their support for her tonight. Deborah was staying at her mother's house for the weekend and would return to her apartment in Tampa Sunday evening.

"I'm not leaving yet," Nathan assured her. "Just walking Gideon out. Actually, why don't you come, too? There's something I need to discuss with both of you—in private."

"A private discussion in the parking lot?" Gideon inquired.

Nathan shrugged. "It's one of the rare times we're all together these days. And this concerns a decision I have to make by tomorrow morning, so this is as good a time as any."

"Does this decision affect us?" Deborah, always the suspicious one, wanted to know.

"In a way, yes."

"Then I want to hear about it. You know how I feel about anyone making decisions on my behalf."

Nathan felt his mouth twist. "Trust me, I know exactly how you feel about that."

She turned and led the way through the exit door to the covered portico for rainy-weather drop-offs. A uniformed police officer stood outside the door. Nathan recognized Dylan Smith even before Deborah stiffened at his side.

"Well, if it isn't the Clan McCloud." Dylan touched his hat in what would probably look like a friendly gesture to anyone who didn't know the history behind his greeting.

"Your uncle the police chief put you on security detail tonight?" Gideon inquired blandly, sweeping the officer with a cool glance.

Dylan was actually a year younger than thirty-year-old Gideon, but he didn't look it. Experience had toughened his features and hardened his expression until there was nothing boyish left about him. Nathan doubted there were many who would be willing to pit their strength against this six-foot-one cop.

Yet Dylan spoke pleasantly enough when he responded to Gideon's barely veiled gibe. "That's right. My job is to keep all the riffraff away from the society crowd here tonight."

"Well, keep up the good work. Maybe you'll get promoted to traffic detail." Gideon made no effort to hide the fact that he hadn't forgotten several ugly confrontations between them in the past. One of those encounters had left Gideon with a black eye and a severely bruised ego.

To Dylan's credit, the sudden tightening of his jaw was the only evidence that Gideon's cutting words had angered him. Turning his back on Gideon, he spoke to Deborah, instead. "'Evening, Ms. McCloud. You're looking extremely well tonight. Very sophisticated and successful."

There was nothing polished about Deborah's response. "Bite me, Dylan."

Before the other man could reply to that suggestion, Nathan said quickly, "That's enough, you guys. Isn't it finally time to put the past behind us and let bygones be bygones?''

Three smoldering glares turned his way. ''No,'' they all said in unison.

He sighed, conceding that he had done all he could to settle that old conflict. ''Whatever. Gideon, where's your truck?''

Without answering, Gideon turned and headed toward the western side of the parking lot. Deborah followed him, though Nathan saw her throw one quick glance over her shoulder toward Dylan. Since Dylan was watching her walk away, Nathan saw their eyes lock—a moment of shared memories, perhaps? Deborah was the one who broke the connection, jerking her head around and hurrying after Gideon.

Nodding cordially to the officer who had once been a thorn in his own side, Nathan followed his siblings, bracing himself for the discussion to come.

Gideon had parked beneath a security lamp, his black-and-chrome pickup gleaming in the yellowish light. It was fully dark now. Though the early October days were still warm, they were growing shorter as winter crept closer. Several of the houses grouped around the golf course were already decorated with orange lights for Halloween.

''What's so important that you had to talk to us tonight?'' Gideon demanded, leaning back against his pickup with his arms crossed over his chest.

Unlike Nathan and Deborah, who had inherited their father's blond hair and blue eyes, Gideon was dark-haired and green-eyed like their mother. And yet in some ways—a trick of facial expression, perhaps—Gideon looked very much like their father, though Nathan knew his brother would not appreciate the comparison.

Nathan drew a deep breath, faced his younger siblings squarely and told them about the call he had received that afternoon.

"Surely you aren't even considering bringing that child here," Deborah said flatly, holding up both hands as if to physically ward off a really bad idea.

Nathan studied his sister's horrified expression. "You think she should be put up for adoption."

"Of course. Face it, Nathan, it's the best solution for everyone, the child included. In California she can be placed with a family who'll raise her far away from the scandal here. People who might never know the circumstances of the child's conception. You bring her here, where everyone knows what went on four years ago, and she'll never live it down. Hell, it's hard enough for *us* to deal with the looks we still get whenever that old gossip resurfaces."

"I can't imagine that anyone would hold the parents' mistakes against an innocent child," Nathan rebutted. He had never known Deborah to be deliberately cruel to anyone, but then again, none of the McClouds were rational when it came to the traumatic events of four years ago.

"It would kill Mother to have that kid shoved in her face every time she goes out in public in her own hometown. It would start the old gossip going again, have her friends tittering behind her back..."

"Some friends, if they would do that," Nathan muttered.

Deborah ignored him. "If you were foolish enough to try to raise her, you would make it impossible for our family to get together for holidays or special occasions. You can't seriously expect Mother to welcome her husband's bastard into the home she shared with him for thirty years!"

"Dad and Kimberly were married by the time Isabelle arrived," Nathan reminded her. "True, they had only been married a few weeks, but Isabelle was not born out of wed-lock.''

"Surely you wouldn't do this to Mother,'' his sister insisted, her voice thick with the pain of a betrayal from which she had never fully recovered.

Drawing another deep breath, Nathan clung to his patience. He reminded himself that Deborah had been young, barely twenty-two, when she'd learned about her father's affair and his young girlfriend's pregnancy. A senior in a large university in another state, she'd had to face the media circus and the avid curiosity of her classmates on her own.

"I didn't say I'm going to bring her here. It's just hard for me to put her up for adoption without even considering all the other possibilities. She's our sister, Deb.''

Deborah took a step backward, clearly rejecting that particular argument. "She's the result of an affair between a middle-aged man and a twenty-five-year-old bimbo,'' she stated angrily. "No one in this town would ever see her differently.''

She was probably right. Not only would it be unfair to bring the child into the household of a footloose bachelor who didn't have a clue about raising kids, it would be wrong to subject her to the gossip that would probably always surround her here. "I guess I just needed confirmation that I'm doing the right thing.''

Deborah's face softened, if only fractionally. "I know you've always had some misguided compulsion to take care of the family and to keep everyone happy and connected. Nathan the Peacemaker—you probably should have been a minister instead of a lawyer, but even when you went to law school it was to please Dad. You couldn't even cut ties with him when he betrayed every value he'd ever stood for. I never agreed with you about that. I never believed he deserved to have even one of us in his life after he deserted us, but I knew you well enough to understand why you felt compelled to make the effort. Even though I still think you were wrong.''

She had never tried to hide her disapproval of Nathan's visits with their father during the past four years. Like their mother, Deborah thought those visits were disloyal. They had wanted Nathan to choose a side—theirs—and never cross that line. ''I didn't approve of his choices any more than you did, Deb. But he was still our father.''

''He abdicated that position when he ran off with Kimberly.''

It was an old argument and a fruitless one. Even if he could change her mind, it was too late now. Stuart was dead.

She seemed to read his thoughts. ''Dad's gone now, and we've all managed to move on. Mother looked more content tonight than I've seen her in a long time. Don't hurt her again, Nathan.''

His chest was starting to hurt—whether from heartburn or heartache, he couldn't have said. He looked at Gideon, who had remained stoically silent throughout Nathan's discussion with their sister. ''I suppose you agree with everything Deborah said.''

Gideon shrugged. ''You do whatever you want. Just leave me out of it.''

Nathan's hand moved toward the inside pocket of his suit jacket, where his wallet now rested. ''I don't suppose you would like to see a photograph of little Isabelle. Neither of you has ever seen her.''

''No,'' they said simultaneously—Gideon's voice flat, Deborah's more passionate.

He dropped his hand. ''Fine. I just thought you had a right to know what's going on with her.''

''You haven't mentioned any of this to mother?''

He gave his sister a look. "I'm not a complete jerk, Deb."

She merely shrugged.

"If the family meeting is over, I'm out of here," Gideon said, pulling his keys from the pocket of the sport coat he'd worn as his only concession to the formality of the event.

"And I'm going back inside. I think I'd like a drink," Deborah said, implicitly daring either of them to try and stop her.

Nathan moved out of her way. He would have offered to escort her back in, but he suspected she'd had enough of his company for now. She was safe enough in the parking lot. There wasn't much crime in Honesty. And Officer Dylan Smith was still very much on duty at the entrance.

Nathan was watching Gideon's truck leave the parking lot when he heard Caitlin's voice behind him. "Are you all right?"

Deliberately blanking his expression, he turned to find her standing only a few feet away.

"I wasn't eavesdropping," she assured him quickly. "I was on my way to my car and I saw the three of you parting. I thought I should check on you when I realized you look…well, you look so tired."

Tired was exactly what he felt. And old, even though he was barely thirty-one. And sad. He'd lost his father. His brother and sister seemed to be drifting farther from him—and each other—all the time, and now he was about to sever all ties with his baby half sister.

What had Stuart done to this family? And could the damage ever really be repaired?

Caitlin took a step closer. "Nathan?"

"I'm fine. As you guessed, I'm tired. I told Gideon and Deborah about the decision I'm facing tonight."

"I take it from your expression that they weren't very supportive."

As always, his first instinct was to defend his family. "You can't really blame them. They're both still getting past everything Dad put them through. And though neither of them is able to admit it yet, they're still dealing with their grief over his death. This just brings everything back for them."

She motioned toward her car, which was parked only a few spaces from the one Gideon had just vacated. "I was just headed home. I've got no plans for the rest of the evening, if you'd like to go someplace and talk. I'm not sure I have any good advice to offer, but I'm a good listener."

"It's a tempting offer—" *very* tempting, actually "—but I think I'll pass tonight. I have to make some arrangements. I'll be leaving for San Diego in the morning. I've canceled my appointments for tomorrow. I hope to be back by Monday, Tuesday at the latest. I hope our scary office manager can rearrange my schedule if I should get detained."

"I imagine Irene can handle just about anything. Um, why are you going to San Diego?"

"I thought I should pay a visit to Mrs. Houston, see if there's anything I can do for her. And I'd like to see Isabelle one more time before…well."

Caitlin laid a hand on his arm, reading something in his tone that had drawn her even closer. "You've decided to go with the adoption plan?"

He tried unsuccessfully to erase a mental image of his father and Kimberly. Despite the scandal surrounding their relationship, Stuart and Kimberly had been happy together, and they had loved their daughter deeply. The vacation in

Mexico had been the first time they had been away from her.

Nathan knew they would never have considered the trip if they'd had any idea they would be leaving the little girl so vulnerable and alone.

Appreciating the moral support Caitlin was offering, he covered her soft, cool hand with his larger one. "Adoption seems like the best alternative for everyone involved. Mrs. Houston and her family will be able to concentrate on her treatments, and Isabelle will be placed in a state-approved, two-parent home. She won't have to be bounced between sitters, constantly uncertain about where she'll end up next."

She nodded, obviously agreeing with his decision and the reasons behind it. "Take all the time you need to settle things in California. Irene and I can keep everything under control at the office until you get back."

"Thanks, Caitlin. I appreciate that. You've been great today."

Her smile was faint and bittersweet. "I understand how difficult family obligations can become."

He was sure she *did* understand. He knew that her widowed mother was confined to a nursing home in Jackson, a tragic victim of an untimely, massive stroke. Caitlin visited her mother at least twice a month, though she'd told him her mother hadn't recognized her in more than a year.

He and Caitlin had both dealt with heartache in their families, and they had both been the ones who'd had to shoulder the responsibilities—Caitlin as an only child, he as the eldest offspring. Despite their differing approaches to work, he and Caitlin actually had quite a bit in common, a thought that had occurred to him on several occasions.

He glanced toward the country club. A steady stream of guests were beginning to emerge. He had no interest in going back inside, but he'd promised his mother he wouldn't leave without telling her good-night.

He swallowed a sigh, along with a futile wish that he was in a cozy tent somewhere in a pristine wilderness with no more pressing decisions than which flies would catch the most trout. He wondered if Caitlin liked camping and fishing.

She gave his arm a little squeeze. "Have a safe trip, Nathan. I hope everything works out for the best—for everyone."

He would have liked to kiss her then, if nothing more than a brush of his lips against her cheek. Just a gesture of gratitude, he assured himself, because she'd been so nice today. But, since their association to this point had not included even casual kisses, he decided the time wasn't right to initiate such a gesture now, even with the most innocent of intentions.

Or were they really that innocent?

He reluctantly released her hand. "Good night, Caitlin."

He waited until she was safely inside her car before he turned, squared his shoulders and moved determinedly back toward the entrance.

After all, he reminded himself grimly, a promise was a promise—no matter how inconvenient. That thought reminded him of the implied promise he'd made to his father when he'd agreed to be Isabelle's executor.

His head was pounding in earnest when he reentered the country club with dragging steps.

Chapter Three

The offices seemed different without Nathan in them. Quieter. More solemn, somehow. For some reason people tended to speak in near whispers—both the clients in the waiting room and the few employees at their desks.

Did Nathan really make that much noise, Caitlin wondered during a brief respite Friday afternoon, or was everyone responding to the tension in the offices due to his extended absence?

Appointments and court dates had been shuffled, reshuffled and rescheduled, and Caitlin was having to work frantically to keep up. Irene worked the organizational miracles Caitlin had come to expect from her, but Caitlin had to admit the efficient office manager was a rather intimidating presence. Nathan's habitual joviality served as a counterbalance to Irene's pragmatism and Caitlin's naturally quiet manner. Without him the office simply wasn't as...well, as alive.

She missed him. And the next time she saw him, she fully intended to let him have it for leaving work dangling this long with little notice and even less explanation of what was keeping him in California.

The few calls they had received from him had been brief, uninformative, and carefully timed so that Caitlin wouldn't be there to talk to him. The messages had all come relayed through Irene or one of the other staff members. Basically they all said the same thing: "Sorry. Still tied up here. Be back as soon as possible."

No personal messages for her, but, then, she hadn't expected any, she assured herself. She simply wanted him to hurry back because she was tired of trying to handle everything here by herself.

Late in the afternoon she sat at her desk, focusing on her computer screen and popping M&M's into her mouth in lieu of the lunch she hadn't had time to eat. Irene tapped on the door and entered carrying a stack of folders. "Here are the files you asked for."

"Thanks. Another wild day, isn't it?"

"It has been…eventful."

Caitlin pushed a hand through her slightly disheveled hair. "You haven't heard from Nathan this afternoon?"

"No, Mr. McCloud hasn't called."

Caitlin bit her lip, making no comment about the heavy disapproval in Irene's voice. The office manager seemed to think Nathan was off on an impulsive vacation, leaving her and Caitlin and the rest of the staff to deal with the resulting chaos. Caitlin couldn't believe that. Nathan might duck out for an afternoon of golf or fishing, but surely he wouldn't leave them in the lurch this long unless something was wrong.

He had told his mother he was taking a few days of well-deserved vacation time. His siblings, of course, knew where he was, but Caitlin doubted they had shared that information with their mother.

Had there been a problem with putting the child up for adoption? Had the girl's guardian changed her mind despite her grave illness? Or maybe Nathan was staying until he was certain the child would be safely placed in a suitable home. That wouldn't surprise her. Despite his sometimes lackadaisical approach to work, Nathan's sense of responsibility to his family was hyperdeveloped.

Or maybe he was simply having a hard time letting Isabelle go.

Caitlin still sympathized with his dilemma, but, oh, was she getting tired, she thought with a sigh, rubbing the back of her taut neck.

To add to her tension level, she had taken on a new case—a medical malpractice claim—that had seemed fairly straightforward at the beginning, but was mushrooming into what could very well prove to be an extremely expensive legal action. She had no doubt that her client had been the victim of malpractice, but such claims were difficult to prove, and the doctor in question was practically a legend in this part of the state. Wealthy, highly visible, socially powerful.

She was beginning to wonder if she'd gotten in over her head. And it didn't help that her partner wasn't around for consultations.

She was developing an incipient headache that threatened to become a migraine. Tapping on her computer keyboard with one hand, she used the other to toss two painkillers into her mouth, washing them down with a sip of cold coffee. The taste made her shudder, but she kept working, refusing to let the stress get the best of her.

Someone tapped on her open office door. Without taking

her eyes from the computer screen, she said, "Whatever it is, just lay it on my desk. I'll get to it as soon as I can."

"I don't really think your desk is the right place for me to put what I'm holding."

Her physical reaction to the sound of Nathan's deep voice rather surprised her. Her heart jumped, her pulse sped up and a quiver went through her.....

Relief, she assured herself. What else could it be?

She hit the buttons on her keyboard to save her work. "It's about time you got back," she said, turning to face him. "I—"

Her words trailed into silence when she saw him. Or, more specifically, when she saw the sleeping toddler he held in his arms, her golden head resting trustingly on his shoulder.

"Irene, hold my calls, please." Releasing the intercom button on her phone, Caitlin leaned back slowly in her chair, still staring at Nathan and the child. She kept her voice low to avoid waking the little girl when she said, "You brought her back with you."

His expression was a complex mixture of sheepishness, defensiveness and what might have been a touch of fear. "Yes."

"Have you lost your mind?"

He grimaced. "Probably. But I really had no other choice."

The funny thing was, she wasn't as surprised as she should have been. Maybe deep inside she had expected this all along.

She sighed. "What happened?"

Balancing the child with a rather endearing awkwardness, he settled carefully into a chair before replying, "She recognized me as soon as she saw me, can you believe that? She's just a baby and it's been months since I saw her last, but the minute I walked into the room, she came running up to me saying 'Nate,' which is what she's always called me."

"That is surprising." The tot hardly looked old enough to talk, much less to remember names and faces.

"I can tell you it gave me a funny feeling when she put her arms up for a hug as if it were only the day before when we saw each other last."

"Was that when you decided to bring her home with you?"

"No. I was still trying to convince myself that it would be better to give her up. Anyway, I spent a couple of hours with her, and then I went to the hospital to visit her great-aunt, Barbara Houston. While I was there, one of the nurses, who seemed quite nice, called me aside to tell me that she and her husband were interested in adopting Isabelle."

He shifted Isabelle to a more comfortable position in his arms. "The nurse said she met Isabelle when the pastor brought her to the hospital to visit Mrs. Houston. She claimed she'd become quite fond of her. And then she proceeded to ask me a few dozen questions about Isabelle's trust fund and whether any of it would be available to whoever adopted her."

Caitlin winced. "Ouch."

"She tried to be subtle about it, of course. She claimed that she simply needed to know the details for Isabelle's sake, that she wanted to be sure the child would have her needs met during her childhood. But I've dealt with greed enough to recognize it when I see it."

"So because one woman was more interested in the trust fund than the child, you decided everyone would be?"

He hesitated, then grimaced. "I know how it sounds, but you didn't see that woman's eyes. There isn't quite a fortune in the trust fund, but the insurance settlement from the tourist helicopter company was sizable enough to draw plenty of attention. No matter where Isabelle ends up, the trust fund is secure until she's eighteen, but some people might think there are ways to get around the safeguards.''

''There are plenty of couples who would love to have a little girl like Isabelle whether or not she has a dime to her name,'' Caitlin reminded him.

''I'm aware of that. But there would be no way for me to know for certain,'' he said stubbornly.

She decided not to bother suggesting that he'd latched on to the first valid excuse he'd found to change his mind about the adoption. He'd probably known from the moment Isabelle had run to greet him that he couldn't give her to strangers, no matter what the repercussions.

''So what are you going to do now?''

He swallowed before he answered. ''I've spent the past few days having myself named her guardian. The process was expedited because of Mrs. Houston's illness, but it still took some finagling. Fortunately, Alan has some influence there.''

Caitlin shook her head in amazement as the reality of what he had done sank in. ''You're her guardian.''

She would have sworn he lost a bit of color, but he nodded gamely. ''I have sole responsibility for her now. As I said, there wasn't anyone else.''

''So now what? You're surely not going to try to raise her yourself?''

''Well…yeah.''

She felt herself sink further into her chair. ''Nathan, you can't. What do you know about raising children? A little girl?''

''Nothing,'' he admitted frankly. ''But I'll learn.''

''Just like that?''

"What other choice do I have?"

"You can—" She glanced at the child to make sure she was still asleep, then lowered her voice to a whisper, anyway. "You can still put her up for adoption. Take a little time to find a nice family you can trust with her safety and her trust fund."

"I figure I'll adopt her myself. I've handled a few adoptions in my time, even a couple for single parents. With the advantage of being her biological half brother, I shouldn't run into any serious problems."

And then what? Caitlin stared at him, trying to imagine footloose Nathan McCloud trading in his sports car for a minivan. Cooking macaroni and cheese, doing laundry, attending PTA meetings....

"You *have* lost your mind," she decided aloud.

"I can see why you might think so," he answered rather stiffly.

"Have you told your family?"

"Not yet. I came here straight from the airport."

"Do you..." She paused while she mentally groped for the right words. "Do you think they'll be able to accept her?"

She watched as he held the toddler closer. "I hope so. They've got good hearts, despite the pain my father caused them. I find it hard to believe they could look at Isabelle and not fall for her, despite the circumstances of her conception."

Caitlin wasn't so sure. Lenore McCloud was a woman who was greatly concerned with her social standing. Having just rebounded from her former husband's betrayal, she wasn't going to easily accept this reminder. Gideon was a taciturn, withdrawn man—a writer who seemed to live more inside his head than in the real world. She couldn't imagine him melting in response to a child's smile.

Caitlin had only met Deborah a couple of times, but Caitlin had gotten an impression of a woman who was impulsive, tempestuous and stubborn—a volatile mixture of her brothers' diverse personalities.

Nathan had a tough road ahead of him.

"I sure hope you know what you're doing."

"Are you kidding? I don't have a clue. I'm open to any advice I can get."

"Don't look at me." She held up both hands. "I know nothing about raising kids—or placating irate family members. I was an only child, remember, and my family actually got along pretty well, despite our other problems."

"You've never told me much about your family," Nathan remarked. "I'd like to hear about them sometime."

She didn't want to talk about her family now. She wondered if it was incredibly selfish of her to be wondering how Nathan's impulsive move would affect her. Professionally speaking, of course, she assured herself—though she knew there was something more to her stunned reaction than that. Something she didn't want to think about right now.

With a drowsy murmur, Isabelle roused and lifted her head from Nathan's shoulder. Her big blue eyes were still heavy-lidded when she looked around in curiosity at her new surroundings, her gaze finally settling on Caitlin's face. "Hi," she said.

A bit surprised by the calm greeting, Caitlin attempted a friendly smile, hoping it wasn't as stiff as it felt. "Hello, Isabelle."

"Who are you?"

"My name is Caitlin."

"Miss Caitlin," Nathan murmured, deeply ingrained Southern traditions kicking in.

"Are you Nate's friend?"

Apparently Nathan hadn't exaggerated when he had gone on about how smart and well-spoken his half sister was for her age. There was hardly a baby lisp in the clear little voice. "Yes, I'm Nathan's friend."

"I'm his sister."

Caitlin couldn't help smiling again at the quiet pride in the statement. "Yes, I know."

"I'm going to live with him now. Aunt Barb is sick."

The desk intercom buzzed before Caitlin could reply. "I'm sorry to interrupt, Ms. Briley, but the call you've been waiting for is on line two."

"You'd better take that." Nathan stood. "Isabelle and I are going to my office to see how much work has piled up while I've been away."

"You probably don't want to know," Caitlin warned as she reached for the phone. "Don't you want to go home for a while before you dive in?"

"I thought I would gather some things to take home with me. I can get some work done tonight after Isabelle's asleep."

"I'm not tired," the child said quickly.

Nathan chuckled. "I didn't say you have to go to bed now. I meant later."

"Okay. Can I get down now?"

"Sure." He set her on her feet.

Dressed in a purple-and-green-striped knit top with purple pants, her feet encased in impossibly tiny white sneakers, her blond curls tumbling almost to her shoulders, the child looked like a life-size porcelain doll. Caitlin couldn't get over how lovely she was. Maybe Nathan was right. Maybe his family would be too captivated by the child to hold her parentage against her. Maybe.

Nathan held out his hand to Isabelle. "C'mon, poppet,

let's leave Miss Caitlin to her call. I'll show you my office.''

Lifting the receiver to her ear and pushing the button for line two, Caitlin spoke absently into the mouthpiece, but her attention was focused on the twosome leaving her office. *Stunned* was hardly the word to describe her feelings at the thought of Nathan bringing a child home as casually as he would have adopted a puppy.

She couldn't even imagine his family's reaction to the development.

Okay, so he had been a little conniving.

Nathan knew very well that Caitlin had never intended to come home with him that evening, but when she had asked, as they were leaving the office, if there was anything she could do to help him out, he'd jumped on the offer so quickly and so fervently that she'd had no chance to back out.

He had assured her that he just needed a little help getting Isabelle set up in his home and had promised he wouldn't keep Caitlin long. Almost before she'd realized what she had agreed to, they were in their cars, Caitlin following as Nathan drove home.

He glanced in the rearview mirror to check on Isabelle, who was belted into a toddler seat behind him on what passed for a back seat in his small car. He'd brought the toddler seat from California; decorated with *Sesame Street* characters, it was the one she'd used in Barbara Houston's car. Nathan thought it was important for Isabelle to have as many familiar things around her as possible to make the transition easier, though she seemed to be adapting to the changes very well thus far.

"You doing okay back there?"

She had been looking out the side window, watching the

passing scenery with the avid curiosity that was so characteristic of his baby sister. Their eyes met in the rearview mirror and she smiled. "I'm okay."

"Are you hungry?"

"A little."

He made a quick mental inventory of his pantry and refrigerator and winced. He didn't have milk. No bread, either. Or peanut butter or fresh fruit or veggies or anything else a growing child needed. Maybe he could call for pizza or something tonight, but that would hardly work for breakfast tomorrow.

Making an impulsive decision, he switched on his turn signal and drove into the parking lot of a shopping center. Noting that Caitlin was still behind him, he parked in front of the supermarket at one end of the center. Caitlin parked beside him.

"I'm really glad you're helping me this evening," he said as soon as they were both out of their cars. "Grocery shopping isn't one of my talents, I'm afraid, and I'm out of everything. You can help me choose the things I'll need to keep on hand for Isabelle."

Still looking a bit confused about how she had become his assistant for the evening, Caitlin wrinkled her nose. "You're looking at someone who eats take-out for nearly every meal. My usual purchases are coffee, bagels and ice cream."

"I like ice cream," Isabelle commented, catching the end of Caitlin's comment as she climbed out of Nathan's car with his assistance.

"And I like ice cream, but we have to buy some healthy food, too." Nathan took her hand. "Surely between the three of us we can gather the stuff to put together some healthy meals."

"I'll help you," Isabelle offered. "I went to the grocery store all the time with Aunt Barb."

Nathan smiled at Caitlin over the child's head. "Sounds like we've got a shopping expert here to help us out."

Caitlin fell into step beside them. "I'm sure we can use all the help we can get."

Rows of silver metal shopping carts waited just inside the supermarket doorway. Nathan lifted Isabelle into one of the plastic seats, then grasped the handle and guided the cart toward the first aisle. Caitlin stayed close by, saying little but seeming agreeable to help with this necessary task.

They looked like a family.

The thought occurred to Nathan abruptly as he and Caitlin strolled down the aisle side by side, pushing Isabelle in front of them. And then, for the first time, he wondered what he would say if someone they knew saw them looking so cozy. He had known when he brought Isabelle home with him that explanations would be inevitable, but it wasn't going to be easy.

"Maybe I should have talked to my mother before coming out in public like this," he murmured to Caitlin, suddenly feeling as if eyes were focused on them from every direction.

"Maybe you should have thought of that sooner," she replied, setting two jars of applesauce in the cart.

"Maybe we'll get out of here without seeing anyone we know."

The look she gave him was skeptical—and rightly so. Honesty wasn't that big, and he had lived here all his life. He rarely stepped out of his house without running into at least one person he knew.

He drew a deep breath and concentrated on the shopping, hoping he wouldn't be spotted by anyone likely to call his mother before he had the chance to talk to her.

Other than his concern about potentially awkward encounters, he might have enjoyed the shopping trip. Isabelle was delightfully serious about helping with the selection process. Caitlin was obviously, if reluctantly, charmed by the little girl—who wouldn't be?—and she revealed a softer side of herself, one that she usually kept hidden at the office.

"Do you like cereal, Isabelle?" she asked, studying a dizzying array of colorful boxes.

"Yes. Cereal's good for breakfast."

Nathan reached for a chocolate-flavored puff cereal, figuring every kid must like that flavor. After all, it was the one he usually bought for himself.

"Not that one, Nate," Isabelle admonished him. "Too much sugar."

Caitlin laughed. Nathan placed his hands on his hips and cocked his head at his sister. "What brand would you recommend?"

Isabelle placed a fingertip against her rosy lips, studying the offerings. "That one," she finally decided, pointing to a box of bite-size wheat squares. "I like those."

Moving down the aisle, they added boxes of flavored instant oatmeal and bags of dried fruit to the cart, both heartily approved by Isabelle. The next aisle held cookies. "I suppose we need to pass these?" Nathan suggested. "Too sugary, right?"

Isabelle frowned. "We need *some* sweets," she said earnestly. "A little doesn't hurt."

He grinned. "Just point to what you like."

Isabelle happily selected a bag of chocolate chip cookies and some pink-frosted animal crackers. He'd have bought out the store at that point, if she'd asked, just because she was so darned cute.

He'd better be careful about that, he thought, or she just might get the idea that he was a soft touch.

Moving on to the canned goods, Nathan stood back and watched while Caitlin and Isabelle debated the relative merits of chicken noodle soup or chicken and stars. He couldn't seem to stop smiling; they made a lovely picture as they focused so intently on the display of red and white cans.

His smile faded when he heard his name spoken from behind him. "Nathan? Is that you?"

His eyes closed in a spasm of emotion. Of all the rotten luck….

He turned. "Hello, Aunt Betty."

She wasn't actually his aunt, not by blood, anyway. She had been married to his father's uncle, which made her his great-aunt by marriage. But she had never let such distinctions deter her. Betty McCloud enjoyed nothing more than bossing around the younger members of her late husband's extended family.

A very large woman—nearly six feet tall and well over two hundred pounds—the seventy-five-year-old former loan officer had a voice like a bullhorn. Several nearby shoppers glanced their way when she asked loudly, "So, what's up? Doing some grocery shopping?"

Resisting the impulse to make a smart-aleck remark to that very obvious question, Nathan merely nodded.

Betty's attention had already turned to his companions. "The law partner, right? Kate?"

"Caitlin," Nathan corrected her.

Caitlin's smile was only slightly strained. "Hello, Mrs. McCloud. It's nice to see you again."

Her hawk-like eyes zeroing in on Isabelle, the older woman asked, "This your little girl? Didn't know you had one. She's a cutie."

Uncertain how to respond, Caitlin looked at Nathan. "I, uh…"

It might not have been the noblest choice Nathan could have made, but he decided to take the easy way out. Escape.

"You know, it was great to see you, Aunt Betty, but we really have to hurry. I'll call you soon and explain everything, okay?"

"Explain what?" she asked, frowning at him.

He merely smiled and pushed the cart so quickly away that Isabelle's fine hair ruffled in the resulting breeze. Her eyes big, she gazed up at him. "Who *was* that?" she asked in a stage whisper.

"That was my great-aunt Betty. Yours, too, I guess."

"She's loud."

Nathan nodded. "I know."

"She thinks I'm Miss Caitlin's little girl."

Nathan avoided Caitlin's eyes. "I know. I'll explain to her later."

"But why…?"

"What kind of fruit juice do you like, Isabelle?" Caitlin asked quickly.

Isabelle seemed to debate for a moment whether to continue her line of questioning or allow herself to be distracted. But then she conceded and requested apple juice.

Staying well ahead of Betty, Nathan practically jogged down the rest of the aisles, tossing food items into the cart until it nearly overflowed. He kept his eyes focused on the shelves, operating on the theory that if he didn't see anyone else he knew, they wouldn't see him, either.

Caitlin helped him pile his purchases on the conveyor belt at the cashier's station. He paid the sizable bill with a bank debit card, then pushed the cart full of now-bagged groceries toward the parking lot. A golfing buddy hailed him just outside the door; Nathan waved and kept moving, successfully avoiding conversation.

"You have to talk to your mother," Caitlin said as they reached their cars. "There's no way you can keep this quiet for long."

"I know." He glanced into the back of his car, which was filled with his bags and Isabelle's. "Think we can put some of these bags in your car? I'm not sure everything's going to fit in mine."

Caitlin hesitated a moment before opening the trunk of her Saturn. He wondered if she had considered parting from him here rather than accompanying him home. "If you have other plans for the evening, I'm sure Isabelle and I can manage by ourselves....."

She sighed and reached for a bag of groceries. "No, I don't have other plans. I'm happy to give you a hand this evening. We are partners, after all."

Partners. Maybe she was trying to downplay the cozily intimate nature of their shopping expedition by reminding him of their business relationship. He couldn't think of any other reason for her to bring it up. But he merely nodded, thanked her and helped her transfer the groceries to her car. He should probably feel at least a little guilty about shamelessly using her this way, but he needed her help too badly.

Chapter Four

It took several trips to transfer all the groceries and belongings into Nathan's house. They unpacked briskly and with little conversation, Isabelle gamely carrying as much as her little arms could hold. Dumping suitcases in the den, they concentrated first on putting away the groceries.

Caitlin lifted an eyebrow at the empty state of Nathan's pantry and refrigerator. "You weren't kidding when you said you were out of groceries, were you?"

He made a face as he stashed milk, eggs and cheese in the nearly empty fridge. "You're not the only one who survives on take-out food."

Isabelle tugged at his shirt. "I'm hungry now, Nate. Can we have hot dogs and macaroni and cheese?"

She had informed them at the supermarket that it was her favorite meal. Nathan had been pleased to hear it; that was a menu even he could prepare. He'd made a vow to himself to learn to cook healthy, balanced meals, but tonight seemed like a good time for something quick and easy.

By the time he had the food ready, all the groceries had been neatly organized and put away. He persuaded Caitlin to join them for dinner, and the three of them ate around the kitchen table. Nathan didn't own a booster seat, of course, so Isabelle sat on a stack of law books to raise her to table height.

By the time she'd finished eating, Isabelle's eyelids were growing heavy again. It had been a long, eventful day for a little girl—for an adult as well, Nathan admitted. He wouldn't mind curling up in a quiet corner for a few hours himself. And not necessarily alone, he added with a thoughtful look at Caitlin, who sat across the table from him, smiling sweetly at Isabelle.

Unfortunately, he had a lot more to do before he could rest that evening. And he doubted Caitlin would be interested in curling up with him, anyway. Especially not tonight.

Bringing Isabelle into his life had changed everything as far as his social life was concerned. When he had considered asking Caitlin out before, he'd been happily unattached. She might have had some hesitation about dating her business partner, but now he was also a single father—and he had no idea how she felt about that.

Caitlin volunteered to clear the kitchen as he carried Isabelle to his bedroom to nap while he prepared the guest room for her use. "I'll leave the door open," he told Isabelle, tucking her into his bed. "Miss Caitlin and I will be in the other room. Just call out if you need anything."

"'Kay," she murmured sleepily, snuggling into his pillows. "G'night, Nate."

"Good night, poppet." He brushed a kiss across her soft cheek, smoothed the covers over her shoulders and straightened. She was still wearing the knit outfit she had traveled in earlier, having removed only her shoes before climbing into bed. Nathan hadn't unpacked her pj's yet, nor her toothbrush or toys or anything else.

He drew a deep breath at the thought of all that lay ahead of him, and then turned toward the doorway to rejoin Caitlin.

Waiting in the den for Nathan, Caitlin looked at the clutter of suitcases and boxes on the floor and wondered exactly how she had ended up here this evening. All she remembered saying was that if there was anything she could do for Nathan and Isabelle...

The next thing she knew, she'd been picking out groceries and eating hot dogs at his kitchen table.

She'd only been in Nathan's house a couple of times. She looked at it now through new eyes, studying the leather and wood furnishings, the wildlife prints and golf-and-wildlife-themed knick-knacks. One wall of the room was dominated by an entertainment centre that included a large-screen TV, VCR and DVD players, a sound system and a video game system. Typical young bachelor's place, she thought of the cozy three-bedroom, ranch-styled house in a neighborhood filled with singles and young marrieds.

"Your life is certainly about to change," she commented when Nathan strolled into the room.

He scooped up a white stuffed owl Isabelle had been carrying around earlier, and studied it with a quizzical expression. "Tell me about it."

"Are you nervous?"

The look he gave her was almost comically expressive. "Terrified."

"I would be, too." She considered talking to him again about the wisdom of the decision he had made, but he looked so tired that she didn't have the heart. Maybe after he'd had some rest, he would see things differently.

She glanced at the bags on the floor. "Need help with these things?"

"Yes, you could help me set up the guest room for Isabelle, if you don't mind."

"Sure. Which things are hers?"

"The black suitcase and carry-on are mine. We'll just leave them in here for now. The two red suitcases and the purple footlocker hold Isabelle's things. Barbara Houston's daughter helped me pack Isabelle's favorites. I told her to dispose of the rest however she saw fit."

Caitlin took hold of the handle of a wheeled red suitcase. "Point me toward the guest room."

He had already hefted the small footlocker off the floor. "This way," he said over his shoulder.

The house was set up with a split floor plan—master bedroom and bath on one end, kitchen, dining room, den and living room centrally located and two smaller bedrooms and a bath at the far end. The doors were all open.

Caitlin noted that Nathan had arranged one of the spare bedrooms as an office with a desk, filing cabinets, bookshelves, computer system and other basic office equipment. It looked very much like the office she had set up in her two-bedroom apartment.

He had done very little decorating in the guest room. The furnishings consisted of a bed, a nightstand, a dresser and a chest of drawers in a warm-toned wood that might have been maple. A blue-and-green plaid spread covered the bed and a beige ginger-jar lamp with a matching shade sat on the nightstand. White blinds covered the single window; there was no curtain to soften the effect. A couple of generic, framed landscape prints hung on the white-painted walls. It was obviously a room that was rarely, if ever, used.

Still holding the footlocker, Nathan paused just inside the doorway. "Doesn't look much like a little girl's room, does it?"

"No," she admitted, "but it has potential. It's a good size, and the furniture is nice."

"Thanks. It's the furniture I had in my room when I was a teenager. Mom donated it to me when I set up housekeeping on my own. She wanted to redecorate her place, anyway."

She released the suitcase and turned slowly in the center of the room. "All you need is a new bedspread, throw pillows, curtains and some colorful framed posters for the walls. The built-in bookshelves are perfect for holding books and toys."

"It sounds like you know just how to fix it up for her."

She frowned warily. "Now, wait a minute. I was only making a few suggestions, not volunteering to decorate."

"But, Caitlin, there's no one else to help me," he said, giving her one of his well-practiced, hopeful-puppy smiles. "I can hardly ask my mother or sister, and what do *I* know about decorating for a little girl?"

"You should have thought of that before you brought one home with you."

When he only kept smiling at her, she sighed and called herself a sucker. "Okay, fine. Maybe I could give you a hand—not that I'm guaranteeing results. I'm no decorator."

"Maybe you could take her shopping in the morning, let her pick out a few things she likes?"

"Oh, I—"

"I have to go talk to my mother," he cut in quickly. "I really need to break the news to her before someone else calls her. I can't take Isabelle with me, obviously, and this isn't something I can tell Mom over the phone."

"In other words, you're asking me to baby-sit while you talk to your mother."

He shrugged, and his expression was sheepish. "I don't have anyone else to ask."

She wished he would quit saying that. She was his business partner, nothing more. It wasn't her responsibility to help him set up a household after making a rash decision that was guaranteed to estrange him from his family.

Because she was feeling stressed and a little defensive—not to mention exhausted from one of the toughest work weeks she'd ever dealt with—she launched into that lecture she had been trying to avoid. "You understand that this is the way your life is going to be if you go through with this? Baby-sitters and family problems and changing your whole life—even your home? Even your career will be affected. You won't have the freedom to work any hours you like, the way you have until now. And we're talking about the next fifteen years. You can't just go back to the way things were when the novelty wears off, especially if you go so far as to adopt her. This little girl is going to have to be your number-one priority until she's completely grown and self-sufficient."

"You think I haven't considered all of that already?" He planted his fists on his hips and stared at her. "This wasn't an impulse, Caitlin. I spent several days in California trying to talk myself out of bringing her here, doing my best to convince myself I wasn't the right person to raise this child. When I said I was terrified, it was more for her sake than my own. Sure, I'll have to change my schedules, give up some freedom, spend less time partying and playing. I can live with that. But as for Isabelle—her whole life is at stake here. Her future."

He was pacing now, his hands flying as he vented. It was probably the first chance he'd had to really talk with anyone since he'd had to make this life-altering decision. "I made a list of all the reasons I shouldn't take this on. It started with the facts that I'm single and have no experience with kids. I reminded myself of the hostility she could face in this town, from my own family, for example. The list of reasons *not* to bring her home with me was several pages long."

"And the list of reasons why you should bring her?"

He squeezed the back of his neck with one hand, his voice quiet. "Pretty short. Only two reasons, actually. She's my sister, and my dad would have wanted me to raise her."

After all the pain he had been through, all the heartache, embarrassment and disappointment, Nathan was still trying to please his father, even after the man's death. Caitlin understood that. She still faithfully visited her mother, even though her mother hadn't looked at Caitlin with a glimmer of recognition in more than a year.

Caitlin could no more turn her back on her mother than she could fly. She couldn't imagine how she might feel if she suddenly found herself responsible for a young sibling. She had a sneaky suspicion she might have reacted much like Nathan had—recklessly taking on more responsibility than was good for her, even at great cost to herself.

She was just glad she wasn't the one who'd been placed in that difficult position. Nathan might be willing to change everything in his life, but hers was right on track.

Because she did sympathize, she said, "Okay. I'll do it."

He seemed to have a little trouble following her transition. "You'll do what?"

"I'll stay with Isabelle tomorrow morning while you talk to your mother. What time do you want me here?"

She could hear the relief in his voice when he replied. "Most of the stores open at ten, don't they? You can pick her up just before then and let her pick out some decorations for her room. Anything she wants to make her feel at home here. You can put it on the company card and I'll pay when the bill comes in.''

''Maybe you'll want to hold off on redecorating until after you talk to your mother.''

He read her unspoken subtext easily enough. ''You think I'll change my mind about keeping her after I talk to my mother?''

Caitlin knew Lenore would do her best to talk her son out of this plan. Could he really withstand her tears, her accusations of betrayal, her pleas and threats? ''I just think it might be a good idea if you—''

''No matter what my mother says, I'm not changing my mind about Isabelle,'' Nathan insisted stubbornly. ''I've already anticipated everything she could possibly say, even if she refuses to ever speak to me again. I would regret that, of course—hell, it would break my heart. But Mom would still have Gideon and Deborah. Isabelle only has me.''

It seemed that there would be nothing anyone could say to change Nathan's mind about this. Having spent the past couple of hours watching him with his little sister, Caitlin realized that their bond was already too strong to be broken by warnings or threats.

She looked at his determined expression with a touch of awe, realizing that she'd underestimated him. She'd never realized quite how forceful he could be. And she hadn't expected him to be so courageously self-sacrificing—for any reason. There was a great deal more to Nathan Mc-Cloud than he had allowed her to see during the past nine months—maybe more than he allowed *anyone* else to see, even those who were closest to him.

''All right. I'll pick her up at ten in the morning,'' she said, committing herself to taking his side in the coming controversy and hoping she didn't regret that decision. "But I warn you," she added in an attempt to lighten the mood, "it's dangerous to send two women shopping with your credit card and no budget."

She was pleased when he gave her a semblance of his enticingly lopsided smile. "So I'll sell my golf clubs, if necessary. I have a feeling I won't be needing them as much for the next, oh, fifteen years or so."

Hard to believe he could keep smiling when he said that. Caitlin swallowed. "I'll try not to go quite that crazy."

"Buy her whatever she wants."

Caitlin frowned at him. "You aren't going to spoil her, are you? You've seen in court what happens when children are overindulged. It ruins them for life, teaches them to expect everyone to give in to their expectations."

"I'll try not to spoil her," he promised, smiling more broadly as he raised one hand in a mock vow. "Just buy whatever she needs to turn this into a nice room. I want to make a good home for her here."

Because the sentiment touched her, even though she was trying her best to retain an emotional distance from this entire situation, she looked away from him and spoke brusquely. "If there's nothing else you need this evening, I'd better head home now. I have a stack of paperwork in my car I need to go through tonight, especially if I'm going to be free for a shopping excursion in the morning."

"Did anything come up at work I should know about?"

"Several things," she replied, thinking of the medical malpractice case she would be working on most of the night. She would have to discuss that with him, of course, but it could wait a few hours. "We'll talk about them later this weekend."

He followed her to the front door. "Irene was giving me some pretty deadly looks before she left the office earlier.

I got the impression she was only being passably courteous because Isabelle was with me, which I could tell was making her crazy with curiosity.''

''She doesn't know yet that you've taken Isabelle as your ward. I didn't tell her why you were in California, only that you were tending to personal business. She probably thinks Isabelle is visiting you for a few days or something. She'll understand better when you explain the situation to her.''

''So she thinks I was in California spending a week at Disneyland while you were carrying the load here?''

''Maybe something like that,'' Caitlin conceded. ''It wasn't my place to discuss your personal business with her, of course.''

''Nice to know our office manager has such a high opinion of me,'' he grumbled.

''Well, you haven't done much to change that opinion,'' she reminded him. ''You either clam up or bolt—or both— whenever she's around. And you have to admit you play havoc with her schedules and routines. You know how obsessive she is about that sort of thing.''

''Do I ever,'' he muttered. ''Wonder what she's going to say when I tell her I've taken in a three-year-old? She'll probably think I should be committed. I'm quite sure she'll think I'm completely unqualified to raise a child, considering her low opinion of me.''

Because Caitlin still wasn't quite convinced, herself, that Nathan had made the right decision, she decided not to comment.

Nathan covered the doorknob with his hand when she reached for it, detaining her for a moment. He was standing so close to her that his arm brushed hers when he turned to face her. His expression was serious again, and his gaze held hers when he spoke. ''Before you leave, I want to thank you for everything you've done for me tonight.''

"That isn't necessary," she said, suddenly self-conscious. "I was happy to give you a hand."

"Don't brush me off. I mean it, Caitlin. I really needed your help this evening—and your company. Bringing Isabelle home alone...well, that was pretty scary for me. Having you here for moral support, even when you were questioning my sanity, meant a great deal to me."

She became even more aware of how very close he stood. Their faces were only inches apart.

The intimacy of their proximity—and maybe something about the way he was looking at her—made her stomach muscles tighten. "That's the sort of thing business partners do for each other," she said inanely.

He smiled then. "No. That's what *friends* do for each other," he corrected. "Thank you for being my friend tonight, Caitlin."

Maybe he intended the kiss he gave her to be nothing more than a friendly peck on the cheek. His lips were warm when he pressed them against her cool skin, just to the right of her mouth. So close to her mouth that their lips almost, but not quite, touched. And the temptation to turn her head just that small amount was suddenly so strong that she jerked backward as though his touch had burned her.

Stumbling awkwardly, her face flaming, she fumbled for the doorknob. "I'll, uh, see you tomorrow."

He moved out of the way so she could make her escape, though she felt him watching her. She felt like a fool as she all but fell out the front door. She didn't look back when she jumped into her car and drove away, but she had the feeling that Nathan watched her until she was out of his sight.

He was probably wondering what the heck had gotten into her. She wondered about that herself. It had only been a friendly kiss on the cheek, after all.

It had to be the very long, stressful week getting to her, she figured, gripping the steering wheel so tightly her knuckles ached. That, combined with the shock of discovering that her partner had suddenly become a single dad, had made her jumpier than usual. Prone to overreaction.

Maybe she had fantasized a few times in the past nine months about what it might be like to kiss her sexy partner, but that had nothing to do with her reaction tonight.

At least, that was what she told herself as she drove a bit too quickly away from his house.

"Purple's my favorite color, Nate. Can I have a purple bedspread?"

"Poppet, you can have any color bedspread your little heart desires, but if you don't hurry and finish your oatmeal, you won't be ready when Miss Caitlin comes to pick you up."

Isabelle dutifully spooned another bite of oatmeal into her mouth. "Why can't you go shopping with us?" she asked as soon as she had swallowed.

"I told you, there's something I have to do this morning. I'll help you fix up your room this afternoon with all the pretty things you and Miss Caitlin buy, okay?"

She squirmed on her stack of law books. "Okay."

Nathan added "booster seat" to the list he had been writing out while Isabelle ate her breakfast. He was fully aware of the magnitude of the favor Caitlin was doing for him today. He made a mental vow that not only would he never impose on her like this again, he would find some way to repay her.

He wanted to get their relationship back on an even footing. Only then could they evaluate what might develop between them in the future—whether it would ever be more than a business partnership or a casual friendship. Obviously, his own circumstances had changed dramatically.

The catalyst of all that change pushed her oatmeal bowl away and squirmed again on the books. "I'm full now."

He set his pen on the pad. "I guess you'd better get dressed, then."

"I didn't get my bath last night 'cause I was so sleepy. Do I take it now?"

Bath? Nathan cleared his throat. "Uh, can you do that yourself?"

Isabelle looked indignant. "I'm almost four," she reminded him. "I can take a bath."

"I'm glad to hear that."

"But I can't wash my hair."

Oh, man. Reminding himself that he'd known what he was getting himself into when he'd asked Alan Curtis to help him get guardianship of his sister, Nathan nodded. "Okay, you take your bath, then I'll help you wash your hair. We'd better hurry, though. Caitlin will be here in an hour."

"*Miss* Caitlin," she corrected him as she climbed down from her chair.

He chuckled. "Miss Caitlin."

Isabelle wasn't ready when Caitlin arrived. Her hair was still damp and she was dressed only in panties and a purple terry cloth robe.

The bath had taken longer than Nathan expected, and he needed a bit more practice at hair washing before he considered himself proficient at the task. He'd had trouble getting the shampoo out of Isabelle's hair without getting it in her eyes. Since then he had been trying to detangle and dry her fine blond hair.

He groaned when the doorbell chimed.

"That's dry enough," he decided, setting the blow dryer

aside. "Run get dressed while I let Miss Caitlin in. And try to hurry, okay?"

"Okay. I'll hurry." She ran full speed toward her bedroom. They had already selected an outfit for the day. It was lying on the bed, ready for her to pull on. Nathan figured she could dress without his assistance.

"I was beginning to wonder if you were going to open the door," Caitlin said when he finally made it to the living room.

Moving aside to let her in, he smiled wryly. "It may take a few days to develop a morning routine here. Isabelle's almost ready."

"Problems?"

"No. We're just running a little behind."

Isabelle entered the room then, her hair tousled around her face, her feet still bare. She had donned her red and white shirt and navy pants, but she carried her socks and shoes in her hands. "I need a little help."

She was such a bright, articulate child that Nathan tended to forget at times how young she was. She was still little more than a baby, really, and her tiny fingers hadn't quite caught up with her clever mind.

He picked her up and set her into a chair, kneeling in front of her. "Okay, Cinderella, let's see if these slippers fit."

Isabelle giggled. "They aren't slippers. They're sneakers."

"That's okay, honey. He isn't really Prince Charming, either," Caitlin murmured.

Nathan gave her a look over his shoulder. "No comments from the wicked witch, please."

Isabelle laughed again. "There wasn't a wicked witch in Cinderella, Nate. It was a wicked *stepmother.*"

"Oh." He kept his eyes on the tiny foot he was stuffing

into a white cotton sock, and decided not to pursue that particular story line. "Well, what story *was* the wicked witch in?"

"Sleeping Beauty. And Snow White. And the Wizard of Oz. But not Cinderella."

He managed to work her foot into a sneaker. "Wow. That was one busy witch."

"They weren't all the *same* witch, Nate. They were different witches."

"Oh. I see I'm going to have to brush up on my fairy tales."

"I suppose Nathan told you our plans for this morning?" Caitlin asked Isabelle.

The child nodded. "We're going shopping for a room."

That made Caitlin smile. "Not a whole room, exactly. Just the things we need to make your room prettier. Is it okay with you if I take you?"

"Do you like purple?"

"I love purple," Caitlin assured her.

Isabelle dimpled and wiggled her now-shod feet. "Then it's okay."

Caitlin reached down to brush a stray lock of hair from Isabelle's face. "Maybe we should brush your hair first? Do you have a barrette or a ponytail holder we can use to hold it back?"

"I'll be right back." Isabelle turned and ran toward her bedroom.

"She seems to have two speeds," Nathan commented. "Very fast and very slow. She's been in slow speed all morning, which is why her hair isn't done."

Caitlin eyed him quizzically. "You were going to do her hair?"

"I've got to learn how," he said with a shrug. "I figure

it can't be too hard to learn how to do a basic ponytail or braid or something.''

She paused a moment, then asked, ''Have you called your mother yet to tell her you want to talk to her?''

''Not yet. I thought I'd call as soon as you leave. She'll be home. She's always home on Saturday mornings. That's when she does her housework.''

''You can't be looking forward to this.''

Major understatement. He decided to let it pass.

Isabelle returned clutching a hairbrush and a barrette with a red fabric bow attached. Her stuffed white owl was tucked beneath her arm. ''Will this bow work? And can Hedwig come with us?''

Caitlin replied, ''The bow is just right. And is Hedwig your owl's name?''

Isabelle nodded. ''From *Harry Potter*. Aunt Barb read the books to me. And I've seen the movie a bunch of times. It's got a scary part, but I like the owls.''

''You like books, Isabelle?'' Caitlin asked as she carefully brushed the child's silky hair back at the top. Nathan watched closely, hoping he could replicate the style.

Isabelle nodded enthusiastically, making her hair tumble out of Caitlin's hands before she could secure it with the barrette. ''Oh, sorry. I like books. I can read a little.''

''Really?'' Caitlin looked at Nathan for confirmation as she patiently gathered Isabelle's hair again.

He nodded proudly. ''She read two books to me on the airplane. They're for beginning readers, and she knew almost every word in them.''

''Isabelle, that's wonderful. You're a very bright little girl.''

Isabelle smiled with an attempt at modesty. ''My aunt Barb taught me. She likes books, too. When she visits me here, I'll read new stories to her.''

Nathan managed not to wince. Isabelle had readily accepted that she would be living with her brother from now on, but she continued to assume her great-aunt would soon recover from her illness and join them. Nathan hadn't had the heart to tell her differently.

Isabelle knew what death was, of course, having lost her parents. But he saw no need to burden her with the truth about her great-aunt's condition for now.

He hoped waiting was the right choice. He suspected there would be many such dilemmas as she grew older. Someday, for example, she would have to learn the details of her parents' scandalous courtship. And he wanted to be the one to tell her, before some malicious kid taunted her with it.

Caitlin handed him the hairbrush, apparently reading his expression. "Isabelle and I have some shopping to do. And you have something you had better do *soon*."

In some ways, she had subconsciously echoed his line of thought. Timing was often critical—and it was definitely time to talk to his mother, before someone beat him to it. "You're right. I'll—"

His doorbell rang before he could finish the sentence.

"You got company, Nate," Isabelle announced needlessly.

"Must be a delivery or something. I'm not expecting anyone." Motioning for them to hold tight a minute, he moved to the door.

The last person he had expected to find on his front step was his mother.

Chapter Five

From where she stood, Caitlin couldn't immediately see Nathan's caller. But she could tell from the sudden tension in his body that it wasn't a pleasant surprise.

A moment later she understood the problem when she heard him say, "Mom. What are you doing here?"

The voice that responded was tight and chilly. "May I come in?"

Nathan looked over his shoulder, his eyes meeting Caitlin's for a moment before he moved out of the doorway. "Of course. Come in."

Lenore spotted Caitlin as soon as she entered. "Hello, Caitlin. I wasn't expecting to see you here this morning."

"I, um," Caitlin glanced at Nathan for guidance. Standing behind his mother, he shrugged helplessly.

Lenore's gaze had already turned to Isabelle. She froze, her carefully made-up face going pale.

"Hello," Isabelle said with her characteristic friendliness. "Who are you?"

"This is my mother," Nathan said quickly. "Mom, this is—"

"I'm sure I know who she is." Lenore pulled her stunned gaze away from Isabelle's face and turned to her son.

Nathan stuck his hands in his pockets, looking more nervous than Caitlin had ever seen him. "She looks like Deborah did at this age, doesn't she?"

It was entirely the wrong thing for him to say, of course. Caitlin grimaced as the older woman stiffened even further.

"How could you do this?" Lenore asked hoarsely.

"Is Deborah my sister?" Isabelle wanted to know, obviously recognizing the reference from things Nathan had told her.

Caitlin quickly reached out to lay her hand on the little girl's shoulder. "Isabelle and I were just leaving. Nathan, we'll see you later."

"Right." He reached out to lightly pat Isabelle's cheek. "Be good for Miss Caitlin, okay, poppet?"

"I will. See you, Nate. 'Bye, Nate's mom."

Caitlin could see Lenore struggling with a response. She wasn't a cruel woman, but this had to be extremely difficult for her. Finally she nodded and muttered, "Goodbye."

Apparently content with the terse response, Isabelle reached out to take Caitlin's hand. "We're going to get a purple bedspread now."

Caitlin touched Nathan's arm as she passed him on the way out—a subtle gesture of support and encouragement. She hadn't been looking forward to this excursion, but she would rather shop with a busload of preschoolers than be in Nathan's shoes right now.

*   *   *

Caitlin's car was loaded to near bulging by the time she returned to Nathan's house. She and Isabelle hadn't quite bought out the local department store, but they had certainly given it their best shot. Shopping wasn't one of Caitlin's usual passions, and she had never spent more than a few minutes at a time in the company of small children, but she enjoyed the outing more than she had expected.

Maybe it was because this particular small child was different from most.

Caitlin had run into a few people she knew, of course. To avoid any problems, she had introduced Isabelle simply as her "young friend," without mentioning Nathan's name. The truth would get out soon enough. She only hoped Isabelle wouldn't have to suffer because of it.

To give Nathan plenty of time, they'd had lunch out. Caitlin believed children should be exposed to good food and nice surroundings early, so she eschewed the usual fast-food places and selected one of her favorite tearooms, instead.

Proving that the previous adults in Isabelle's life had subscribed to Caitlin's philosophy, Isabelle displayed very nice manners as she and Caitlin dined on soup and sandwiches. Sitting in a booster seat provided by the restaurant, a snowy napkin draped over her lap, Isabelle thoroughly charmed the staff and the other diners with her contagious smiles and precocious conversation.

"She reminds me of Shirley Temple," an older woman at an adjoining table informed Caitlin. "Those big blue eyes and sweet little dimples—and the way she behaves. So poised and polite for a child her age."

Uncertain how to respond—since she, of course, had had nothing to do with Isabelle's manners—Caitlin smiled and murmured something inaudible.

She drove straight back to Nathan's house after they finished the ice cream they had ordered for dessert. Surely enough time had passed that it would be safe to go back, she reasoned.

Excited about the prospect of decorating her room, Isabelle practically bounced in the safety seat Caitlin had borrowed from Nathan. The little girl babbled a mile a minute. Fortunately the only responses required were a few nods and murmurs. Caitlin was becoming increasingly distracted by her concern about what had transpired between Nathan and his mother.

"Is Nate's mom still here?" Isabelle asked as Caitlin parked in the driveway.

"No, her car's gone," Caitlin replied with some relief.

"She was sad."

The quiet comment surprised Caitlin. It was the first time Isabelle had mentioned Lenore since they'd left earlier. She had assumed the child had already forgotten the brief encounter. "What makes you think that?"

"Her eyes were sad. I think she was nice, though."

"She can be very nice," Caitlin agreed, though she didn't want to say much more. She didn't know if Isabelle would ever even see Lenore again. "Let's get Nathan to help us carry all this stuff in."

"We got a bunch of stuff," Isabelle commented happily, looking at all the packages piled around her—not to mention the ones squeezed into the trunk, Caitlin thought.

"Yes, we do." Reminding herself that Nathan had encouraged her to buy whatever Isabelle wanted, she helped the child out of the car and held her hand as they walked to the front door.

Though Nathan was smiling when he opened the door, the expression in his eyes made Caitlin's breath lodge painfully in her chest.

"Well?" he asked. "Do I have any money left?"

''Nathan—''

He cut off her concerned question with a quick, ''Later.'' And then he focused on Isabelle. ''So, did you find anything you like?''

The child immediately launched into a breathless monologue, listing not only everything they had purchased that morning, but also nearly everything else they'd seen. Responding with apparent fascination, Nathan helped them carry in boxes and packages, hauling everything straight to Isabelle's room.

He teased about the amount of purchases they had made, laughed when Isabelle said something funny, asked questions and made appropriate comments, but Caitlin sensed that a part of him had simply shut down. His smile was as bright and charming as ever, but a light had gone out in his eyes. She had heard that phrase before, but she'd never quite understood what it meant until now. Nathan's usually gleaming blue eyes were dark, and their expression was heartbreakingly empty.

Darn it, she hadn't wanted to get this deeply involved in her partner's personal problems. But looking at Nathan now, she knew she couldn't pull back without trying to encourage him.

The best way to help now seemed to be with manual labor and upbeat conversation. Within a couple of hours, Nathan's bland guest room had been transformed into a lovely setting for a little girl. The bed was covered with a lavender-and-white gingham comforter over lavender sheets and a white eyelet dust ruffle that just brushed the floor. Throw pillows in gingham, solid lavender and white eyelet rested invitingly against the headboard. White eyelet panels hung at the windows, and the beige ginger jar lamp had been exchanged for a white china lamp hand-painted with clusters of violets.

The built-in bookshelves now held books, toys and Isabelle's collection of Disney figurines. Colorful framed posters depicting several of those same characters replaced the dull landscapes on the walls.

On the mirrored dresser sat a pretty little white-painted jewelry box and a purple glass music box—items Isabelle had seen on display at the store and had fallen in love with. Caitlin had bought them for her, charging those purchases to her own card, rather than Nathan's. Her lecture about not spoiling the child had hovered at the back of her mind, but she hadn't been able to resist when she'd seen how longingly Isabelle gazed at the music box that played ''When You Wish Upon a Star.''

A purple fabric-covered butterfly chair was tucked into one corner of the room, an inviting place to curl up and read or listen to the purple-cased radio/CD player that now rested on the nearby chest of drawers. That had been one of the items on Nathan's list of recommended purchases. A music lover, himself, he probably wanted to share the pleasure with Isabelle. The rest of her belongings were neatly stowed in the room's good-size closet.

''It's beautiful,'' Isabelle breathed when they declared the room finished. Clutching her stuffed owl, she stood in the center of the room, turning in circles to admire every inch of her living quarters. ''It's perfect.''

''It does look nice,'' Nathan agreed. He smiled at Caitlin. ''You did a great job.''

She replied self-deprecatingly. ''Most of this was displayed together as a grouping. Isabelle and I just pointed, charged and had it bagged.''

''I picked out the posters,'' Isabelle said, motioning to each as she named the subject. ''Belle, Ariel, Jasmine and Mulan. There were a lot more at the poster store—I almost got Pocahontas and Esmerelda—but I liked these four the best.''

''These are perfect,'' Nathan assured her. ''I really like Jasmine,'' he added, indicating a fiery-haired mermaid.

Isabelle rolled her eyes. ''That's not Jasmine, that's Ariel.''

''Oh.'' He grinned at Caitlin. ''Nice clam shells.''

Caitlin cleared her throat loudly. ''Isabelle, are you thirsty? Would you like some fruit juice?''

''No, thank you.'' The child was still obviously entranced with her room. She wandered over to the bookshelf to make a minute adjustment of a figurine—one of the stars of *The Lion King,* Caitlin believed, though she was hardly an expert on modern-era Disney characters.

''Tell you what.'' Nathan tugged lightly at Isabelle's hair. ''Miss Caitlin and I are going to have some coffee in the kitchen while you finish admiring your room. If you're tired, you and Hedwig can climb up on the bed and see if those pillows are as comfortable as they look.''

''I'm not tired,'' Isabelle assured him, quickly stifling the yawn that had escaped while he'd spoken. ''But Hedwig might be.''

''Then I'm sure he would appreciate a little rest. Owls like to nap during the daytime, you know.''

Isabelle had already kicked off her shoes and was climbing onto the bed when Caitlin followed Nathan out of the room.

Nathan urged Caitlin to sit at the kitchen table while he made the coffee. He didn't meet her eyes as he measured coffee into the basket, added water, then pulled out mugs, creamer and sugar while the coffee brewed. He talked the whole time, but he kept the conversation focused on Isabelle.

"She seemed to really enjoy the outing," he added, using a paper towel to wipe a countertop that was already spotless. "And the lunch—did some woman really say she looked like Shirley Temple?"

"Yes. Nathan—"

He opened a cabinet door and rummaged inside. "Do you want some cookies or something? We have chocolate chip and animal crackers."

"I remember. But, no, I don't need any cookies, thank you. Isabelle and I had ice cream for dessert. What—"

"Coffee's ready. Just cream in yours, right?"

"Right. Are you ready to talk yet?"

His hands went still for a moment, his back very stiff and straight. And then he finished pouring coffee into the mugs. "Almost."

She waited, sitting quietly as he placed one steaming mug in front of her and then took the seat opposite her, his own mug clasped loosely between his hands. He seemed to have no interest in actually drinking the beverage.

Caitlin sipped her own only to give her something to do while he decided what he wanted—or needed—to tell her. She was sure the coffee tasted fine, but Nathan's stark expression kept her from enjoying it.

He sighed. "My talk with my mother didn't go well."

"I gathered that already."

There was another pause before he spoke again. "She told me I've broken her heart, and she isn't sure she can ever forgive me."

"You're her son, Nathan. She loves you."

"I know. But right now she doesn't ever want to see me again."

Caitlin's fingers tightened spasmodically around her mug. "She said that?"

"Words to that effect."

"She didn't mean it. She's hurt. And worried about what everyone will say when word gets out that you've brought your father's child home with you. I'm sure she's embarrassed about having the old gossip crop up again."

"I understand all of that, and I told her so. I even tried to apologize for causing her pain, even though I really felt I had no choice. She didn't want to hear anything I had to say."

"Pain has a way of shutting down hearing. You've dealt with enough ugly divorces to understand that."

Staring into his mug, Nathan nodded. "My head understands that. But my heart thinks I deserve better than to be thrown out of her life for doing no more than taking in a little girl who had nowhere else to go."

"I didn't say your mother was being fair. I said her reaction isn't completely unexpected."

"I'd hoped when she saw Isabelle—how sweet and vulnerable she is—maybe my mother could forget..."

"When she looked at Isabelle, she saw your father. And her own past, if Isabelle looks as much like Deborah as you said. I'm sure it was a shock to her. But still she managed not to say anything hurtful in front of Isabelle."

"No. She said she didn't wish any ill to the child, but she doesn't want to have anything to do with her. She doesn't want Isabelle in her home, and she doesn't want to visit me in mine as long as Isabelle is here."

"And what did *you* say?"

The hesitation was a bit longer this time. "I tried to be patient. I had made a promise to myself that I wouldn't lose my temper or say anything I would regret later. I was just going to let her say whatever she needed to say and hope she would come around eventually."

"But...?"

He sighed again. "I'm not very good at holding my tongue. I sort of lost my temper."

Caitlin groaned. "Oh, Nathan. What did you say?"

His expression turned defensive. "I reminded her that she was just given a fancy award for her work with children's charities, and I thought it was the height of hypocrisy for her to be willing to throw this child out in the streets because she's a social embarrassment. I said anyone who would blame an innocent little girl for events that happened before she was born had a heart of stone. And I might have said something along the lines that she was letting *me* down by not standing behind me when I most need my family's support."

He'd had a right to speak his mind, of course, but perhaps it would have been better if Nathan had stuck to his original plan of letting his mother do all the talking during that first encounter. Still, he didn't seem to have said anything that was ultimately unforgivable. "Give it time. Maybe she will come around."

He scowled. "Maybe right now I don't care if she does or not."

"You don't mean that."

"At the moment I do. But I'll get over it. I just don't know if she will."

Because he seemed to need the reassurance, Caitlin reached out to touch his hand where it lay so lifelessly on the table. "You knew this was a possibility, Nathan. You said you were prepared to face it for Isabelle's sake."

"I am," he assured her. "I still believe Isabelle needs me more than my mother does. I'll have to be content to be a family of two from now on."

"No regrets about the decision you made?"

Nathan glanced toward the doorway in the direction of Isabelle's room. "You saw how happy she looked in there.

She's already had her life turned upside down twice in the past year. The only reason she's adjusting so well this time is because she already knew me and had a good relationship with me. Do you think she would have settled in so easily with strangers?''

Caitlin thought Isabelle was extremely resilient, but she couldn't say with any certainty that she would have happily adjusted to a family she didn't know. Isabelle adored Nathan, and she had talked about him constantly during their outing.

Nathan was Isabelle's anchor, now that fate had cast her adrift again. And Caitlin was slowly coming to believe that his courageous and self-sacrificing decision to bring her into his home had been the only real choice he'd had. Caitlin had only spent a few hours with the child and already she knew that deliberately walking away from Isabelle would be difficult.

Caitlin could hardly expect Lenore to welcome Isabelle with open arms, but Lenore should know her son well enough to understand that he'd done what he felt he had to do. Was it so easy for Lenore to turn her back on her own son when Nathan had been unable to do so with his half sister?

"Maybe she will come around in time," she repeated lamely. "In the meantime…"

"In the meantime, I have my own life. A life that includes Isabelle now."

Caitlin nodded and started to remove her hand from his. Before she could pull away, he covered her hand with his free one. "You've been really great today. I don't know what I would have done without you."

Something in his voice raised her mental warning flags. And maybe the way he was looking at her, with a new warmth in his eyes that ignited an answering spark in her.

A spark she fully intended to douse before it blazed out of control.

It wasn't that hard to figure out what was going on here. Nathan was feeling overwhelmed and cut off from the support of his family. She was the one person who was on his side in this conflict. They had to be very careful about mistaking gratitude and desperation for something more… personal.

"There's no need to thank me again," she said lightly, trying to pull her hand away. "I enjoyed the day, actually. It was nice to get away from work for a few hours."

His fingers tightened on hers. His hand was as warm as his gaze, and she felt the spark inside her flare dangerously.

She had worked out the reasoning behind his behavior, but how was she supposed to explain her own? If there was one thing she did *not* need, it was a messy involvement with her business partner. Especially now, when his own emotions were so precarious, his life so complicated.

She had always known that work and personal lives should be kept separate. And she had a policy of not dating men with children—not that she had dated much in the past few years, she had to admit. She'd been too busy, too focused on her education and career, too wary of having anyone else intrude on her plans. But when she had dated, she had carefully avoided single fathers.

Nathan was now the equivalent of a single father, as well as her business partner, so…

She gave a firm tug at her hand, pulling it into her lap. "I should probably go now."

The way he looked at her let her know that her expression had revealed at least some of what she was thinking— and a touch of panic, perhaps. He kept his next comment business related, probably in an attempt to calm her. "You were going to catch me up on what happened at the office while I was gone.''

She had already stood to carry her mug to the sink. ''We can talk about work later.''

''You said there were several things you needed to discuss with me.''

Keeping her eyes on the mug she was rinsing, she replied, ''Nothing that won't keep. I'll probably spend the rest of the weekend doing research, so you probably won't hear from me. If you need me, call, okay? You have my numbers.''

''Caitlin.''

He had moved so quietly she hadn't realized he'd risen from the table. His voice came from directly behind her.

She nearly jumped out of her shoes.

Laughing softly, he placed his hands on her shoulders. ''Sorry, I didn't mean to startle you.''

She stared blindly out the window over the sink. She didn't really see the tiny backyard with its big shady trees; her attention was entirely focused on the man who stood so close behind her that she could feel his warmth against her back.

''Caitlin,'' he murmured again, the laughter gone from his voice now.

She turned her head very slowly, looking at him over her shoulder. Their eyes locked, and the heat between them flared so high she felt her cheeks flame in response. It was an instinctive, primal reaction—one that overpowered the logical, cautionary lectures she had just given herself. At this moment she was having trouble remembering why she shouldn't give in to the urge to kiss him, when it was something she'd been wanting to do for some time now. And when it was so very obvious that he wanted to kiss her, too—no matter what his reasons.

Would one kiss be so bad, she wondered even as his mouth moved toward hers—if only to satisfy their curiosity? She could already feel her lips tingling in anticipation of that first moment of contact.....

''Nate? I got thirsty.''

The sound of Isabelle's voice from the doorway caused Nathan to jump back as if he'd been caught attempting something illegal. His sudden release of Caitlin's shoulders made her sway and clutch at the sink for support.

Nathan's voice seemed about half an octave higher than usual when he said, ''You want a drink, poppet? Sure, no problem. What would you like?''

Though she looked a bit puzzled by his behavior, Isabelle merely opened the refrigerator door and pointed to the apple juice.

If a neon sign had suddenly appeared on the ceiling, Caitlin couldn't have gotten the message more clearly about why they *shouldn't* give in to their curiosity. All the reasons she had listed earlier were still valid; putting them out of her mind did not make them go away.

''I'd better leave,'' she said, moving toward the door. ''I have a lot of work to do this weekend.''

Nathan didn't try to detain her this time.

''Tell Miss Caitlin thank you for taking you shopping and helping us decorate,'' he said to Isabelle.

Caught off guard by Isabelle's response, Caitlin nearly had the breath knocked out of her when the child locked her arms around Caitlin's waist. ''Thank you, Miss Caitlin.''

Looking down at the top of the little girl's golden head, Caitlin swallowed an unexpected lump in her throat. Getting *way* too involved here, she chided herself even as she wrapped her arms around Isabelle's shoulders. She needed to escape soon and then spend the rest of the weekend settling back into her own routines, leaving Nathan and Isabelle to establish their own.

While she sympathized with how alone Nathan must be feeling right now, he had gone into this with his eyes open. It wasn't up to her to help him figure out how to live with the choice he had made. She didn't want to be callous, but she had her own problems.

"You're welcome, Isabelle," she murmured. "I'll see you later, okay?"

She made her break while Nathan was busy pouring juice for Isabelle. A bit cowardly, perhaps, but it seemed like the best idea at the time.

The sooner she was out of there, the sooner she could get back to her own carefully planned life.

Because throwing herself into her work had always been her way of escaping difficult personal problems, Caitlin drove to her office in the restored old house Nathan had purchased when he had gone into business for himself. No one else was there on a Saturday afternoon, of course. There would be no one to interfere with her concentration. For the rest of the day, she was thinking about nothing but business.

She had just managed to put Nathan and Isabelle to the back of her mind and immerse herself in medical malpractice research when she heard a woman's voice coming from the waiting room. "Caitlin? Are you here?"

She almost groaned out loud. She'd been so preoccupied when she'd entered earlier that she must have forgotten to lock the door behind her. Great security. She stood and smoothed her hands down the casual blouse and slacks she had worn for her day of shopping and work.

"I'm here," she said, moving toward the doorway.

To Caitlin's shock, Lenore McCloud stood in the center of the empty waiting room.

This time it was all Caitlin could do to keep the groan from escaping. It seemed that she hadn't evaded Nathan's personal problems, after all. One of them had followed her here.

Because surprise had rendered Caitlin momentarily speechless, Lenore spoke first. "I saw your car in the parking lot when I drove past. I hope I didn't frighten you when I called out."

"No, I was just a bit startled, since I wasn't expecting anyone. Um, is there something I can do for you, Mrs. McCloud?"

As immaculate as always in a leopard-print silk blouse and trim brown slacks, not a hair out of place, Lenore looked at Caitlin with a taut expression. "I think you know what I want to talk to you about."

As much as she would have liked to tell Lenore that she did not want to get involved, Caitlin said, instead, "Why don't you have a seat, Mrs. McCloud? Would you like a cup of coffee? I made a fresh pot when I got here a little while ago."

Lenore declined the coffee, but she did take a seat on one of the waiting room couches, perching stiffly on the very edge. Caitlin settled into a nearby chair. "You're upset that Nathan has taken responsibility for his little sister," she said to get the conversation started.

The word *sister* made Lenore's features tighten even more, if possible. Caitlin had chosen the word deliberately as a subtle way of stressing the blood bond that had influenced Nathan's decision. "I am more than 'upset.' I'm devastated that my son is ruining his life."

Ruining *his* life—or hers? Caitlin wondered cynically.

All she said was, "I don't think the situation is quite that drastic."

"Of course it's drastic! Nathan is only thirty-one, and he should be concentrating on his own future. He has this firm to consider. It's just getting solidly established and gaining respect in legal circles. I credit you in great part for that, of course."

"Thank you, but—"

"And it isn't only his career he's putting at risk. What will this do to his social life? He shouldn't have to worry about baby-sitters and day care and the other responsibilities and expenses of raising a child. And when he is interested in starting a family of his own, what kind of effect will this have? What woman would want to become involved with a man who is solely responsible for raising a small child, especially when that child was at the center of a statewide scandal?"

Caitlin cleared her throat. She certainly didn't want to become embroiled in a conversation about Nathan's love life—present *or* future! "I know Nathan has given a great deal of thought to all of these issues—"

"Nathan doesn't give a great deal of thought to anything," Lenore cut in bitterly. "He's impulsive and reckless—just like his father. He makes these grand gestures, and then he expects other people to bail him out. Just like when he started this firm. Several people tried to convince him he wasn't ready to strike out on his own, that he should work for another firm for a few years and gain experience and maturity, but he wouldn't listen. Then, as soon as the workload here became too demanding, he brought you in and dumped much of the responsibility on you."

"That's hardly an accurate description of our partnership," Caitlin felt obliged to protest. "Nathan pulls his weight and then some. He certainly does things in his own creative manner, but he's a brilliant attorney. He couldn't have made the firm so successful in such a short time if he weren't. He's the personality of the firm. I'm the organizer and detail person. It's a fair distribution of our talents.''

Her eyes almost feverish, Lenore leaned forward a bit further on the couch, making Caitlin worry that the older woman would tip onto the floor. ''Nathan listens to you, Caitlin. He respects you. He won't listen to my advice about this because he thinks I can't be objective—and maybe he's right. But you're an uninvolved party. If you talk to him, tell him what a mistake he's making—''

This time it was Caitlin who interrupted. ''I *have* spoken to him, Mrs. McCloud. Nathan has made his decision. He isn't going to change his mind because of anything I say—or anyone else, for that matter.''

Lenore shook her head. ''You can convince him that it's in the child's best interest to find another family for her. Nathan's not qualified. He isn't prepared. He doesn't understand everything that's involved in raising a child to adulthood. Especially on his own, with no one to help him...''

''You can help him.''

The quiet comment made Lenore recoil. ''No. I can't.''

''I understand how difficult this is for you, but Nathan needs you, Mrs. McCloud. Granted, you and I may not completely understand the commitment he has made, but you have to admit that his reasons were actually quite noble. He has a kind and generous heart, which he probably inherited from you, since your charity work is so well-known, especially on the behalf of local children.''

''That isn't going to work,'' Lenore announced sternly. ''It's true that I'm not a vicious woman, but it's simply too much to expect me to help my son spend the rest of his life paying for his father's selfish mistakes. I won't do it.''

"She really is a sweet little girl."

"You aren't going to help me, are you?"

Caitlin twisted her hands in her lap. "I can't agree to try to talk Nathan into giving Isabelle away. Whatever hesitations you have—or even that I might have—I believe he's more aware of the ramifications of his decision than you seem to think. He might have acted impulsively, but it wasn't blindly. He loves his little sister, and he's going to do what he thinks is best for her."

"And when you find yourself running this business entirely by yourself because Nathan's personal life is too hectic?"

Caitlin almost winced. Lenore had come too close to describing the past week. "I'm sure Nathan will learn to juggle work and child raising. Single parents do it all the time."

"My son is *not* a single parent!" Lenore stood abruptly. "It's obvious that you're on Nathan's side—"

"I'm not on *anyone's* side," Caitlin objected. "I am simply not getting involved in your family dispute."

"So you say. Just don't tell anyone I didn't warn you about the trouble headed your way."

"Mrs. McCloud—"

But the older woman had already reached the door. She let herself out with a slam that was somehow still dignified.

Caitlin clenched her hands in her hair and let the growl that had been building inside her escape on a frustrated exhale.

Just what had Nathan gotten them *both* into?

Chapter Six

Late that night Nathan stood beside Isabelle's bed, gazing down at the tiny figure burrowed into the blankets. Her golden hair spilled over the pillows, and her breathing was slow and even. Hedwig the owl kept wide-eyed vigil at her side.

There was a certain satisfaction in standing there watching her sleep, confident that she was safe, well-fed, warm and content. He couldn't imagine what it would be like to be sitting alone in his house tonight, not even knowing where his little sister was or who was watching out for her.

He still clearly remembered the first time he had seen Isabelle. It had been on his first, awkward visit with Stuart and Kimberly in California, three months after Isabelle's birth.

Stuart had tried to stay in touch with his other offspring, but Nathan was the only one who had taken his calls. Nathan had made that trip to San Diego thinking it would be

a one-time visit, an opportunity to sit down with his father
and talk frankly about the devastation Stuart had left behind
within his first family. And maybe to seek a little advice
about how Nathan, as the eldest son, should deal with those
repercussions.

He had known even then that some people might find it
odd that he'd sought counsel from the very man who had
caused the problems in the first place, but Nathan had always valued his father's opinions. Stuart's betrayal had
shaken Nathan's faith but hadn't erased all the memories
of those earlier, happier years.

Nathan had figured he and his father both deserved one
last face-to-face confrontation, even though his siblings
hadn't agreed. Gideon wouldn't even discuss the trip, and
Deborah had angrily announced that she had no interest in
anything Stuart had to say about his actions. Prickly and
apprehensive, Nathan had arrived on his father's doorstep.
Fifteen minutes later he'd been sitting in Stuart and Kimberly's sunny living room with baby Isabelle on his lap.
She had gazed up at him with wide-eyed fascination and a
dimpled, toothless smile. He had become a big brother
again, as devoted to this baby sibling as he was to Gideon
and Deborah. He could no more disclaim Isabelle than he
could the brother and sister with whom he'd been raised.

It had been mostly because of Isabelle that he had traveled to California several more times after that first visit.
He had grown fonder of his little sister, and he'd rebuilt a
relationship of sorts with his father—admittedly not the
same as before, but still a bond of blood and shared experiences. He'd even come to like Kimberly and to accept
the fact that Stuart was happier with her and Isabelle than
Nathan had seen him in years in Mississippi.

And then it had all ended in a fiery helicopter crash in
Mexico.

Nathan had grieved deeply for his father—a grieving made more painful by the fact that he hadn't been able to share this pain with those he loved best. His mother hadn't been able to discuss her late husband's death. Gideon had become even more withdrawn and remote than before, and Deborah had retreated both physically and emotionally from her family, keeping her feelings locked behind a barrier of hurt and anger.

Oddly enough, it had been Caitlin who had been most available to Nathan during that initial shock of grief. She had been his partner only a few months at that time, but she'd sensed his need to talk about his father, and she'd proven to be a good listener. He'd been careful not to take too much advantage of her sympathy, but the couple of times he had unloaded on her, he had always felt considerably better.

And now he had turned to her again. And once again, she had been there for him when no one else was. It was becoming as hard for him to imagine his life without Caitlin as it was to picture himself giving his little sister to strangers.

He just wished he knew how Caitlin felt about him. There was something about the way she had looked at him when he'd almost kissed her earlier that had made him believe she wanted to kiss him, too. It hadn't been the first time he'd sensed that the attraction he felt for her was mutual.

Had Isabelle not entered the kitchen when she did, Nathan would have finally satisfied his curiosity about what it would be like to kiss his pretty, gray-eyed partner. He strongly suspected that first taste would have only whetted his appetite for more.

He wondered now why he had waited so long to work up the nerve to make his move. He should have asked her out weeks ago. Now, before he could even take her to dinner, he would have to learn how one went about hiring a dependable baby-sitter.

Leaning over to brush a kiss over the top of Isabelle's silky head, he reminded himself that he didn't regret bringing the child home with him. But he was certainly aware of how much more complicated his life had become.

Caitlin wasn't sure what to expect when she arrived at the office Monday morning. She hadn't seen Nathan Sunday, though she had spoken with him on the phone a couple of times when he'd called with business-related questions. He told her he had stayed home all day trying to wade through the stacks of memos and messages that had piled up during his week-long absence, and he needed clarification about a few things.

Caitlin had asked about Isabelle during the first call, of course. Nathan told her the child was fine, playing happily in her room with the few favorite toys she had brought with her from California. Because she had spent so much of her short life in the company of adults, she was used to entertaining herself.

The second time he called Caitlin, several hours later, he'd sounded a bit more frazzled. As well behaved as Isabelle was, she was still a young child whose life had been uprooted too many times. She had become a bit fretful and clingy as the day advanced, wanting to make sure she had Nathan's attention—perhaps subconsciously needing reassurance that this home would be a permanent one.

Caitlin had answered his business questions, then couldn't resist asking, "Do you need any assistance there? I could come help you entertain her for a little while....."

Nathan had politely but firmly declined the offer. "You've done enough this weekend. I'm sure you have things you need to do, and I have to learn to deal with these problems on my own, anyway.''

Even though she agreed with that sentiment, she'd felt a bit guilty after hanging up. Silly, really. There was no reason at all why she should feel responsible for Isabelle *or* Nathan.

Her arms filled with the work she'd carried home for the weekend, she entered the McCloud and Briley Law Offices Monday morning not sure whether Nathan would even be there. She'd forgotten to ask him whether he'd arranged for day care, but she doubted he'd been able to set up anything that quickly.

Mandy, the latest in a line of receptionists who had come and gone just in the nine months Caitlin had been partner, looked up from her desk with a perky smile when Caitlin walked in. ''Good morning, Ms. Briley. I made coffee.''

It was with some effort that Caitlin returned the smile. Mandy made hands-down the *worst* coffee Caitlin had ever tasted. She couldn't imagine how Mandy managed that feat, since they bought the coffee premeasured in filter packs that only required adding a specified amount of water, but somehow when Mandy touched the coffeemaker the results were always unfortunate.

But since it was difficult to find good help for an entry-level job at an entry-level salary, and since Mandy had other assets—punctuality being one of them—Caitlin couldn't complain about the coffee. ''Any calls for me yet?''

The offices didn't officially open for another ten minutes, so she wasn't really surprised when the receptionist shook her head. ''Not yet. But I'm sure there will be a flood of calls starting at eight.''

''No doubt.'' When Caitlin was not in court or meeting

with clients, she was usually on the phone. "Has Nathan called in?"

"Not since I got here." Mandy leaned forward and lowered her voice conspiratorially. "Is it true Mr. McCloud just found out he's a father? I heard that little girl who was with him Friday is his daughter."

Caitlin couldn't help staring at the younger woman. She was both amazed and dismayed that the gossip mill was already churning out wild fabrications, only days after Nathan returned from San Diego.

Before she could speak, Irene's chilly voice came from the doorway that led back to the offices. "Mr. McCloud has become the guardian of his young half sister, who was recently orphaned. And I'm sure he would appreciate it if his employees refrained from gossiping about him—at work or away."

Her usually rosy cheeks going pale, Mandy snapped straight upright in her seat. "I didn't say anything bad about him. I was just repeating what I heard."

"Please don't repeat whatever you might hear in the future."

"Yes, ma'am." Mandy looked greatly relieved when the telephone buzzed, giving her a chance to snatch up the receiver and escape into her duties. "Good morning, McCloud and Briley Law Offices."

Without waiting to find out who was calling, Caitlin headed for her office. Irene stayed at her heels, carrying a thick file. "I have all the information for your first appointment this morning. He's scheduled to arrive at eight-thirty."

Caitlin unloaded her own heavy burden on her desk. "Thank you. Um, did Nathan explain the situation to you about his sister?"

"I'm afraid my information came through gossip, as

well," Irene admitted a bit sheepishly. "Mr. McCloud's aunt is in my Sunday school class. She said she had seen him at the grocery store with the child and very quickly figured out who Isabelle was."

Betty must have called Lenore almost immediately after she'd put the facts together, Caitlin realized, thinking of the expression on Lenore's face when she had first seen Isabelle. It hadn't been at all kind of Betty to break the news to Lenore before Nathan had a chance to talk to his mother. Nor to talk about Nathan's personal life to the ladies of her Sunday school class.

"Was my information incorrect?" Irene asked with an uncharacteristic touch of uncertainty.

"No, you heard correctly. Nathan has taken his little sister as his ward."

"Perhaps I shouldn't have corrected Mandy's misconception? Maybe it would have been better if I had chided her for discussing her employer without telling her the real story."

Realizing that Irene must be misinterpreting her frown as disapproval, Caitlin smoothed her expression and said, "No, Mandy and the others should know the facts. Nathan certainly isn't trying to hide his new relationship with his sister. It all happened so quickly that he hasn't really had time to discuss the situation with anyone."

"So this will be a permanent arrangement?"

"Yes, it will. And I'm sure it will require some adjustment on all our parts until he settles into a routine—just as it did last week."

Irene looked as though she would have loved to further discuss the developments in Nathan's life, but innate professionalism made her keep her questions and comments to herself, other than to say, "I'm sure we'll all do our best."

"Of course. Now, the most pressing matters we need to address this morning are…"

"Having a staff meeting without me?" Nathan asked as he strolled through the door, looking like the model of a rising young executive in his sharply tailored dark suit, his dark-blond hair neatly brushed away from his smiling face. Tagging behind him was a tiny blond sprite wearing a vividly colored plaid jumper and carrying a bulging purple backpack.

Nathan winked at Caitlin, then greeted the office manager more formally before saying, "Isabelle's going to be hanging out with us today. I figure she can spread out her stuff in the break room while I'm with clients. She brought coloring books and crayons and toys to keep her entertained. I don't have to be in court today, so I'll be able to keep a pretty close eye on her."

"And what about tomorrow?" Caitlin asked. "You are scheduled to be in court in the morning."

Nathan glanced at Isabelle. "I haven't quite—"

"Perhaps I should show Isabelle to the break room," Irene suggested. "I believe there's some fresh orange juice in the fridge," she added. "There's also a TV, if you would like to watch *Nickelodeon*."

Isabelle looked questioningly at Nathan, who nodded reassuringly. "Go with Mrs. Mitchell, poppet. I need to talk to Miss Caitlin for a minute. I'll be right here if you need me, okay?"

"You won't leave?" she asked, looking at him anxiously.

"I promise I won't leave," he said, holding up his right hand in a vow. "Miss Caitlin will tie me to her desk if I try."

"I'll even sit on him, if necessary," Caitlin agreed, making Isabelle smile.

Caitlin's own smile lasted only until Irene and Isabelle were out of sight. "Well?" she asked then, "what are you going to do tomorrow?"

"I'm not sure," he admitted. "I'll only be in court tomorrow morning. I suppose Mandy or Loretta could keep an eye on her until I get back. It's not as if she's much trouble, after all."

"Nathan, you can't bring a little girl to a law office every day. Even if she didn't interfere with business, it isn't a good environment for her. What do you expect her to do, color and watch television all day?"

"Okay, I know I have to make other arrangements for her."

Caitlin reached for the local telephone directory. "You should call some day care centers."

Nathan shifted his feet on the tasteful carpeting. "Day care?"

"Unless you know someone who's available for private child care?"

"No," he conceded.

"Actually, you should find a good preschool program. Isabelle needs to be mentally challenged. After all, she's already starting to read. She's obviously incredibly bright for her age."

"Preschool?" Nathan looked intrigued. "Sounds better than day care."

"Definitely something to consider. Look in the yellow pages. You've got a little while before your first appointment. Mine's going to be here in just a few minutes."

"Oh. That was a hint for me to leave, right?"

Caitlin had already opened her client's file. "You're so clever."

"I'll just go to my office to make some calls."

"Good idea. See you later." She kept her eyes on the

file until he'd closed the door behind him. And then she sat for several long moments gazing after him and remembering the way he had winked at her when he'd entered. Not to mention the shivery little feeling that wink had caused to ripple through her. And then she frowned, shook her head and reprimanded herself for letting thoughts of Nathan interfere with her concentration. Again.

Caitlin had made one good friend outside of work since she'd moved to Honesty nine months ago. A neighbor in her apartment complex, Lindsey Newman was a sales representative for a local manufacturer, and she traveled quite a bit. She and Caitlin tried to get together when Lindsey was in town. There weren't that many single women their age in Honesty, and Caitlin enjoyed spending time with Lindsey.

They met early Monday evening at their favorite restaurant. Without stopping to change, Caitlin drove there straight from the office. Her dark-red hair gleaming in the indirect lighting of the popular, but low-key restaurant, Lindsey greeted Caitlin with a broad smile that pushed shallow dimples into her fair cheeks. "Hey, stranger."

Setting her purse on the floor beside her chair, Caitlin returned the smile warmly. "It has been a while since we've managed to get together, hasn't it? To be honest, this is the first night in ages that I've had a chance to just relax a bit—even though I have a huge pile of paperwork to go through when I get home."

"I still say you're a hopeless workaholic."

"Says the woman who just spent nearly a month on the road selling fishing lures to every little sporting goods store between here and Austin."

Lindsey chuckled. "What can I say? Apparently fishing is the hottest hobby going right now. Retailers are practically lining up for FlashPopper Lures, and I need to be there to fill the demand if I'm going to bank enough commission money to take that European vacation I've always wanted to take.''

"So *who's* the workaholic?''

"Ah.'' Lindsey held up a finger. "But the difference is that I'm working with the specific goal of taking a long, leisurely vacation. You, on the other hand, are working for the express purpose of attracting more work.''

"When I figure out what you just said, I'm sure I'll have a snappy comeback.'' Caitlin ordered a glass of white wine and a shrimp cocktail from their flirtatious young waiter, then waited while Lindsey selected wine and shrimp toast for her appetizer. "How was your trip?'' she asked when they were free to chat again.

Lindsey wrinkled her nose. "Let's just say there aren't a lot of hot spots in places like Bald Knob, Arkansas— although I did find a very nice Cajun restaurant there.''

They talked a few more minutes about the off-the-beaten-path places where Lindsey marketed her wares, and then their appetizers arrived. Caitlin had just dipped a fat shrimp into the spicy sauce when Lindsey asked, "So what's this I hear about your sexy partner adopting a little girl?''

Caitlin dropped the shrimp. Fortunately, it landed on the dish rather than on her lap. She recovered it carefully. "Where on earth did you hear that? You've only been back in town since last night.''

"Are you kidding? Everyone's talking about it. I went to the health club for a workout this afternoon, and two of the aerobics instructors were talking about him at the juice bar. One of them used to date him, apparently. Or wanted to date him, I'm not sure which. Anyway, word has gotten out that he's adopted a little girl. Some people think she's his illegitimate daughter. Most believe she's the child his father had with that campaign worker a few years ago.''

''That's the correct version. She's his half sister, Isabelle. He hasn't adopted her yet, but he is her legal guardian now.''

''I know Stuart McCloud and his wife died in that terrible accident earlier this year, but I thought the mother's family had taken in the child.''

''Her maternal great-aunt took her, but she's gravely ill now and can't take care of Isabelle anymore. There wasn't anyone else to take her. It was either Nathan or the state of California.''

''Poor little girl. She's had a tough time of it, hasn't she?''

''Very. She's young enough that she doesn't entirely understand all of it, of course, but it has still been difficult for her.''

''How's Nathan's family taking it? The word through the grapevine is that his mother freaked out.''

Caitlin grimaced as she flashed back to that uncomfortable conversation with Nathan's mother. ''She isn't exactly pleased with him.''

''I bet. I remember very clearly what it was like around here when that scandal broke. It was a media circus, and poor Mrs. McCloud was humiliated.''

''I heard all about the debacle, of course. I had actually planned to vote for Stuart McCloud for governor.''

''You and another 52 percent of the voters polled before the affair with the young campaign worker and the resulting pregnancy hit the news. He probably would have been elected.''

''Very likely.'' Caitlin ate another shrimp, savoring the taste even as she concentrated on the conversation.

''So…?'' Lindsey prompted.

''So what?''

"So how's Nathan working out as a daddy?"

Caitlin's neck muscles tightened. "He's a very good big brother."

"It's certainly going to change his social life. The aerobics instructor has completely lost interest in dating him, even though she thinks it's sort of sexy that he's raising a little girl. But she admits to being the high-maintenance type who wouldn't want to share his attention. And, anyway, she doesn't do runny noses."

Caitlin curled her lip. "How honest of her to admit her shallowness."

Lindsey sipped her wine, then asked over the rim, "How do *you* feel about runny noses?"

"What's *that* supposed to mean?"

Lindsey waited until the waiter had replaced the appetizers with their main courses before explaining. "I was just wondering if Nathan's responsibility for his little sister makes him any less attractive to you."

Caitlin stabbed her fork into her entree. "Don't start that again."

"You're going to deny it again?" Smiling smugly, Lindsey took a bite of her salmon.

Caitlin set her fork down with a thump. "How many times do I have to tell you that Nathan is my business partner and nothing more? I don't think of him the way you're implying. I never have."

Lindsey rolled her eyes. "Oh, sure. You spend eight hours a day with a guy who's certifiably drop-dead gorgeous, and I'm supposed to believe you've never even noticed? And then I suppose you have some land you want to sell me?"

Feeling a bit grumpy now, Caitlin picked up her fork again. "Well, obviously, he's a good-looking man. I'm not blind."

Lindsey made a show of wiping her brow. "I'm glad

you admitted that. I was beginning to worry about your eyesight.''

"Still, my relationship with Nathan is strictly professional.''

"Hmm. I heard you were spotted grocery shopping with him and his little girl.''

Caitlin's fork hit the plate again. "Where did you hear *that*?''

"Oh, around.''

Shaking her head in disbelief, Caitlin murmured, "This is unbelievable.''

"Frankly, that's what I thought. I know you're not all that fond of shopping. At least that's what I always believed. And then I heard you spent most of Saturday picking out sheets and curtains.''

"Is there no privacy in this town?''

"I had to stop by the cleaners on the way home from the health club. Mrs. Albertson, who owns the cleaners, was shopping in the same department store as you were on Saturday. She was very intrigued that you were taking care of Nathan's little sister that morning. Mrs. Albertson thinks Nathan's going to be looking for a wife to help him raise that little girl. And she thinks you two make a lovely couple.''

"I'm losing my appetite.''

"Sorry. Just thought you would want to know what's being said around town.''

It was probably the reason her friend was such a successful sales rep, Caitlin mused. Lindsey could walk into a roomful of strangers and know everyone's story within the first fifteen minutes. She was the sort of person other people simply enjoyed talking to.

Caitlin usually did, too—until tonight, when the subject was a bit too close to home.

"I'm not romantically involved with Nathan McCloud,''

she said distinctively, keeping her voice low so she wouldn't be overheard. "We're simply business partners. And friends, of course, in a casual way."

Lindsey smiled in surrender. "Okay, I know there's nothing really going on. Even though I think you're crazy not to make a move on the guy. If I'd thought I had half a chance with him I'd have gone after him, myself, a long time ago."

Caitlin found the mental picture of Lindsey and Nathan together unexpectedly disturbing. It was only because she didn't think they would make a very good match personalitywise, she assured herself, though she couldn't think of any specific reason why they wouldn't get along.

She tried to keep those thoughts hidden when she said, "So, why didn't you?"

"Well, he did flirt with me," Lindsey acknowledged. "But no more than he does any other woman within range of his lethal smile."

Lethal was an apt description of Nathan's smile, Caitlin mused, especially when he turned on the high voltage. She was no more immune to it than any other woman, though she prided herself on keeping her reactions well suppressed. Most of the time, at least.

"Besides," Lindsey continued, peering at Caitlin through her lashes as she toyed with what was left of her dinner. "Seemed to me the only woman Nathan's really interested in is his business partner."

"You're delusional."

"Actually, I've often been described as very perceptive and insightful," her friend responded cheerily. "And there's definitely *something* there between the two of you— as I think I've mentioned before."

It was true that Lindsey often teased Caitlin about her sexy business partner. So why was Caitlin feeling more self-conscious and defensive this time? Deciding to prove that she could give as good as she got, she said, "I still say that if you're so taken with him, you should do something about it."

Lindsey sighed with apparent regret. "Too late now. Back when it was just him, I might have been tempted. *Was* tempted, actually. But now that there's a kid involved…"

"You mean you're no longer interested in him because he's become responsible for Isabelle?" Surely she had misunderstood.

But Lindsey nodded. "Maybe it makes me as shallow as the aerobics instructor, but I can't see myself getting involved with a man with a little girl. Way too much pressure involved in that situation for my comfort."

Caitlin couldn't imagine why she was suddenly feeling rather indignant on Nathan's behalf. Women who had once practically thrown themselves at his feet were suddenly scratching him off their eligible-bachelor lists. After all, didn't she have her own rule about single fathers? And hadn't she been cautioning herself about not getting too involved with Nathan and Isabelle?

But it was different with her, she tried to reassure herself. She hadn't pursued him *before* he had Isabelle, either.

Lindsey seemed to sense that it was time to change the subject. "Tell me some more funny stories about your new office manager."

That new conversational gambit and its offshoots took them through dessert. Though Caitlin was greatly relieved that they had changed the topic, Nathan and Isabelle remained at the back of her mind. One particular remark kept echoing through her thoughts—the one Lindsey had repeated about Nathan being on the lookout for a wife who could help him raise his little sister.

It was a prophecy Caitlin couldn't seem to shake, no matter how hard she tried to dismiss it as idle gossip.

Chapter Seven

Nathan had Isabelle with him again when he showed up at the office late Tuesday morning. Studying the uncharacteristic shadows beneath his eyes and the lines around his mouth, Caitlin pulled him into the file room to ask, "What's wrong? I thought you were going to find somewhere to take Isabelle during working hours."

His answer came out in a growl. "I called around. There are two excellent preschools in this town. Both of them depend on my mother for fund-raising and enlisting volunteer pools."

"You don't mean…"

He nodded grimly. "When the administrators found out who Isabelle was, they suddenly discovered there were no openings."

"That's appalling."

"That's unacceptable." Irene stood in the doorway of the file room, her steely eyes glinting, her crimson hair seeming to flame with ire. "I'm sorry, Mr. McCloud, but I couldn't help overhearing. Did I understand you to say that two preschools turned down your application because they didn't want to risk offending your mother?"

Nathan cleared his throat, as intimidated as always by Irene, especially when faced with her temper. "That's exactly what happened."

She tapped one orthopedically clad foot on the carpet, her mouth set in a grim line. "Which school was your first choice?"

"I've heard Miss Thelma's is the best. But—"

She turned with military precision. "I'll take care of it. In the meantime, you need to get ready for your court appearance this morning. Your sister will be fine here until you get back. Mandy and Loretta can take turns watching her."

"Thanks, but…"

His voice faded when he realized he was talking to an empty doorway. The look he gave Caitlin then was almost comical. "You really think—"

"I think Isabelle will be enrolled in preschool before lunchtime," Caitlin said, amused despite the gravity of the situation.

"If anyone can do it, it will be Irene." He rubbed the back of his neck. "I just hope if Isabelle does get in, she'll be treated the same as the other kids."

"She will be," Caitlin predicted. "For one thing, they won't be able to help falling for her once they spend time with her. And you *are* an attorney. They're well aware that you could file a lawsuit if there's any hint Isabelle is mistreated. And, finally, they might be a little worried about annoying your mother now, but they're *really* not going to risk making Irene mad again."

"You have a point there," Nathan conceded with a weak semblance of his usual smile.

"I can't help noticing that you look tired this morning. Are you okay?"

"I was up most of the night preparing for my case today," he admitted. "I was a week behind, of course. And by the time I'd made dinner last night and cleaned up the kitchen and washed a couple of loads of clothes and given Isabelle her bath and read her bedtime stories, it was already sort of late. Then between work and worry about getting her into a quality day care program, I managed only a couple of hours sleep."

She thought of all the single working mothers who had to deal with those very burdens, often unappreciated. And then she thought of the women who were no longer interested in Nathan precisely because of the chores he had just listed. And of the woman who had predicted that he would soon be looking for someone to share those chores with him.

"You need a housekeeper," she blurted in sudden inspiration.

"A housekeeper?" he repeated, his hand going still at his neck.

"Of course. Someone to do the cooking and laundry and housework. You've managed to get by with once-a-week cleaning help until now, but with Isabelle there, you need daily help. If you're really lucky, you'll find someone who can do double duty as a baby-sitter when necessary. It won't be cheap, of course, but I'm sure it will be worth it."

"You know, that's a good idea. As soon as I have time, I'll place an ad or call a housekeepers' agency or something."

"I'll handle that for you, Mr. McCloud," Irene said as

she entered with his briefcase. "I have several connections with housekeeping services. Sorry for eavesdropping again," she added perfunctorily. "Now you really must leave or you'll be late for court. And I've placed a call to Miss Thelma. I'm expecting her to call me back shortly. I intend to let her know exactly what I think of the way she treated you, especially you being a lawyer and all."

Caitlin watched as Nathan's hand fell to his side. "You, um—"

Irene shook a finger at him. "You really must go, Mr. McCloud. You know how irritated Judge Coleman gets when anyone causes a delay in his schedule. Don't worry about a thing here. I'll take care of everything."

Caitlin smiled when Nathan looked rather helplessly in her direction, and then she made shooing motions with her hands. "What are you standing there for? Go, go."

Looking more than a little bemused, he went.

Irene shook her head after Nathan had departed. "Imagine a woman deserting her son in his time of need, regardless of the circumstances," she muttered. "I'm not usually one to get involved in the personal lives of my employers—"

"Of course not," Caitlin murmured, watching the indignant office manager in fascination.

"But if we're going to keep this office running smoothly, it's obvious that I'm going to have to give him a hand with getting his routines in order, both here and at home."

"I'm sure Nathan appreciates your help," Caitlin assured her, suppressing a smile at the memory of Nathan's dazed expression when he'd left. "Do you really think you can find him a housekeeper?"

"Oh, yes. As a matter of fact, I believe my sister, Fayrene Tuckerman, would be interested in the position. She retired from housekeeping a few years back, but she's been at loose ends ever since her husband died last year. She's very organized and efficient, and she's quite fond of children, so this could be just the opportunity she's been looking for. I'll call her and ask if she's interested.''

''Your *sister?* Um, Irene, maybe—''

But the woman was already gone, intent on her mission of having everything in her universe back under control. If getting Nathan's home life organized meant that the office routines would go smoothly again, then she considered it her duty to see to it.

Things were getting more interesting around here all the time. But Caitlin, like Irene, was becoming rather anxious for a normal routine.

Nathan was rapidly losing control of his life. Ever since he had received that telephone call from his father's attorney, he had been on a roller coaster of changes and emotions, and he felt as if someone else was guiding the ride.

By the time he returned from court Tuesday afternoon, after spending several frustrating hours in front of a judge who had never liked him and a jury that seemed to be completely uninterested in anything except getting out of the courtroom as quickly as possible, he was wiped out. He arrived at his office to find that not only was Isabelle enrolled in a preschool program, but he was now the employer of a full-time housekeeper. Irene Mitchell's sister, no less.

''Please tell me she was pulling my leg,'' he said to Caitlin as he stood in her office, his back pressed against her closed door. ''Please tell me she hasn't hired her sister as my housekeeper.''

Caitlin closed the divorce file she'd been studying and looked at him sympathetically. ''I tried to convince her to wait until you returned. She said she saw no need to waste time. She said you could hire her sister on a temporary basis, and if it didn't work out you could find someone else."

"Right. Like I'm going to have the nerve to fire her sister. Especially if the woman is anything like Irene."

"Actually, I believe *you're* the one on probation," she murmured with a glint of mischief in her eyes. "If Fayrene Tuckerman doesn't like you, she's free to leave your employ."

He raised both arms in a gesture of sheer frustration. "What made Irene think she has the authority to hire a housekeeper for me?"

"She heard you say you didn't have time to interview anyone yourself just now. She considers it her job to assist you by handling tasks you don't have time to tackle. Irene is a very efficient office manager."

"This isn't going to work. You have to do something."

Her eyebrows rose. She tapped one hand on her desk, a sign that she was becoming annoyed. "*I* have to do something?"

"Exactly. You're the one who got me into this."

"And how, exactly, do you figure that?"

"You hired Irene in the first place."

"Of all the—" She slapped both hands on her desk and stood. "All I've done is try to help you while still keeping this firm afloat. *You're* the one who has brought the personal complications into the office."

He grimaced, knowing she was right. If there was one person who was blameless in all of this, it was Caitlin, who had gone out of her way to help him. He moved closer to her, his tone apologetic when he said, "You're right. I'm sorry."

Only slightly appeased, she sniffed. "You *should* apologize. I hired Irene because you weren't there to help me interview the applicants. I still think she's a great office manager. Okay, she's a little overenthusiastic about it, but she means well. She's simply trying to help.''

"You're right. I'm being a jerk. But still…"

"I understand you're uncomfortable with the present situation. But you have to admit Irene's sister is probably a superior housekeeper."

"That's exactly what I'm afraid of. I'll probably be afraid to move in my own house. I'll leave footprints on the carpet or something."

"I doubt it will be that bad."

He wished she sounded a bit more confident. "Will you meet her with me?"

"You're a big boy, Nathan. There's really no need for—"

"I need you," he cut in. He'd intended to say the words lightly, but they came out a bit more seriously than he'd planned. He cleared his throat. "I would really appreciate it if you would be there when I meet her for the first time— just for moral support."

After a moment she sighed. "All right. When?"

"Irene said her sister would be at my house at six this evening."

"Fine. I have a meeting with a client tonight, but it's not until eight. That should leave plenty of time for me to hold your hand while you meet your new housekeeper."

Though he knew she was being sarcastic, Nathan liked the idea of her holding his hand. He contented himself with leaning over to give her a quick kiss on the cheek. He was delighted when the gesture made her blush to the roots of her hair. "Thank you."

She stepped away from him so quickly she bumped hard into the corner of her desk. "You're welcome. Shouldn't you go check on Isabelle?"

"Last time I looked she was sound asleep in the break room."

"Then you'd better go see if she's still sleeping. I have a couple dozen calls to make in the next few minutes."

"Right. I'll let you get to it, then." Relishing the lingering taste of her soft skin on his lips, he let himself out of her office.

Caitlin felt as though her cheek still tingled when she parked in front of Nathan's house that evening. And then she told herself she was being ridiculous. Of *course* her cheek wasn't still tingling just because Nathan had given her a friendly peck of gratitude. If she didn't get these silly fancies out of her mind, she was going to make herself crazy.

She didn't know what was wrong with her lately, but she was more than ready to get back to the way things had been a couple of weeks ago, when she and Nathan had been nothing more than business partners who kept their hands—and their lips—to themselves. Along with their personal problems.

So what was she doing coming to his house this evening to help him interview his new housekeeper?

Apparently she had arrived before Fayrene Tuckerman. But it was only a quarter to six. If Fayrene really was like her sister, she would arrive promptly on the hour.

Nathan opened the door when she rang the bell. He had changed out of the suit he'd worn for work and into a pair of snug-fitting jeans and a soft-looking, butter-yellow pullover. She noted immediately that the color was perfect for his lightly tanned skin and sandy hair and that the fabric looked invitingly touchable.

Strictly an observation, of course.

It wasn't that she actually *wanted* to run her hands up

the front of that lovely soft shirt or to slide her fingers into his thick, gold-streaked hair, she assured herself, knowing even then that she lied. Still, she could think about how nice it would be without actually doing anything about it.

"Thanks again for coming tonight," he said, ushering her inside and closing the door behind her. "Isabelle's in the den, watching cartoons. She just finished her dinner. Can I get you anything? Coffee? Iced tea? Soda?"

"No, thank you." It annoyed her that her words came out a bit too primly. She was trying too hard to keep this encounter polite and impersonal. She cleared her throat and attempted to speak more casually. "Have you made a list of questions for Mrs. Tuckerman?"

"Sort of a mental list." He cocked his head as he studied her, still standing in the entryway. "I've never seen that dress on you. Is it new?"

Her automatic response was to smooth her hand down the skirt of the green knit dress she had worn for her meeting. Since when had Nathan been interested in her wardrobe? He'd never seemed to notice such things before, other than his habitual observations about how nice she looked— something he said to nearly everyone every morning. Casual compliments were a staple part of Nathan's conversations, as automatic for him as breathing.

"Yes, it's new."

"It looks really good. The color makes your eyes shine. Have I ever mentioned that you have really beautiful eyes?"

Okay, *way* too personal. That was the kind of remark that made her go sort of shivery inside, which was definitely not the way to stay detached this evening. She dragged her gaze away from his face and glanced in the direction of the den. "Isabelle's watching TV? I'll go say hello to her."

"Why does it make you so uncomfortable when I compliment you? Do you think I don't notice how pretty you are?"

That brought her attention back to him. "Now how am I supposed to answer that?"

"It was a fairly straightforward question, I think." He reached out to toy with a strand of her hair, studying it as if he were trying to memorize the color and texture, though she sensed his attention was fully focused on her reactions to the questions he was asking. "Every time I try to tell you that I find you attractive, you get all gruff and flustered. Is it because you don't know if I'm serious or because you aren't interested in hearing it?"

"I think it would be better not to talk about attraction at all," she said, and this time her tone was downright schoolmarmish.

"Why?"

She smothered a sigh. Did he have to make everything so difficult? "Because it could get sticky. We're business partners. Colleagues."

"Friends," he added.

"Friends," she conceded. "But that's all."

His fingers slid into her hair at the back of her neck. His face was very close now, his eyes boring so deeply into hers that she imagined he could see every wayward thought she was trying so hard to hide. "Not quite all," he murmured.

Before she could move away, his mouth was on hers. And then she *couldn't* move away.

She wanted to believe it was shock holding her immobile and not the fact that she had been wanting this kiss for so long. She wanted to believe it, but she knew better. She was perfectly capable of moving away, but, oh, heavens, she didn't want to.

His mouth moved coaxingly on hers. His lips were warm and firm and skillful. Exactly as she had fantasized—and feared—his kiss would be. As she had feared even more, she knew their relationship would never be quite the same from this point on.

That same realization was in Nathan's eyes when he drew back. Maybe a hint of the same what-have-we-done alarm.

The chime of the doorbell made them both almost jump out of their shoes.

"That must be the housekeeper," Nathan said, his voice husky.

"You let her in. I'll, uh, go check on Isabelle."

Caitlin almost bolted from the entryway. There was no way she could meet Irene Mitchell's sister without first splashing some cold water on her face.

Maybe it was because his brain was still rattled from kissing Caitlin that Nathan wasn't as sharp-witted as usual when he saw the woman standing on his doorstep. "Irene?" he said blankly. "What are you—"

"Irene is my twin sister," the thin-faced, flame-haired woman replied crisply. "I'm Fayrene Tuckerman. I assume you're Nathan McCloud?"

"Yes, I—"

She stepped past him, holding her handbag in front of her, and looked around the entryway in assessment. "Lovely house. Shouldn't be too difficult to keep it up."

"Well, it's—"

"The kitchen is this way, I presume?"

He shouldn't have been surprised that she guessed correctly on the first try. "Yes, it's—"

She was already moving, leaving him no choice but to follow behind her.

"Mrs. Tuckerman—"

"You may call me Fayrene. Ah. Nice kitchen. Good appliances. Efficient positioning. We'll want to move the coffeemaker and toaster over to this counter, of course, and I'm sure the cabinets and drawers could be rearranged, but it's very workable. Where are the washer and dryer?"

"Through that door. Can I—"

Because she had poked her head into the laundry room, her voice was a bit muffled when she overrode him again. "I'll need a brighter light in here. And a surface for pretreating stains and folding laundry. A small table should fit nicely into that corner. Please see to that quickly. With a small child, stains are a constant battle."

"Yes, I've noticed she—"

Fayrene closed the laundry room door and turned to face him. "I live only fifteen minutes from here, so I should have no problem being here by six forty-five each morning to prepare breakfast for you and the little girl. Is that early enough?"

"Plenty early. I—"

"I'll have dinner ready by six, and I'll leave shortly after that unless you have plans and need me to stay later to watch the child. I'm available most evenings except Sundays and Wednesdays, when I attend church services. And every third Tuesday evening of each month, my bridge club meets, so you'll need to make other arrangements if you have plans. If six is too early for you to eat, I'll prepare the meals and leave them in the refrigerator so you'll only have to warm the food when you're ready. I expect my duties to include cleaning, laundry, cooking and childcare, but I don't do yard work or exterior windows."

"I wouldn't expect you to—"

"My sister said the little girl starts preschool tomorrow. When does she need to be dropped off and picked up?"

"The program starts at 8:00 a.m. and ends at 2:00 p.m. After that, there's a day care program until early evening for the students with working parents."

"I'll pick her up at two. No need for her to stay later if the remainder of the afternoon is merely day care. I can do errands as necessary while I'm out, such as picking up the cleaning. I'll need a safety seat for my car, of course. I assume she still uses one."

"Yes, at her age and weight she's still required to ride in a safety seat."

"Very wise. I'm appalled at the number of people who allow children to ride in a vehicle completely unrestrained. Aren't they aware that those precious little bodies are thrown like missiles in accidents? And as far as the excuse that their children don't like being restrained—poppycock. Parents are supposed to be adults, not playmates. I don't believe in taking any risks when it comes to a child's safety."

Okay, he liked that philosophy. He wanted to know that Isabelle would be watched over by someone who made her safety a top priority. "I completely agree. But—"

"I really should meet the child now, don't you think? She needs to get comfortable with me before I pick her up at Miss Thelma's tomorrow afternoon. I assume you'll be taking her there on her first morning of school?"

"Yes. I'm sure there will be some paperwork they'll want me to fill out."

Because he had become so accustomed to having her interrupt him, he was almost surprised when she allowed him to complete that comment. And then, when she still didn't speak, he realized she was waiting for him to follow through on her suggestion—or had it been a command?— that he take her to meet Isabelle.

He motioned toward the doorway, trying to regain at

least a semblance of control over this bizarre interview. "Isabelle's in the den with my business partner. Shall we?"

She nodded and swept through the doorway.

Caitlin and Isabelle were seated cozily on the big leather sofa in the den, watching a cartoon on television. Isabelle had apparently been educating Caitlin about the names of all the characters on the animated series. Nathan had heard her chattering as he'd approached the room.

Caitlin looked up when Nathan and Fayrene entered. Her expression when she spotted the woman looked very much the way his own must have earlier.

Before she could make the same embarrassing mistake he had made, he spoke quickly, "Caitlin Briley, this is Irene Mitchell's twin sister, Fayrene Tuckerman."

Caitlin stood to greet the woman. "It's very nice to meet you. I didn't realize you and Irene were twins."

Fayrene nodded, but her attention was already focused on Isabelle. Her rather stern face softened with a smile warmer than Nathan had ever seen from her sister. "You must be Isabelle."

Isabelle blinked. "You're Ms. Mitchell's sister?"

"Yes, her twin sister. That's why we look alike."

Isabelle cocked her head. "You don't look *exactly* alike," she decided. "Your smile is different."

Nathan decided he had better intercede before the conversation turned too personal. "Isabelle, Mrs. Tuckerman is going to come help us out around here. She'll pick you up at preschool tomorrow and stay with you until I get home from work."

"You won't mind that, will you, Isabelle?" Fayrene smiled confidently. "We'll have a very nice time."

Isabelle glanced at Nathan. "You'll come home after work?"

She still needed a great deal of reassurance that he

wouldn't be leaving her, he realized. He tried to give her that security with his smile. "Of course I'll come home, poppet. I'll be anxious to hear all about your first day at preschool."

She nodded and looked back at Fayrene. "Okay. What's your name again?"

"The last family I worked for thought it was amusing to call me Mrs. T. You may do the same, if you like."

Definitely not like her sister, Nathan realized then. Although identical in appearance and equally intimidating at first impression, they were quite different in other ways. And while he was still wary about taking yet another new person into his life and his home, he was becoming convinced that he couldn't have found a more qualified housekeeper. Now that Isabelle had given her seal of approval, it seemed they were all set.

Caitlin seemed to come to the same conclusion. "It was very nice to meet you, Mrs. Tuckerman."

"Mrs. T.," Isabelle whispered loudly, tugging at Caitlin's dress.

Caitlin smiled before adding, "I really should be going now. I have a meeting tonight."

Nathan took a step toward her. "I'll walk you out."

She didn't meet his eyes when she said, "That's not necessary."

"Certainly you should walk her out," Fayrene said to Nathan. "Isabelle and I will get to know each other. Do you like hot cocoa, Isabelle?"

The little girl nodded eagerly. "Especially with marshmallows."

"Then come with me to the kitchen and we'll see what we can find. While I make the cocoa, you can tell me how you feel about going to school tomorrow."

Isabelle willingly skipped out of the room at Fayrene's

side, already beginning to chatter. Nathan and Caitlin were left standing in awkward silence, he trying to read her expression and she seemingly intent on keeping him from doing so.

The memory of the kiss they had shared hung almost palpably in the air between them.

Chapter Eight

Caitlin had every intention of making her escape as quickly as possible. She needed to do a great deal of thinking—away from Nathan.

"There's really no need for you to walk me out," she said. "You wanted me to meet Mrs. Tuckerman and I did. I heartily approve of her, by the way. You're lucky she was available."

Ignoring her less-than-subtle hint, he moved to the doorway, where he paused and motioned for her to precede him. Short of dashing past him and trying to outrun him to her car, there didn't seem to be any way to avoid having him walk her out. Holding her head high, she swept past him, keeping her gaze focused ahead.

Nathan stayed close behind her, his voice low when he said, "Can you believe how much she looks like Irene? Gave me a shock when I answered the door."

"I felt the same way when you and she walked into the den. I had no idea Irene had an identical twin sister."

"They even dye their hair the same color. Wonder whose idea that was?"

"Who knows?" She started to reach for the front door-knob, but Nathan beat her to it, opening the door with a chivalrous flourish.

Hearing the door close behind them, she felt an urge to babble as she strode down the landscaped walkway toward her car. "It's starting to get cooler at night, isn't it? And beginning in a couple of weeks, when we turn our clocks back an hour, it will be dark almost by the time we close our office. Hard to believe it's almost winter already."

She was fully aware that she sounded like an idiot, but Nathan politely refrained from treating her like one. "This month *is* passing quickly," he agreed. "Probably because so much has been going on. So many big changes."

His words made her rather wistful. Things had been so much easier a month ago. Back before Nathan had brought Isabelle home and had pulled Caitlin into his life because there had been no one else to turn to.

Before he had kissed her.

She tried to keep her attention focused on the conversation she had started, banal though it may be. "Guess you'll be going trick-or-treating in a couple of weeks?"

He chuckled. "I always do that, anyway," he boasted, though she didn't believe him. And then his amusement faded. "It's the holidays after Halloween that concern me."

She nodded somberly, thinking of how difficult those holidays would be for him if he was still estranged from his family, which certainly seemed likely at this point. She was sure he had always considered Thanksgiving and Christmas as times to spend with his mother and siblings. She was just as sure that he would not spend those celebrations with them now if Isabelle wasn't welcome to join them.

Because she simply didn't know what to say about his family dilemma, she decided to let his comment pass. She pulled her car keys from the outside pocket of her black leather purse. "I'll be in court in the morning, so it will probably be tomorrow afternoon when I see you. I hope Isabelle's first day at preschool goes well."

"I'm sure she'll do fine. She's a pretty remarkable kid."

"Yes, she is. I haven't spent much time with children, but I can tell that your little sister is very special."

"Thank you." He seemed genuinely pleased by her words, as proud, she thought, as any new father. "I think so, too."

She pushed the button that automatically unlocked her car and opened the door. "Well, I'll see you tomorrow. Good night."

"I would like to kiss you again."

The quiet words made her cling to her car door for support. "Please don't say that."

Nathan took a step closer to her, his voice just loud enough to reach her ears. "Not saying it doesn't make it any less true."

Shaking her head, she pressed against the car as if instinctively trying to put as much physical distance between herself and Nathan as possible. Her heart was pounding again now, as swiftly as it had been before, when he'd stunned her with that unexpected kiss.

"You're just overwhelmed by everything that has happened in the past week. You're feeling cut off from your family and grateful because I've tried to help you."

"It isn't gratitude, even though I *am* appreciative of all you've done. I felt this way before Alan Curtis called. I just hadn't gotten around to doing anything about it yet, though I certainly intended to.''

"I really wish you wouldn't. It's too...complicated.''

"Would you have reacted differently before Isabelle moved in with me?''

Thinking of the women who *would* back off because of his new circumstances, she shook her head. "This has nothing to do with Isabelle. I don't believe in office dalliances. They're risky and awkward and ultimately messy. It's best to avoid those complications whenever possible.''

"I'm not talking about an 'office dalliance,'" he replied, obviously taking exception to the term she had chosen. "Yes, I'm physically attracted to you, but it's more than that. I care about you.''

Sheer panic made her heart jump and then start pounding even harder. At least she assumed it was panic and not anything more dangerous. "Let's...not talk about this now. As you said, there's a lot going on in your life and at work now. It's the wrong time to start something else.''

"So we should just pretend nothing happened? Go back to being nothing more than business partners?''

"We are nothing more than business partners," she muttered in exasperation. "And I, for one, would like to get back to business!''

"Damn, you have beautiful eyes," he mused, gazing at her meltingly.

Groaning, she jerked the car door open. "I have a meeting to attend. And after that I have a good four hours of research to do on the medical malpractice case, which we still haven't had time to discuss yet.''

"I'll discuss it anytime you like. How about here at my place after your meeting tonight?''

She frowned, refusing to be swayed by his wicked smile. "We'll discuss it at the office. Now that your personal life is in order, there's no reason we can't get back to having our business discussions in the conference room.''

''I'll count the minutes until I see you again.''

She didn't know what had suddenly put him in this cheerful, teasing mood, but she didn't trust it for a minute. ''Stop that,'' she snapped. ''I'm not falling for your notorious charms, so there's no need to waste them on me.''

''Thank you,'' he said with mock gravity. ''I find you charming, too.''

A low growl escaped her. Before she completely lost what little composure she had left, she slid into her car and shut the door with a loud snap. Nathan stepped back, his thumbs hooked in his jeans pockets, and watched her drive away with what, in her rearview mirror, looked suspiciously like a smug grin.

It seemed each passing day of the next week made Nathan more aware of how different his life had become.

Though Mrs. T. worked miracles on the home front, taking the load of cooking, laundry and housework off his shoulders, he still made a point to spend as much time as possible with Isabelle in the evenings. He listened to her stories about school, heard about the new friends she was making there and admired the colorful artwork and carefully drawn alphabet sheets she brought home every day.

Each night he read her a bedtime story and tucked her into bed. Every morning he woke her with tickles and kisses so that she began each new day with a smile. Even without the extra chores, his life away from the office revolved around Isabelle.

His mother and sister were barely speaking to him. His brother didn't seem to be particularly angry with him, but had further distanced himself, saying simply that he didn't want to get involved. Nathan's friends thought he had lost his mind.

"You're really going to try to raise a kid by yourself?" his most-frequent fishing buddy, Jim Horner, had asked incredulously. "Dude, are you nuts?"

"So what would you have done?" Nathan asked over the gas pump where they had met by accident. "Put your own little sister out into the streets?"

His friend, an unmarried firefighter with notoriously reckless courage and a heart as big as his oversized four-by-four truck, was taken aback by that question. "I don't know," he said finally. "But I sure wouldn't have had the guts to bring her home with me. What is she—five? Six?"

"She's three. Almost four."

Jim practically shuddered. "Man, she's just a baby."

"Pretty much."

"So do you have someone to help you with her? Like a nanny or something?"

"I've hired a housekeeper who helps with child care during the day, but not a full-time nanny. I don't need that right now."

"What about your free time? You still going to be able to go play golf anytime you want? Or head to the coast for a long fishing weekend? Or drive down to N'Awlins for a long party weekend?"

"Obviously not." Nathan replaced the gas nozzle on the pump and twisted the gas cap back into place. "I can still take the occasional afternoon or Saturday morning for a golf game, but I'll need to set it up in advance now so I'll have time to arrange for a baby-sitter."

Jim digested that information in apparent dismay. "Man."

Nathan shrugged. "Things change, pal. Guess it's time for me to grow up and settle down."

Jim laid a heavy hand on Nathan's shoulder and gave him an exaggerated soulful look. "Dude, you're a better man than I am."

"Knock it off," Nathan had growled in exasperation. "I did what any big brother would do—you included, whether you admit it or not."

"So you say. Give me a call someday when you've got a baby-sitter, okay? We'll go play a few holes—see if being a daddy has made you soft."

The other pals Nathan encountered during that week reacted in similar ways, all of them expressing their shock at his new circumstances. Even the guys he knew who were married with children of their own seemed stunned by his actions, saying they couldn't picture him as a single parent, especially of such a young child.

As for his women friends...

It was true he hadn't dated much lately. Specifically since he'd started looking at Caitlin through different eyes several months ago. But he was still rather surprised by the way women reacted to his new responsibilities. It seemed the single ones fell into two camps: those who wanted nothing to do with a man raising a child and those who made it clear that they would be delighted to audition for the position of stepguardian.

The latter group seemed to believe the commitment he had made to his half sister signaled that he was ready to embrace the joys of marriage and fatherhood. He didn't know how he felt about those things at this point, but he was damned sure he wasn't interested in sampling them with the few women who so eagerly offered their services.

Married women seemed intent on offering him parenting advice—some of it conflicting. That was mostly what he encountered when he dropped Isabelle off at preschool each morning. Everything from critiques of her wardrobe and

hairstyles to questions about whether he was making sure
she ate right and brushed her teeth regularly.

He didn't particularly appreciate being treated like an
idiot, but he always managed to answer politely—so far, at
least—because he didn't want to jeopardize Isabelle's still-
precarious standing in the exclusive preschool. He could
only hope that it would eventually become apparent that he
was managing to take care of her well enough on his own.

The older residents in town were far less supportive.
They were the ones who had felt most betrayed by their
local political hero's scandalous behavior four years ago.
The ones who had encouraged the longtime community
leader to run for governor. Who had contributed to his campaign funds and worked tirelessly in his headquarters. The
ones who knew and respected Lenore McCloud and sympathized deeply with the humiliation she had suffered at
her profligate husband's hands.

Those people thought Nathan had been cold and unfeel-
ing to bring the offspring of his father's affair into the same
town where poor, dear Lenore was still living and volunteering so selflessly.

A few of his older acquaintances suggested that he
should have found a nice family somewhere else—prefer-
ably in California—and paid them a generous monthly sti-
pend to raise Isabelle. That would have been much wiser,
they assured him sternly. He had tersely informed them that
he did not regret his choice, would not consider changing
his mind and that he hoped they—and his mother—would
eventually come to terms with his decision and accept Isabelle for the special child she was. All in all, it was an
exhausting week.

And then there was Caitlin.

If he had suddenly developed a highly contagious disease, she wouldn't have avoided him more diligently than

she had since he had kissed her. Yes, she was very busy at work—as was he—but she could have made a few extra minutes for some personal time with him. She didn't. Aside from asking about Isabelle every day, she treated him like a co-worker who was little more than a stranger to her away from the office.

She was beginning to tick him off.

Every time her behavior made him question whether she had been honest about not being personally interested in him, he had only to mentally replay their kiss for reassurance. She was interested, all right. She just didn't want to be. He had his work cut out for him.

Helping her with her complicated medical malpractice case seemed to be the most immediate way to stay actively involved in her daily routines. They met at least once daily to discuss their cases, and that one seemed to be growing more complex with each passing hour.

"Dr. Ripley's attorneys are really starting to rub me the wrong way," Caitlin muttered on Wednesday afternoon, a week and a day after The Kiss. "They treat me as though I have no idea what I'm doing."

"I've dealt with these guys before, a couple of years ago when I first started out." Sitting beside her at the paper-littered conference table, Nathan tossed a condescending letter aside. "They treat everyone that way."

"They're so obnoxiously confident that we'll decide to fold. That we'll be so intimidated by their reputation and resources that we'll be afraid to take them on in court."

"They have good reason to expect so," Nathan said with a shrug. "Few small firms *have* been successful in challenging them. Face it, Caitlin, we don't have the same resources. You should know how expensive and time-consuming a medical malpractice case can become, especially against a physician as wealthy and as aggressively represented as Ripley.''

''Are you saying I shouldn't have taken the case? You know we're in the right here, Nathan. And you know none of the bigger firms would even talk to poor Mr. Smith.''

''For the very reasons I just mentioned. It's too tough a case. The outcome is too unpredictable, and the commitment too long-term when you consider all the inevitable maneuvers and appeals.''

''Assuming they don't agree to a decent settlement before it gets to court.''

He tapped the letter she and her client had found so offensive. ''They've offered a settlement, remember?''

He fully expected her reaction—a disdainful sniff accompanied by that temperamental flash of silver in her eyes. ''It's not only unacceptable, it's insulting. Mrs. Smith *died.*''

''Which she might well have done, even if Ripley hadn't misdiagnosed her. Her cancer was already well advanced.''

Even though she knew it was his job to point out all the counterarguments, her eyes still flashed again. ''At least she'd have had a chance. Ripley took that away from her when he brushed her off as a hypochondriac and prescribed sedatives instead of medical tests. The guy has a nasty habit of assuming most women's ailments can be treated with antidepressants. She isn't the first who has had to find another doctor.''

''Hearsay. You'll have to show proof that he is more likely to misdiagnose women than men. And you'll need at least one recognized expert to testify that Mrs. Smith's cancer, if caught earlier, could possibly have been cured. And, finally, you'll have to convince a jury that Ripley was flagrantly negligent in his treatment of Mrs. Smith and not honestly misguided by her atypical symptoms.''

"We have two women—acquaintances of the Smiths— who came forward and claimed Dr. Ripley treated them for depression when they really had something else. And a former employee—a nurse—who says she left because she didn't like his attitude toward his female clients."

"I've read their statements. There's reason to believe that at least one of those former patients *did* suffer depression, in addition to the neurological disease that was diagnosed later. And you can bet Ripley has evidence to support his claim that the nurse is a disgruntled former employee with an ax to grind against him."

Her voice was terse now. "You're saying you wouldn't have taken the case? That you think it's as hopeless as all those other firms did?"

He just loved it when she got that righteous-crusader-for-justice look on her face. He smiled and draped an arm around her shoulders. "I didn't say that. You've got a hell of a fight ahead of you, but you aren't alone. You have my full support. I think we can get a better offer from these jerks."

It was probably her relief at his encouragement that made her smile at him before she remembered to react to having his arm around her. She shifted her weight in an attempt to move away. He promptly tightened his arm.

"Nathan." There was a warning in her voice that he chose to ignore.

"I've missed you this past week," he murmured, looking at her sternly set mouth. "We've hardly had a minute to be alone together."

"This isn't that minute." She scooted a couple of inches sideways, but he simply moved with her, keeping her within the circle of his arm. "Nathan, stop it. Someone could walk in at any time. They could get the mistaken idea that something is going on between us."

As far as he was concerned, something was going on between them. As far as certain parts of him were concerned, it wasn't nearly enough.

"Have dinner with me tonight. Just the two of us."

She shook her head. "You need to be with Isabelle."

"I've been with Isabelle every night for the past two weeks. She won't mind spending a few extra hours with Mrs. T. Isabelle has become very fond of her."

"I still don't think it's a good idea."

"You have other plans?"

She hesitated just long enough to let him know she didn't. Caitlin wasn't the type to make use of expedient lies. "No. But I still have to decline. I told you last week that I don't want to get entangled in a potentially awkward personal involvement with my business partner."

He touched a fingertip to her lower lip. "Are you sure it isn't already too late for that? Because as far as I'm concerned, there's already a potentially awkward personal involvement. I can't turn off my feelings for you just because you don't consider this a convenient time."

"It isn't the timing. It's the circumstances."

His attention was fully focused on her mouth now and the memory of the way it had felt and tasted against his. A jolt of sensation went through him when she nervously moistened her lips with the tip of her tongue, leaving her mouth damp and soft. "If I kissed you now," he asked whimsically, "would you sue me?"

A slight quiver went through her lips then, almost as if she could already feel him against them. "I, uh—"

Oh, yeah. She wanted him to kiss her again. Forcing himself to be content with what he hoped wasn't sheer self-delusion, he dropped his arm and moved away. "You're right, of course. This isn't the time or the place."

Seemingly taken aback by his capitulation, she hesitated

a moment, then briskly began to gather her paperwork. "I'll start compiling a list of potential expert witnesses. And I'll draft a letter to Dr. Ripley's attorneys, letting them know that our client finds their settlement offer unacceptable."

"Sounds good."

"Okay. See you later."

It was a blatant dismissal—or a strategic retreat. He decided to let her get away with it, but not before saying offhandedly, "Come to think about it, Mrs. T. couldn't baby-sit for me tonight, anyway. She goes to church on Wednesday nights. So maybe you and I will have dinner another night."

Caitlin frowned, obviously trying to decide how to answer without committing herself to anything.

"Isabelle's been asking about you," he added. "She wants to know when you're going to come see her again."

Cheap shot, he knew, but hey, he was a lawyer. He would utilize any strategy that had a reasonable chance of success.

The look Caitlin gave him was heavy with reproach. "That's really not fair."

"I know," he said cheerfully. "But it's true, nonetheless. She *has* asked about you."

"I would like to see Isabelle again," Caitlin admitted somewhat reluctantly. "But—"

"Then have dinner with us soon. I'll behave. And Isabelle can be our chaperone."

"Oh, *that's* reassuring."

"We'll make it very soon," he said, speaking with a confidence that implied the matter was settled. And then he left the room, before she had a chance to reply.

He knew when not to push his luck.

Most Saturday mornings found Caitlin at the office at her usual time. She rarely met with clients on weekends and she even more rarely asked any of the staff to work those days, but she always got a great deal accomplished. At least, she did when she wasn't interrupted, as she had been by Nathan's mother a couple of weeks earlier, or distracted, as she was by her thoughts of Nathan on this third Saturday in October.

She had been sitting at her desk for more than half an hour, a cooling cup of coffee at her elbow, a mind-numbingly dry and complex legal description in front of her. She wasn't a real estate attorney, so she was following the description with difficulty, comparing it painstakingly to another deed one of her clients was disputing. Her full concentration should have been focused on directions and degrees, but instead her thoughts kept wandering.

Maybe she should have worked at home today, she mused. True, she wouldn't have had all the office resources at her fingertips, but at least in her apartment she wouldn't be surrounded by reminders of Nathan. She wouldn't hear the echoes of his laughter in the other rooms or picture him standing beside her desk, looking at her with that unnerving new gleam of awareness in his eyes.

She wondered what he and Isabelle were doing today. And whether Isabelle was really settling into her preschool program as well as Nathan believed. Whether Isabelle really missed seeing her. And, most annoying of all, she kept wondering whether Nathan was thinking of her today as often as she thought of him.

She groaned and buried her face in her hands. What was wrong with her? She was acting like a schoolgirl with an embarrassing crush on a classmate!

"Whatever you're reading must be really boring," Nathan commented from the doorway. "You look as though you're falling asleep at your desk."

She jumped, her hands falling to the desktop with a thud, her shoulders straightening. It was a measure of her distraction that she hadn't heard anyone enter the offices. Again.

They really should invest in a better security system.

"I wasn't expecting you this morning," she said, then noticed his little blond shadow. "Hello, Isabelle."

She was caught by surprise a second time when the little girl dashed across the office and launched herself into Caitlin's lap. Her arms filled with warm, soft, sweet-smelling child, Caitlin rested her cheek for a moment against Isabelle's fine hair.

This, she thought, could become addictive.

After a moment Isabelle wriggled back to look into Caitlin's face. "Where have you been, Miss Caitlin?"

Caitlin smiled wryly. "I've been busy, I'm afraid. And so have you, I hear. How's preschool?"

"It's good. I've got a new friend. Her name is Kelsey. And I like Jessica and Tiffany and Justin, too, but I don't like Danny, because he pulls my hair and says I got holes in my face. I told him he's stupid because he doesn't know the difference between holes and dimples, and he pulled my hair *again!* So I said I wouldn't be his friend, and then he pouted like a baby."

Caitlin followed the breathless diatribe with some difficulty, giving Nathan a quizzical look over the top of Isabelle's head. She wasn't quite sure what to say, except a lame, "I'm glad you're making new friends."

Nathan stepped forward and laid a sheet of yellow construction paper on the desk in front of her. "Isabelle made this for you at school."

She smiled when she studied the gift. It was an endearingly lopsided crayon drawing of a woman with a big red smile, glued-on brown yarn hair, and clothes fashioned from mismatched scraps of fabric, ribbons and buttons.

"It's a picture of you, Miss Caitlin," Isabelle said earnestly.

"It's lovely." Caitlin touched a fingertip to one flyaway twist of yarn hair. "Thank you, Isabelle, I'll treasure this."

Nathan hefted the bulging purple backpack he carried higher on one arm. "Come on, poppet, Miss Caitlin's busy. Let's go set up your toys in my office and you can play while I catch up on some correspondence."

"I brought my travel dollhouse," Isabelle informed Caitlin. "It's got furniture and a family and a car and a little dog and a cat. Nate bought it for me at the toy store. You want to see it?"

"It sounds really cool. I'll come see it in a little while, okay?"

"Okay." Isabelle bustled out of the room, obviously eager to play with her new toy.

Nathan lingered in the doorway for a moment. "She wasn't able to bring many toys with her from California. I didn't think it would hurt to buy her a few new things occasionally."

"Neither do I," she replied with lifted eyebrows. "And there's certainly no need to justify your purchases to me."

He smiled wryly. "Maybe I'm just seeking reassurance. I'm sort of playing this by ear, you know."

"And you seem to be doing just fine."

"Thanks." He glanced at the pile of documents on the desk in front of her. "I won't disturb you any longer. I'll be in my office if you need anything."

Caitlin glared in frustration at the doorway after he left. Because of her pervasive thoughts of Nathan, she hadn't been able to concentrate on work *before* the interruption. Now that she was so aware of Nathan and Isabelle only a couple of rooms away, she was afraid concentration would be even more difficult—if not impossible.

Her work had always been so important to her, taking precedence over nearly everything else. The pursuit of career success had been her one driving ambition since she was ten years old. Already tired of living in an endless series of dilapidated trailers and apartments while her good-hearted but impractical father had drifted from one dead-end job to another, she had decided that her future would be different.

Studying the parents of her classmates, she had determined that a solid career was the best measure of security and stability. Her father had reinforced that belief, telling her repeatedly that she had the opportunity to make something more of herself than he had accomplished in his own life.

It hadn't been easy. Lacking family resources, she had funded her college education with scholarships, grants and a series of jobs. Her father—overweight and a heavy smoker—had died of a heart attack three months after her college graduation. Her mother, who had always struggled with high blood pressure, had suffered her stroke during Caitlin's second year of law school and had never recovered from the massive brain damage. Had Caitlin been easily distracted or discouraged, she never would have made it this far.

So why was she having so much trouble now, when everything had been going so well? What was it about Nathan that he could slip past emotional barriers that no other man had been able to bypass? A couple of guys had tried, but she had never been swayed from her ultimate goal—full partnership in a solid, secure, successful practice. Maybe here in Honesty with Nathan or perhaps in an older, larger firm somewhere else.

Because of her mother's condition, it was convenient for now to be here, only an hour's drive from the nursing home, but she was still open to offers. She had always believed she was free to pick up and leave at any time, with proper notification to her partner, of course, and suitable arrangements for her mother. She wasn't at all comfortable with the sensation that insidious little tendrils were twining around her ankles—or her heart, perhaps?—making her feel that it wouldn't be as easy to leave this place as she had previously believed.

She was fully aware of the contradictions in her emotional reasoning; the almost-obsessive need to be free to leave even as she worked ceaselessly toward long-term security. Maybe a psychologist could analyze that dichotomy; she simply accepted it as a result of her childhood experiences. She was as afraid of emotional bonds as she was of career obstacles.

Nathan and Isabelle definitely represented at least one of those fears.

As if to recall her attention to matters at hand, one of the documents on her desk ruffled in a gust of temperature-controlled air from a ceiling vent. Great, she thought with a scowl. Now she'd drifted off into philosophical soul searching instead of the painstaking scrutiny of property descriptions.

Vowing to be more productive for the rest of the day, she directed her attention fully to the papers in front of her.

Chapter Nine

Caitlin managed to work uninterrupted for another hour. After making a final note on the yellow legal pad in front of her, she closed the case file. Might as well take a break, she thought, stretching casually.

Maybe she would pop into Nathan's office for a couple of minutes. She had promised Isabelle she would look at her dollhouse. It would be rude not to follow through on that promise.

Nathan's door was open. She heard his computer keyboard clattering as she approached. She had almost reached the doorway when she heard Isabelle singing very quietly— a nursery rhyme, perhaps? Pausing in the doorway, she took in the scene. Nathan was hard at work at his desk, his brow creased in concentration, and Isabelle sat cross-legged on the carpet, contentedly arranging furniture in a colorful plastic dollhouse.

It was a sight that made her feel like sighing for some strange reason.

Isabelle spotted her first. Ending her song in midline, she broke into a smile. "Did you come to see my dollhouse, Miss Caitlin?"

"Yes, I did." She glanced apologetically at Nathan, who had looked away from his computer. "I'm sorry, I didn't mean to interrupt your work."

He pressed a couple of buttons to save and close his file. "I can finish this later."

Feeling as though she were the intruder this time, she entered the office and knelt in front of Isabelle's dollhouse. It really was an intriguing toy; constructed of heavy-duty plastic, it was hinged to fold into a carrying case when not in use. Each room was equipped with whimsically shaped plastic furnishings. A red plastic convertible held a cheerful-looking family of four—father, mother, brother and baby sister.

"This is really nice." Caitlin picked up a pink plastic sofa to admire more closely. "I'm sure you've been having fun with it."

Isabelle touched a chubby finger to each plastic figure. "This is Bob. He's the dad. This is Susie. She's the mom. The kids are Mike and Annie."

"I like the names you've chosen."

"They're people in stories I like."

"I see." Caitlin replaced the couch and gave the little car a push. "It's a very fine play set, Isabelle."

"Thank you." Isabelle made an adjustment to a yellow chair, the pride of home ownership glowing on her little face.

Nathan glanced at his watch. "It's almost noon. I bet you're getting hungry, poppet."

Isabelle rubbed her tummy. "I am hungry."

"So am I. How about it, Caitlin, want to make it a three-some for lunch?"

"Oh, I—"

Isabelle jumped up and caught Caitlin's hand in hers, gazing entreatingly up at her. "Come have lunch with us, Miss Caitlin. Please."

So unfair. There was no way she could resist the look in those big blue eyes. "Well, I suppose I could join you for a quick lunch."

The little girl's smile was ample reward for Caitlin capitulation.

Because it was nearby and offered an extensive children's menu, they selected Jolly's Deli for their lunch destination, taking Nathan's car. A popular establishment close to the main shopping areas, Jolly's was as crowded as Caitlin had expected, but she knew the service to be fast.

As she had also predicted, she knew quite a few of the other diners and Nathan was acquainted with even more of them. She was keenly aware of the attention focused their way as they stood in line to order, Isabelle standing between them holding their hands. Many locals knew who Isabelle was now, of course, and they expressed their interest with sidelong stares and behind-the-hand whispers.

She could only imagine what the gossips must be making of seeing her with Nathan and Isabelle again. Even before Isabelle's arrival, Caitlin knew there had been idle speculation about her relationship with Nathan, which was understandable, she supposed. Both of them young, single and unattached, spending so much time together at work. Now…well, the grapevine would probably have them engaged by sundown.

Since there was nothing she could do about potential

rumors, she decided to hold her head high and enjoy her lunch.

There were few awkward moments during the casual meal, mostly because Isabelle provided entertainment with stories about her preschool adventures. Caitlin listened attentively to the child, but she would hate to be tested later on anything Isabelle said.

Caitlin's attention kept wandering to Nathan, who sat more quietly than usual at the other side of the table. She had the feeling that while he was outwardly enjoying the meal and the conversation, he was actually watching her, too.

It was inevitable, of course, with all that surreptitious watching, that their eyes would eventually meet. And hold. Though she was aware that Isabelle was still babbling, and she could still hear the chatter and clatter of the crowded restaurant around them, she couldn't seem to focus on anything but the gleam in Nathan's deep-blue eyes.

How strange that she could suddenly almost feel the pressure of his lips against her. She had been prone to relive The Kiss at odd moments, but this was the first time she had drifted into fantasy right out in public. Especially in front of Nathan. Not to mention Isabelle.

"Nate? Hey, Nate?"

Still looking into Caitlin's eyes as though he could see the disturbing thoughts behind them, Nathan responded absently to Isabelle's prodding. "What is it, poppet?"

"Isn't that your mom?"

The innocent question made both Caitlin and Nathan start, their gazes breaking apart. Following the direction of Isabelle's pointing finger, Caitlin spotted Lenore McCloud at the same time the other woman noticed them.

Carrying plates filled at the salad bar, Lenore and another woman were headed toward a table not far from the one where Caitlin sat with Nathan and Isabelle. Lenore's steps faltered, her face going taut with pained recognition.

Caitlin had the unsettling sensation that the noisy restaurant suddenly went quiet around them, though she knew that was exaggeration. She also knew, however, that many pairs of eyes waited to see how Lenore would react to this awkward encounter.

They all should have known, of course, that Lenore was nothing if not socially conscious. Though her eyes had gone flat and opaque, she managed a cordial nod. "Nathan. Caitlin."

Isabelle took no offense at the slight. "Hi, Nate's mom," she said with her brightest Shirley Temple smile. "We're having lunch."

Her gaze darting quickly around them, Lenore cleared her throat and replied, "Yes, so I see. Enjoy your meal." She gave Nathan a look of reproach before turning to her companion. "We'd better claim our table before someone else does, Maxine."

Caitlin noted that Lenore chose a seat that placed her back toward their table. Glancing at Nathan, Caitlin saw the flash of pain in his eyes. He so obviously hated this distance between his mother and himself, but he was just as obviously at a loss as to how to bridge it.

Remembering the adamancy in Lenore's voice when she'd insisted she could never accept Isabelle, Caitlin wasn't sure there was any solution to the impasse.

They finished their lunches quickly. Isabelle seemed to be unaware that the mood had changed, but Caitlin was all too conscious of the difference in Nathan. He had been rather quiet before his mother's appearance, but he was positively subdued now. She hated seeing him this way, but she could think of nothing that would cheer him up.

Fortunately, Isabelle was very good at that sort of thing. By the time they returned to the office, Nathan was smiling again, if only for his little sister's sake.

Settling Isabelle with her dollhouse again, Nathan followed Caitlin into her office. "Do you have much more to do today?"

"Not much. Another couple of hours, maybe. You?"

"Maybe a half hour to finish that file I was working on before lunch. Just as well. I'm not sure Isabelle's dollhouse is going to hold her attention much longer."

"She really is a very well-behaved little girl. No pouting or tears, no tantrums, no whining."

"Except for the tantrums, I've seen a little of all of the above from her, but not much." His smile looked a bit weary around the edges. "She's a normal three-year-old, Caitlin, but she is a good kid, on the whole."

"No question about that." She hesitated, then tentatively laid a hand on his arm. The muscles beneath his long-sleeved rugby shirt were rock hard with the tension she had sensed in him since they'd left the deli. "Are you okay?"

"Who, me?" He flashed a semblance of his usual cocky grin. "I'm always okay."

Giving him a repressive frown, she said, "You know what I mean. I know the scene with your mother bothered you."

His mouth quirked wryly at her choice of words. "My mother would *never* cause a scene. She was as calm, collected and polite as she would have been with any distant acquaintance—or even with a bitter enemy—in such a public venue."

"I know that must have hurt you."

"It breaks my heart," he answered simply. "But I don't know what else to do about it."

"Would you like me to try to talk to her again?"

He covered her hand with his own. "Thanks, but I don't think it would help. My mother is the most stubborn woman I've ever met. Strike that. The *second* most stubborn woman. My sister still holds top prize."

"I just wish there was something I could do to help." Caitlin had discovered that she really hated seeing the empty look of pain in Nathan's beautiful eyes.

Even as that thought occurred to her, she saw his eyes light with a soft gleam. His fingers tightened around hers. "I can think of a few things you could do to help me feel better."

She sighed and started to move away. She should have known he wouldn't be serious for long. Nathan's typical response when things got too intense was to start wise-cracking and flirting.

As always, his flirting made her self-conscious. "I suppose we had better get back to—"

The rest of her words were smothered beneath his mouth.

She couldn't believe he was kissing her right there in the office. With no warning, no provocation, no chance for her to resist. And she *would* have resisted, she assured herself even as she tilted her head slightly to accommodate his kiss, if only he had given her some forewarning of his intentions.

His arms went around her, pulling her closer. She rested her hands on his chest so she could push him away—in just a minute.

Hi tilted his head and deepened the kiss. Her fingers curled into his shirt, and she wasn't pushing him away. Didn't want to.

She parted her lips and kissed him back—and it had nothing to do with sympathy or wanting to soothe his pain or anything else but pure desire. She'd been wanting to kiss him again ever since the last time, damn it. And it was even better than she remembered.

Nathan was the one who finally raised his head.

For just a moment she would have sworn he was at a loss for words. Characteristically, he recovered almost immediately. "Have dinner with me tonight."

Trying to pull her resolve together, she shook her head. "Isabelle—"

"Can stay with a sitter for a few hours. Mrs. T. has volunteered several times."

Still shaking her head, she moved a couple of steps away from him, laying a hand on her desk as if to draw strength from its solid surface. "No. We have to stop this. Now."

Nathan made a sound that closely resembled a growl. "I really should add you to that list of stubborn women. I'd say you run neck-and-neck with my mother and my sister."

"I haven't changed my mind about us," she said, knowing she sounded as obstinate as he accused her of being. "I still think it would be a mistake for us to confuse friendship and natural attraction for something more."

"I'm not at all confused," he assured her easily. "I simply want a chance to spend some time with you. Alone."

"Definitely not a good idea. It seems like every time we're alone together lately, well…" She felt her cheeks warm before she finished lamely, "Things get out of hand."

Nathan laughed. While she couldn't help being relieved that he was smiling again, she didn't like feeling that it was at her expense. "I rather like it when things get out of hand," he said.

The old Nathan was definitely back—at least for now. Maybe she should be pleased with herself for finding a way to cheer him up, even if unintentionally. Instead, she tried to speak firmly and with unmistakable finality. "I am not getting involved with you, Nathan."

He reached out to touch a fingertip to her lower lip,

which was still warm and moist from kissing him. "Caitlin. You already are."

Turning away from him so quickly she almost stumbled, she spoke more gruffly this time. "Go check on your sister. She really shouldn't be left alone this long."

"This issue between us is far from settled."

She only sighed in response to his warning. "Just go away, Nathan. I have work to do."

She was relieved when he turned and left the office, leaving her to settled into her desk chair and bury her face in her hands. She was not unaware that he had left her in the same despairing position he'd found her in earlier.

Sunday would have been Stuart McCloud's sixtieth birthday. Nathan was painfully aware of the significance of the date from the time he woke that morning.

He couldn't help feeling a bit nostalgic as he dragged himself into the laundry room to wash a load of Isabelle's play clothes, then moved into the kitchen to start breakfast. Birthdays had always been a big deal in the McCloud household, with special breakfasts, parties and elaborate gifts. Stuart was the one who had insisted each birthday be celebrated. Simply surviving another year was an accomplishment in itself, he had said many times.

Stuart had fallen six months short of surviving his own sixtieth year.

Nathan gazed pensively out the window over the sink. It was a dark, gray morning. Looked as though it might start raining any minute. Isabelle was still sleeping. He had let her stay up a bit later than usual watching videos last night since he'd known she could sleep in today.

Though he hadn't been a faithful churchgoer for the past several years, he supposed he should start taking Isabelle to Sunday school. Problem was, the only church he had ever attended was the one in which his mother was an extremely active member. Maybe he'd better look into a few others. He wouldn't want to ruin his mother's longtime pleasure in her church.

The smell of scorching batter brought his attention back to what he was supposed to be doing. He flipped the pancakes quickly, frowning at the charred edges. Okay, so he would eat these.

He remembered lazy weekend mornings when *he* had been the one to sleep in. He would then read the paper while sipping coffee and munching cold pizza or whatever else he might find in the fridge. Maybe head out midafternoon with his golf clubs or a fishing rod, a cooler of beer and whatever buddy had been available at a moment's notice. On other Sundays he'd had lunch with his mother, sometimes joined by his brother and sister.

If he had wanted to stay out until midnight on weekends—or all night—he'd been free to do so. If he'd been in the mood for a woman's company, all he'd had to do was pick up the phone.

How his life had changed.

Because he was still in that strangely melancholy mood, and feeling just a little lonely, he covered the plate of pancakes to keep them warm and reached for the telephone.

His brother answered on the fourth ring, just when Nathan was beginning to think Gideon wasn't in the mood to answer the phone today. He didn't worry about waking him—Gideon was always up at sunrise. He said his brain was sharper in the mornings.

Which didn't mean he was a cheerful riser. "What?" he barked into the phone.

"Sorry," Nathan said. "Bad timing?"

"Rough scene," his brother replied. "Been at it since five and I've only managed two paragraphs."

Nathan knew better than to ask how close Gideon was to deadline. Saying the word *deadline* to Gideon McCloud was like saying *kill* in front of a trained attack dog. Always elicited a snarl, at the very least.

He settled for asking carefully, "Anything bothering you?"

"Other than intrusive early-morning phone calls, you mean?"

"Other than that," Nathan agreed equably.

"No, nothing's bothering me in particular. What's up with you? Why did you call?"

"I just felt like checking in. I haven't talked to you in a couple of weeks."

"Still got the kid?"

"You know I do."

"Pretty weird, bro. You raising a kid, I mean."

"I know. But she's a pretty cool kid. Why don't you have dinner with us one night this week and find out for yourself?"

"We've had this discussion. I don't need any more siblings. The two I've got are trouble enough—you calling me during prime working hours, Deb nagging me every few days to try to talk sense into you."

"Deborah's been calling you about me?"

"Yeah. Even though I keep telling her I don't have any influence over your actions. Never have. Never wanted to."

Though their personalities were very different, they had been closer than this once, Nathan mused, remembering summer days of swimming and skateboarding, autumn afternoons of basketball and football, spring weekends of baseball and tennis. Gideon had always been rather quiet and introspective, content to spend hours in his room with piles of novels and notebooks for his own scribblings, but he'd withdrawn even more into himself as he'd left his teen years.

Nathan had tried countless times to identify the turning points in his brother's life, any specific causes for the changes in him. But whatever traumas there had been, if any, Gideon kept them to himself. To their parents' dismay, he dropped out of college his junior year. A year later he'd sold his first short story. Almost four years after that his first novel had seen print.

His early readership had been small but loyal; his earnings, modest, but sufficient for his simple tastes. And now he seemed to be poised on the brink of breaking out into a larger market. His tightly plotted and eccentrically cast novels were becoming more popular through enthusiastic word-of-mouth from his core of longtime readers. If Gideon was excited about the new direction his writing career was taking, he kept that to himself, as well.

"You remember what today would have been, don't you?" Nathan asked quietly, wondering if the date had had anything to do with Gideon's difficulty writing that morning.

Gideon's reply was curt. "I remember."

"You want to talk about it?"

Gideon had been estranged from their father even before Stuart had left the family, but Nathan couldn't believe his brother hadn't suffered in some way from Stuart's death, even though he had steadily refused to discuss his feelings. Nathan didn't think it was healthy to keep feelings so deeply bottled up. He'd been trying for years to maintain open lines of communication between himself and his younger brother, even though he usually felt as though he was the only one making any effort at all to reach out.

He couldn't remember the last time Gideon had called him. He couldn't help wondering if he would ever hear from his brother again if he didn't initiate the call. The thought that they could actually drift that far apart made him even sadder than he had been before he'd placed this call. Maybe dialing his brother's number hadn't been such a good idea, after all.

"No, I don't want to talk about it." Gideon's reply was adamant. A heavy silence followed it.

Nathan tried to think of something more to say. "Maybe when you get a little extra time we can get together for a game of racquetball. It's been a long time since I've stomped you."

"A *very* long time," Gideon retorted. "As I recall it, I whupped your butt the last five or six times we played."

"Yeah, well, I've practiced a bit in the past year or so since you last defeated me. I might just surprise you."

"Could be. I'm out of practice. Haven't been to the gym in a while."

"So you want to get together for a game sometime?"

Gideon's hesitation was long enough to make Nathan believe his brother was looking for a reasonably civil way to reject the offer. Instead he said, "Yeah, okay. We'll do that sometime."

It certainly wasn't an enthusiastic response, nor had he made any specific plans, but he hadn't closed the door Nathan had so tentatively opened. Nathan took some encouragement from that. "Great. Give me a call sometime."

"Sure. Is there anything else, or can I get back to work now?"

"Go back to work. I just wanted to say hi."

"Okay. See you around." Just as Nathan was preparing to hang up, Gideon added gruffly, "Thanks for calling."

A dial tone sounded in Nathan's ear almost before Gideon finished speaking. Nathan stared for a moment at the receiver, disproportionately pleased by his brother's parting words, yet wondering if they had really meant anything.

Was Gideon really glad that Nathan stubbornly kept in touch or was it just something he'd said automatically, trying to be polite? And yet, when had Gideon ever done anything just to be polite?

He punched in a new set of numbers before he had a chance to talk himself out of doing so. His sister was not an early riser, and the hoarseness of her voice let him know he had awakened her. "Hi, Deb, it's me. Sorry if I called too early."

He could envision her pushing her blond hair out of her face, frowning and struggling to sound awake and coherent. "I wasn't asleep," she lied blatantly. "What's wrong, Nathan?"

"Nothing's wrong. I just wanted to talk to you a minute."

"What about?"

"I just talked to Gideon. He said you'd been calling him about me."

"I only called him twice," she replied a bit defensively. "I wanted to know if he'd made an effort to talk you out of ruining our mother's life, but he said it was none of his business what you do. I knew you wouldn't listen to me, but I thought maybe you'd listen to Gideon if he would make the effort."

"Deborah, I'm not doing anything to ruin Mother's life. Stop being so melodramatic."

Her indignant huff sounded clearly through the phone lines. "You're wrong, of course. Mother is pretty much devastated by what you've done. She told me that every time she goes out in public she dreads the possibility of running into you. And she wonders if everyone who knows what you've done is staring at her and talking about her."

"Deborah, all I've done is take in a little girl who had nowhere else to go. My own sister—and yours, I might add. I can understand Mom having a little trouble dealing with the circumstances of Isabelle's conception, but I am having trouble understanding why *you* are taking such a hard line. You've always liked kids, Deborah. I can't imagine that you would seriously advocate putting any little girl out on the streets, especially your own flesh and blood."

"That's not fair," she protested, the quiver in her voice betraying that his criticism had hurt. "I'm hardly advocating any such thing. I wholeheartedly agree that a good home should be found for her—just not there, right under Mother's nose."

"So you're saying I should move away? Just sell my firm and settle quietly somewhere else, where none of you will ever have to risk seeing me again?"

"Damn it, Nathan, you make it sound as if we've thrown you out of the family! *You're* the one who initiated this situation. You've made your choice between your family and a new family, just like—"

Her words stopped abruptly, leaving a brittle, painful silence in their place.

"Just like Dad did?" Nathan leaned heavily against the kitchen counter. "That's what you and Mom are thinking? That I've betrayed and abandoned the family, the same way Dad did?"

"You've made it quite clear that you've chosen Kimberly's daughter over us," his sister replied stiffly. "You just said that you're willing to move away with her and never see the rest of us again."

"Like Dad did." Nathan shook his head in frustration. "Deborah, you can't really believe the situation is the same. Dad was a married man who betrayed his family for another woman—a woman who knew he already had a family and fell in love with him, anyway. I've never said I approved of the choices they made, but they were adults. They had plenty of other options. Isabelle's just a baby. She had absolutely no say in anything that happened to her.''

Trying to keep his voice low despite the intensity of his emotions, he straightened and began to pace with the phone. ''Yeah, I could have given her up. That's what I went to California to do. The only person I talked to who was interested in adopting her wanted my professional advice about how to get around the legal safeguards of a little girl's trust fund.''

Deborah was silent for so long he wondered if she had thrown the phone aside. Was she even listening?

When she finally spoke, her tone was uncharacteristically subdued. ''I'm sorry, Nathan. I know you believe you did the right thing, and I know it hurts you that your family hasn't been more supportive. But, I need more time, okay? I just can't deal with it right now. Especially not today.''

So she, too, was aware of the date. ''I haven't left the family, Deborah,'' he said, his tone more gentle now. ''I haven't betrayed anyone, including Mom. And I haven't chosen Isabelle over any of you. I just couldn't abandon her—any more than I could any of the rest of you.''

''Maybe I'll understand that someday. I don't know if Mom ever will.''

''I'm trusting that she'll come around eventually. She needs time, too. I understand that.''

''Just—do your best to keep from hurting her any more, will you?''

Remembering the look on his mother's face when she had spotted them at the deli, Nathan winced. ''I'll try,'' he said, but short of actually moving away he didn't know how to guarantee that they wouldn't end up in the same place again. Honesty just wasn't that big a town.

"Are you doing okay, Deb? Are you happy?"

Her reply was so dispirited that it made his chest ache. "Who, me? I'm fine. No problems here."

"Is there anything I can—"

She cut in with a flat, unamused laugh. "Don't you ever get tired of being the big brother all the time, Nathan? Take care of your other little sister—this one can take care of herself."

She didn't give him a chance to quiz her any further. Muttering some excuse about having things to do, she brought the call to an abrupt end.

Nathan's head was hurting when he hung up the phone. Maybe calling his siblings hadn't been such a good idea, after all. He didn't seem to have accomplished anything.

"Sorry, Dad," he murmured. "I tried."

Dragging her stuffed owl behind her, Isabelle padded into the kitchen, bare pink toes flashing beneath the hem of her long pink nightgown. Her blond hair was tousled, her eyes still heavy-lidded when she smiled up at him. "My tummy woke me up. It's hungry."

He had to smile at that, of course. Lifting her into his arms, he gave her a hug and a kiss on the cheek. "Good morning. How do pancakes sound for breakfast?"

"Pancakes sound yummy."

Chuckling, he set her in her booster seat and moved to pour milk and orange juice into glasses. He just wished it was this easy to make his other siblings happy.

Chapter Ten

Lindsey Newman lowered the two-page letter she had been reading and studied Caitlin over the top of it. "Wow," she said.

Sprawled on her sofa, Caitlin nodded. "I know. Wow."

"If this opportunity comes through, it could be very big for you."

"I know. Los Angeles. Well, I never expected an opening like this to crop up so soon."

Lindsey tapped the letter. "This must be some good friend to recommend you for something like this."

"Tom and I were good friends in law school," Caitlin admitted. "He graduated a year ahead of me and pulled some strings to get into his uncle's firm in Los Angeles."

Lindsey's eyebrows lifted. "How good a friend was he?"

"We dated a few times. And, okay, maybe he was a little more involved than I was. He wanted to get serious, but I convinced him I wanted to establish my career before I became too deeply involved with anyone.''

''It's obvious he hasn't completely given up on the idea. I bet he figures that if he can get you on the partnership track in his uncle's firm, there would be no reason why the two of you couldn't get together.''

No reason, Caitlin mused, except that she wasn't interested in Tom that way. Never had been and couldn't foresee that she ever would be. She *was,* however, intrigued by the implication that he could get her an interview in his long-established and very successful law firm. After all, this was exactly the kind of break she had been hoping for—wasn't it?

''Are you going to let him arrange an interview for you?''

''I thought I would try to set something up with him after the first of the year.''

''Why so long?''

''I have too much going on here to possibly get away before then. The malpractice case alone is taking hours of my time, and I've barely gotten started on that one.''

''Mm. It wouldn't have anything to do with you being perfectly content right here, would it? Maybe you really like being a partner in a smaller firm. And maybe you aren't interested in this Tom guy because you have a more interesting fella here.''

''Don't start, Lindsey.''

''I still can't believe you turned Nathan down when he asked you out.''

Caitlin wished now that she hadn't admitted in a weak moment that Nathan had asked her to dinner. That was what came from having only one close girlfriend, she thought ruefully. Eventually Lindsey learned everything there was to know about Caitlin's life.

"*You* would have turned him down."

"Sure—because of the kid. But you're just chicken."

"Cautious."

"Same thing."

Caitlin let that pass.

"So," Lindsey asked, "have you told him you might have a chance with the big L.A. firm?"

"No. The letter was in my mail when I got home from the office yesterday. I haven't seen Nathan since."

"Are you going to tell him?"

"Certainly I will, if I decide to go to L.A. for an interview. But there's no need to mention it yet. Nathan has enough to worry about for now."

"He won't like it. He'll try to talk you out of going."

Caitlin shrugged, not quite meeting her friend's eyes. "He could find another associate easily enough."

"Something tells me it wouldn't be losing a business partner that would concern him most."

"What is it with you trying to match me up with Nathan?" Caitlin asked in frustration.

Lindsey grinned. "Hey, I just hate to see a prime young male go to waste."

Her smile faded a bit then. "And, besides, I really don't want to see you move to L.A., either."

"There's certainly no guarantee that I'll move to L.A. I don't even have an interview yet, remember? Even if I should get an interview, that doesn't mean I would get an offer. And even getting an offer doesn't mean I would accept if it didn't feel right."

Lindsey shrugged. "I just know you'll get any position you go after. Any firm would be crazy not to want you."

"Thanks, but you're hardly objective."

"There is that." She set the letter on a table and stood. "I'd better get ready for my sales trip tomorrow. I've got another load of laundry to do tonight—or I'll have to risk being in a car accident wearing ragged underwear, something my mother always warned me against.''

Caitlin stood to walk her friend to the door. ''Do us both a favor—don't have a car accident even wearing brand-new underwear.''

Lindsey laughed. ''I'll do my best.''

Caitlin's telephone started ringing almost as soon as she closed the door behind Lindsey. Somehow she knew whose voice she would hear when she answered and she was right.

''How's it going, beautiful?'' Nathan asked cheerfully.

She settled into a chair, curling her feet beneath her. ''Is this an obscene call?''

''It can be. Want me to talk dirty to you?''

''Why don't you tell me why you called?''

''I just wanted to hear your voice.''

She toyed with a tassel at the corner of a small tapestry throw pillow. ''That sounds like a line.''

''It isn't, you know. I really did just want to talk to you.''

''Anything in particular you want to discuss?''

''Not specifically. How about you? Anything interesting going on in your life today?''

Her gaze was drawn to the letter still lying on the coffee table. ''No. Nothing exciting. You?''

''Not a lot. Isabelle and I went to the park this afternoon. That was an experience.''

''I'm sure it was. Did you have fun?''

''Yeah. Even though I was dismayed by how many people let their kids run wild in places like that. Some of those kids were hellions—pushing, shoving, breaking in line, screaming when they didn't get their way. I can tell I'm going to have to be careful about making sure Isabelle hangs out with the right friends. I wouldn't want her to start imitating some of those brats.''

Caitlin couldn't help smiling. He sounded so much like an indignant parent and so different from the carefree bachelor he had been so recently.

Her amusement faded when he said after a slight pause, "Today would have been my father's sixtieth birthday."

"It must have been a difficult day for you."

"A bit. Dad loved birthdays. He always insisted on balloons and a cake. Even after he left, I tried to make a point of calling him on his birthday, though neither Gideon nor Deborah did, of course."

"At least you have the comfort of knowing you acknowledged the occasions while your father was still living. I wonder if Gideon and Deborah regret not doing so when they had the chance."

"Maybe. I talked to both of them today. Gideon said he was having trouble concentrating on his work, and Deborah seemed sad. I'm sure both of them were affected by the date."

"They didn't talk to you about their feelings?"

"Hey, I was just glad neither of them hung up on me."

"They're still that resentful about you taking Isabelle?"

"Gideon says he doesn't care one way or another, as long as I leave him out of it. He's leaving the door between us unlocked, if not fully open. Deborah, well, maybe she's coming around a little. I think she listened when I talked today instead of tuning me out."

"That's a good sign, I suppose."

"Perhaps. To be honest, I don't know what's going on with Deb now."

And it was driving him crazy, she thought. "Did you talk to your mother today?"

"No. I was afraid hearing from me, especially today, would only upset her."

"I'm sure she misses you."

''She knows where to reach me.'' He hesitated a moment, then sighed. ''I'll call her again soon. I didn't give up on Dad and I won't give up on my mother.''

''You're a good son, Nathan. And a good brother.''

''Thanks. It means a lot to me for you to say that.''

Because they were straying too close to personal feelings again, Caitlin redirected the conversation. ''What's Isabelle up to now?''

''I put her in bed twenty minutes ago, at eight. She was tired from playing at the park, and she has to get up early for school tomorrow.''

''I hadn't realized it was so late. Lindsey just left. She and I were visiting and the time slipped away from me.''

''How is Lindsey? I haven't seen her in a while.''

''She's fine. Traveling a lot with her job.''

''Next time you see her, tell her I said hi.''

''You could always call her and tell her yourself,'' Caitlin said a bit too casually. ''She always says you're kind of cute.''

He chuckled. ''Thanks, but not interested. Lindsey's nice, but she's not my type.''

''Oh? I didn't know you had a type.''

''Oh, yeah. My type has shiny brown hair, beautiful gray eyes, a clever mind, a sharp tongue—and the sweetest mouth I've ever tasted.''

Her face was hot by the time he finished speaking, and it wasn't the only part of her in danger of overheating. He'd caught her off guard that time, unprepared for the hormonal rush his words evoked. ''Nathan…''

''I can't keep pretending I don't have these feelings for you, Caitlin. Because I know you're worried about it, I've tried to keep my thoughts to myself, but it's just not working.''

"You're still upset about your family. You're turning to me for support."

"I felt this way before Isabelle came to live with me. I've told you that before. I don't know if you simply don't believe me or if you're afraid to believe me."

"I'm not afraid of you," she said automatically.

"Aren't you?"

Not of *him,* perhaps, but the way he made her feel...well, that terrified her. She bit her lip and sat in silence, holding the phone to her ear.

After a moment Nathan spoke again. "I'm not trying to upset you, Caitlin. If you want me to keep pretending, I'll do my best. But I can't promise I won't slip every once in a while."

She still couldn't think of anything to say.

"Just tell me one thing," Nathan prodded.

"What?" she asked warily.

"Do you really have no feelings for me? Other than just friendship, I mean."

She wanted to say right then that friendship was all she felt for him. Tried to say it and mean it.

She couldn't make herself form the words. Probably because she knew they would be a lie.

There was satisfaction in his voice when he spoke again. "I knew it wasn't all one-sided."

"Okay, maybe I feel...something. But I don't know if it's—"

"Let's not look for definitions right now," he suggested. "Let's just play it by ear, shall we?"

"I'm not sure what you mean by that."

"Just what I said. No expectations. Let's just see where it leads, okay?"

"I, um—"

"I know you're really swamped with this malpractice

case right now, so I won't ask for too much of your free time—what little you have. But someone gave me tickets for a symphony concert next Saturday night. You like that sort of thing, don't you?''

"Well, yes, I—''

"We'll concentrate on work during the week and Saturday night we'll focus on us. Okay?''

"Well, I suppose—''

"Great. I'm looking forward to it.''

Caitlin frowned, trying to decide exactly what she had just agreed to. Before she could try to pin him down, he said, "I won't keep you any longer. Like I said, I just wanted to hear your voice. Good night, Caitlin. Sleep well.''

Sleep well? She doubted it. She had a sneaking suspicion she would be plagued by disturbing dreams of Nathan. And it wouldn't be the first time.

She leaned over to pick up the letter her classmate had sent from Los Angeles. Tom seemed quite confident that he could get her an interview with the senior partners in his big firm, though he was only on the junior partnership track for now. He was willing to make sure she got on that track with him, he wrote. No strings, he had added, though she knew he had still harbored feelings for her when he moved to California.

She had been very fond of Tom, a serious, intelligent, ambitious young man with a fascination for history and the law. They'd had a lot in common and had shared many pleasant times together.

She had found him attractive. Enough so that she'd spent a few weekend getaways with him. But when it had become clear to her that he wanted more, she'd backed away. She had told herself she wasn't ready for a serious relationship, that she wanted to concentrate solely on establishing her

career, and that she didn't want to get in the way of Tom
doing the same with his uncle's firm in L.A. But the truth
was, her feelings for Tom had simply never been strong
enough to keep them together.

What she felt for Nathan bore absolutely no resemblance
to the gentle affection she had held for Tom.

Tom had been undemanding, supportive, as intensely focused on his own career as she was on hers. He had connections to several prominent firms, entertained fantasies
about someday being appointed to the Supreme Court and
had never protested her long working hours because he had
worked longer hours.

Tom hadn't slipped off on lovely afternoons for golf or
other play, wouldn't have been content for long in a two-
partner firm in a small Southern town and certainly
wouldn't have let his personal life intrude on his business.
Nathan, on the other hand, let *everything* interfere with
business. He came with baggage and ties that would make
any sane woman think twice about getting involved with
him.

So why did the thought of joining Tom in a firm in L.A.
leave her apathetic, when her palms were sweating at the
very thought of attending a symphony performance with
Nathan?

Caitlin was relieved when Nathan stayed true to his word
and allowed her to concentrate on work that week. Maybe
there was a touch more warmth than usual in his morning
greetings, but she doubted anyone else noticed. And if the
smiles he gave her were slightly more intimate than before,
causing a shiver of reaction to course down her spine each
time…well, maybe that was only in her imagination. No
one else around them seemed to find anything out of the
ordinary about their interaction.

Since both of them were busy with work, spending long hours in court, with clients, on the phone, or buried in research, they didn't actually see much of each other during the early part of the week. Caitlin found herself looking forward to each of those fleeting encounters a bit too eagerly. Even the briefest and most mundane conversation between them left her with an increased pulse rate and an odd warmth somewhere deep inside her.

When had this happened? At what point, exactly, had she stopped looking at Nathan as merely an attractive business associate? When had she started thinking of him as a potential partner in the bedroom as well as in the courtroom? Was there a particular moment when her feelings had changed or simply a gradual increase in her awareness of her reactions to him?

And what on earth was she going to do about it?

By Wednesday afternoon she was having major mood swings, one minute telling herself she would be crazy not to at least give them a chance to explore the feelings between them, the next telling herself she would be insane to even consider such a possibility. Did she really want to risk ruining a great working relationship—not to mention having her heart broken—if this whole thing turned out to be as disastrous as she feared?

And Nathan was certainly in no position to start a hot and heavy affair! He had Isabelle to think about now. She had to be his first priority.

So that was it. They had to resist these perilous impulses. She was sure the feelings would pass soon enough, letting them get back to the more comfortable relationship they had had before. Friends. Very good friends, she amended. She cared about him, of course, but there was no need to bring sex into the equation.

Now if only she could convince her recalcitrant hormones to stop kicking into overdrive every time he smiled at her.

Nathan hung around the office a bit later than usual Wednesday afternoon. He knew he really should head home. This was Mrs. T.'s choir practice night, and he didn't want to delay her unnecessarily. But for some reason, he found himself procrastinating when it came time to leave. He'd heard the clerical staff clear out a short while earlier. Even Irene had already gone home. He and Caitlin were the only ones in the offices, and she was involved in an intense conference call that could last a while longer.

It wasn't that he dreaded going home, he assured himself. Mrs. T. would have a delicious meal waiting there for him. Isabelle would greet him with hugs and giggles and amusing stories about her day at preschool. He would play with her for a couple of hours, read her a story or two and tuck her into bed. Maybe spend another two or three hours watching the tube and reading through some paperwork before turning in.

Very exciting path his life had taken lately, he thought wryly.

Leaning back in his desk chair, he let his thoughts drift backward to the week before Alan Curtis had called. He remembered watching Caitlin walk across his office with her smooth, graceful strides. Remembered flirting with her and making her blush. Remembered thinking he had plenty of time to charm his way into her bed—and perhaps into her heart.

He suspected she'd been in his heart since the day she had first come into his office with her smoky-gray eyes, her very respectable résumé, and her burning ambition.

He didn't regret bringing Isabelle into his life, he reassured himself. Given the same decision, even knowing first-hand how his life would change, he would do nothing differently.

But that didn't mean he had absolutely no regrets. He wished he had asked Caitlin out while he'd still had more free time. And he wished he could have taken care of the youngest member of his family without losing the older ones.

He missed his mother. While he hadn't seen her every day before Isabelle moved in, he had talked to her on the phone most days. Just a quick call to say hello, make sure she was okay. To share a funny story, maybe, or hear about her many community activities.

He didn't want to believe his relationship with her was over.

He recalled the assertion he'd made to Caitlin that he hadn't given up on his relationship with his father and he wouldn't give up on his mother. And then he reached for the phone.

"Mom?" he said when she answered. "It's Nathan."

There was only a slight pause before she replied, "I haven't forgotten the sound of your voice."

"I'm glad to hear that," he said lightly. "I've missed hearing yours."

"I miss you, too, Nathan."

"Then why are we acting this way? Why can't we get past this?"

"You know why."

"Are you really telling me you don't want to see me again?" His voice was very quiet now, his throat tight as he waited for her to answer. "Do I mean that little to you?"

"Please don't be cruel." Pain throbbed in her low voice, making him realize exactly how deeply he had hurt her. "You know very well that I love you, Nathan."

She had loved his father, too—more than he, or perhaps

even Stuart, had known until the marriage ended. Nathan understood that now, but it still hurt that she was comparing his actions to her unfaithful husband's. "I love you, too, Mom. And I would like to see you again."

Another long pause, and then… "Perhaps you could come by the house some afternoon for a cup of tea. You can slip away from the office for an hour or so, can't you?"

He knew, of course, why she had suggested tea rather than dinner. She was making it clear that she was inviting *him* to her house and not his ward.

He bit his lip, trying to decide how to respond. Maybe he should take advantage of any small gesture; maybe if he and his mother opened a dialogue, she could better understand the position he had been placed in.

Maybe someday soon she could even be around Isabelle and see a sweet little girl instead of her husband's betrayal.

"Sure, Mom. That would be great."

He could hear the relief in her voice when she responded, "How about tomorrow afternoon? Do you have any free time then?"

He glanced at his calendar and winced. "Um, I'm afraid I can't make it tomorrow."

"I understand if you have to work. I thought you might be free because you usually have a light load on Thursday afternoons."

He cleared his throat. "Actually, I'm supposed to be at Miss Thelma's tomorrow afternoon. Isabelle's class is having a Halloween party and parents are encouraged to attend."

He had the odd sensation that the telephone receiver suddenly grew cold in his hand. "I see," she said.

"I wouldn't want Isabelle to be the only one there without someone to perform for. I think they're singing a song or something. And there's a carnival after the program, with booths and games and treats. The parents are expected to help out for a little while.''

His stumbling explanation seemed to only make the situation worse. ''Yes, well, perhaps another time.''

''I hate to keep harping on this, Mom, but Isabelle's an important part of my life now. I can't pretend otherwise. I'm going to have her for the next fifteen years or so. Couldn't you...couldn't you think of her as my adopted daughter, or something, and forget about her parentage? You wouldn't shun an adopted child, would you?''

''Do you think I haven't tried to think of her that way?'' Lenore demanded, her words practically vibrating through the lines. ''I can't. At least not yet. Please, Nathan, I can't talk about this now.''

He sighed. ''I'll call you next week, Mom.''

She murmured something inaudible and disconnected the call. Nathan hung up the phone and leaned back in his chair, staring blindly out the window.

Chapter Eleven

He didn't hear her come in. Caitlin paused just inside the open doorway of Nathan's office, struck by his pose and his distant expression.

Just the fact that he sat so motionlessly was disconcerting enough; Nathan was never still for long. And there were so many complex emotions swirling in his eyes that she couldn't begin to guess what he was feeling. Worried? Sad? Lonely?

Maybe he was just tired. She could identify with that, since she hadn't been sleeping well this week.

Of course, her reason for losing sleep was sitting right here in front of her.

"Nathan?"

Still looking deeply distracted, he turned his head to look at her. "Hmm?"

"I'm getting ready to leave for the day. Are you staying awhile?"

"No." He pushed his chair away from the desk and stood. "I'm leaving."

She had seen him just before lunch, and he'd been grinning and cutting up then. His mood seemed to have taken a full hundred-eighty-degree turn. She took a few steps closer to him, trying to read his expression. "Rough afternoon?"

He shrugged. "Not really. Settled the Compton case."

"Was Mr. Compton satisfied?"

"I think so. I finally convinced him he couldn't count on getting any more money if we went to court."

"You should be pleased. I know you were concerned about taking that case to court."

"Yeah, I'm glad it's over."

It was obvious to her that his settled case was the last thing on his mind. "Everything else going okay?"

He pushed his mouth into a smile. "Sure. How about you? I thought you'd be tied up a while longer on the conference call."

"We were able to wrap it up pretty quickly. I'll go over my notes with you sometime tomorrow."

"I'll make time in the morning, if you're free then. I have to leave for a couple hours tomorrow afternoon. There's a Halloween program at Isabelle's school. I think they're singing or something. She wants me there to watch."

"Need me to cover for you here?"

"Thanks, but I've cleared my calendar for a couple of hours. I had a week's notice about the program."

"I'm sure Isabelle will be thrilled to have you there."

"My first appearance as a parental unit. How do you think I'll do?"

Was he worried about that? "I think you'll do just fine."

His smile became a bit more genuine. "Thanks for the vote of confidence."

"You're welcome." She returned the smile, then started to turn toward the door.

He caught her forearm, swinging her back around to face him. "I'm afraid I just can't resist..." he murmured right before his mouth came down on hers.

There was something about his kisses—something that emptied her mind, robbed her willpower, weakened her knees and accelerated her pulse rate. Something more addictive than any drug could possibly be.

She wrapped her arms around his neck. She hadn't actually planned to do so, but she didn't try very hard to resist the impulse. The move brought them closer, their bodies pressed together from chest to knee.

The rather primly tailored navy suit Caitlin had worn like a coat of armor that day seemed to become suddenly thinner as Nathan's hands swept over her back and hips. She could have almost sworn she felt the warmth of his palms directly on her skin, though she knew that was impossible. Wishful thinking, perhaps.

His hair was soft and thick when she plunged her hands into it. His mouth was warm and hungry when her tongue tangled with his. His body was lean and hard beneath his conservative business clothing. Growing harder by the moment, she couldn't help noticing as his hands slid down her hips and held her more snugly against him.

He had already made it clear that he wanted her. This merely reinforced his words. She had already known she wanted him. It was becoming harder all the time for her to deny it—to herself or to him.

He tugged at her jacket, pulling it off her shoulders and down her arms, revealing the thin, sleeveless ice-blue shell she wore beneath. Another tug, and the shell came free from the waistband of her straight navy skirt. A moment later she knew exactly how it felt to have Nathan's hands on the bare skin of her back.

It felt fabulous.

She tilted her head, letting her lips rub softly against his. And then she arched into him when he brought his hands around beneath the shell to cup her breasts through the thin fabric of her bra. His thumbs rubbed her nipples, making her shiver in his arms.

"Nathan," she murmured into his mouth.

He drew his hands from beneath her top to cup her flushed face between them. His eyes were such a dark blue—gleaming sapphires—when they locked with hers. His voice was a hoarse growl when he asked, "Do you have any idea how badly I want you?"

Since their lower bodies were still plastered tightly together, she nodded. "I have a pretty good idea."

His hands lowered to her shoulders and stroked slowly down her forearms. "I have a pretty good idea it's not all one-sided."

There was no sense in denying her feelings now, not when she was draped all over him, her nipples hard against his chest, her hands fisted in his shirt to keep him close to her. "It's not one-sided."

He smiled and brushed a kiss against the tip of her nose. "It seems like it has taken months to get you to admit that."

Probably because it had, she mused wryly. She must have started falling for him the first time she met him, when he'd smiled at her and said, "I would be deeply honored if you would consider being my partner, Caitlin Briley."

He lowered his head to kiss her again, gently this time. Lingeringly. The tenderness of the embrace affected her even more deeply than the passion of before. She melted against him.

The kiss changed again, flaring hotter and needier. If he had lowered her to the floor then, she wouldn't have uttered a syllable of protest. He could have tossed aside the navy suit and taken her right there in the office, and she would have given herself to him with utter abandon.

She would have sworn he was tempted to do just that. She could almost feel the urge ripple through him, so strong he trembled with it. For just a moment they seemed poised on the brink of something momentous. Life changing. Irreversible.

Nathan was the one who came to his senses first. She wasn't sure whether she was more relieved or disappointed when he lifted his head, slowly bringing the kiss to an end. "Damn," he said.

It took her a few beats to catch up. "What?" She cleared her throat. "What's wrong?"

"I have to go home. It's Mrs. T.'s choir night."

Recalled abruptly to her senses, she shook her head and took a step backward, putting some distance between them.

"You have to go home to Isabelle," she said, very slowly returning to reality.

"Come with me. Have dinner with us."

"No. I— No." She simply wasn't ready for a cozy family meal with Nathan and his little sister.

He looked as though he would have liked to argue, but he reluctantly accepted her answer. "All right. We're still on for the symphony Saturday night, right?"

"Yes." It would be rude to back out on that commitment now, since he had already made arrangements.

"Great. I've been looking forward to it all week."

Picking up his overstuffed briefcase, he nodded toward the door. "After you, partner."

She made an attempt to pull her dignity together. Lifting her chin and squaring her shoulders, she turned to leave his office.

"Caitlin?" His voice sounded oddly amused.

"Yes?" she asked, glancing over her shoulder.

He scooped her jacket off the floor and dangled it from one finger. "I doubt that you want Irene to find this here in the morning."

Her cheeks burned. Snatching the jacket away from him, she shoved her arms into it.

She didn't even want to *think* about Irene finding her clothes scattered around Nathan's office.

A steady stream of monsters, wizards, superheroes, princesses, cartoon characters and movie villains rang Caitlin's doorbell Thursday evening. Though she had heard reports that trick-or-treating had been falling out of favor nationwide, the tradition was still thriving in Honesty. Most of her visitors were children from the large, family-friendly, town house apartment complex in which she had lived since moving here, but there were also quite a few from the modestly priced housing development that began on the next block.

Having been forewarned by the neighbors about the number of trick-or-treaters to expect, she had bought several big bags of candy. As was the apartment complex practice, she left her outside light burning as a signal that she welcomed ghostly visitors. Her apartment was at the end of a block of town houses, so it seemed to be one of the first stops.

Though some of her older neighbors had complained that they wished the practice could be banned and that they worried about crime and vandalism from roving packs of unsupervised teenagers, Caitlin rather enjoyed the evening.

She'd spread her work out on her coffee table, tuned the TV to a classic-TV-comedy-series marathon and popped up and down to answer the door.

The children were adorable in their costumes, their eyes shining from behind masks or through layers of makeup. Proud parents hovered self-consciously in the background, whispering instructions, "Say trick or treat. Tell the nice lady thank you." Most of the kids displayed very nice manners, and Caitlin decided not to let the ruder, usually older ones spoil her pleasure in the evening.

The doorbell had almost completely stopped ringing by seven-thirty, which was a relief since she was almost out of candy. She was considering turning off the light and calling it an evening when the bell chimed again.

She should have turned off her light after the last group of trick-or-treaters fifteen minutes earlier. But since she hadn't, she stood, picked up the nearly empty bowl of candy and opened her door.

A dashing duo posed on her doorstep. A tall, lean Superman in blue tights and red cape stood with his arms crossed nobly over his chest, while a petite blond Supergirl bounced at his side, looking as though she might very well take off and fly. "Trick or treat, Miss Caitlin!"

With an effort, Caitlin drew her gaze from Nathan and smiled down at Isabelle. "Maybe you two should come inside. It isn't often I get a visit from Superman and Supergirl."

Isabelle wasn't wearing a mask, but she wore a fairly heavy coating of blue eye shadow, rosy blusher and pink lipstick. Caitlin couldn't help smiling as she pictured Nathan inexpertly applying the face paints. Isabelle skipped into the living room, hauling a bulging treat bag filled with candy. Nathan followed, apparently completely at ease in his own costume.

He should have looked ridiculous, Caitlin thought in bemusement. Instead, he was gorgeous. A tall, lean, sandy-haired, blue-eyed hero. Funny, she had never fancied herself as Lois Lane—until now.

"You really go all out for this holiday, don't you?" she asked him quizzically as she snapped off the outside light to put an end to the festivities for the evening.

He chuckled. "This was Isabelle's idea. I've been letting her look at some of my old comic books, and Superman and Supergirl are her favorites."

"You have a comic book collection?" she asked without surprise.

"Not a particularly valuable one. Just my favorites from when I was a kid—maybe a hundred editions."

"Oh. Just a hundred," she teased, making him grin.

"Nate wasn't sure he wanted to dress up, but I told him it would be more fun if we both did," Isabelle confided. "Look how much candy I got, Miss Caitlin. Tons and tons."

"Very impressive." Caitlin emptied the half dozen remaining pieces of candy in her bowl into Isabelle's treat bag. "There you go. Be sure and let Nathan go through everything before you eat it, okay? Just to make sure it all looks safe and tightly wrapped."

"I will. Nate already made me promise."

"I've refreshed myself on basic trick-or-treat protocol," he added.

Caitlin gave him a thumbs-up of approval before asking Isabelle, "Have you had a good time today?"

"Oh, yes!" The child launched immediately into a breathless litany of the events of her day, beginning with breakfast, rambling through her morning preschool classes and continuing through the Halloween program and carnival that had followed. She concluded with a detailed itinerary of the houses where they had stopped for trick-or-treating—all belonging to friends of her brother, she added.

Caitlin listened politely, though her gaze kept wandering to Nathan. He did look fine in those tights, she thought with a stifled sigh.

Barely pausing for breath after her monologue, Isabelle added, "I got to go to the bathroom."

Nathan groaned. "Isabelle."

"Well, I do!" she insisted, wide-eyed.

Caitlin smiled. "I happen to have a bathroom. Let me show you where it is."

Isabelle took her hand. "Okay."

Leading the little girl to the first door on the right in the hallway, Caitlin reached in to turn on the light. "Do you need any assistance?"

"No, thank you. I can do it."

Amused by the child's brusquely independent tone, Caitlin stepped out of the doorway. "Call out if you need anything."

Isabelle firmly closed the door between them. Chuckling, Caitlin stepped back into the living room and was immediately enveloped by a pair of strong male arms.

"Ever kiss a superhero?" Nathan asked.

"I can't say that I have," she replied, letting her hands slide up his chest, pausing to trace the stylized "S", then moving up to circle his neck. "But it might be an interesting experience."

"I'll try to make it a little better than 'interesting,'" he promised as he lowered his mouth to hers.

The kiss was *considerably* better than interesting. It was well on its way to becoming spectacular when they heard the bathroom door open, indicating that Isabelle would rejoin them momentarily. Reluctantly Caitlin extricated herself from Nathan's arms and stepped backward.

Giving her a rueful look, he pulled his long red cape around him.

Caitlin turned to entertain Isabelle for a moment, helping the child rearrange her own costume, asking a few more questions about the school Halloween carnival, laughing at Isabelle's description of her teachers' stint in a dunking booth. After a couple of minutes Nathan stepped forward. "We'd better go, kiddo. We have to fight injustice and evil all around the world."

"Actually," Isabelle confided to Caitlin, "I have to go to bed. I have school tomorrow."

Caitlin leaned over to kiss her soft cheek. "I'm glad you came to my door tonight, Isabelle. It was a very nice treat for me."

Isabelle threw her arms around Caitlin's neck and snuggled her painted little face into Caitlin's throat. "Thank you for the candy, Miss Caitlin. I love you."

Oh, God. Caitlin felt unexpected tears threaten. She wrapped her arms around Isabelle's fragile little body and squeezed gently, her watery gaze meeting Nathan's over the child's head.

He gave her a lopsided smile that seemed to say, "Now you understand why I couldn't give her up."

She had understood his reasoning all along, of course. She simply didn't know if she was ready to make such a permanent commitment herself.

Nathan restrained himself to a kiss on her cheek as he passed her on the way out the door. "See you tomorrow."

"Be careful out there fighting crime, Superman," she murmured, then closed the door behind him and leaned her forehead against the wood.

She wished she had a few superpowers of her own—the ability to see the future among them.

Straightening, she spotted the folded letter she had

tucked into a basket on a cherry side table close to the door. She still hadn't told Nathan about hearing from Tom, or about the possibility that she could be interviewed for a fast-track position in Los Angeles.

She didn't know what was holding her back. Maybe she didn't know what she would tell him if he asked if she really wanted that interview.

Because Nathan got held up in an unexpected client meeting Saturday, barely getting away in time to make the symphony performance, he arranged by phone for Caitlin to meet him at his house. That way, they agreed, he would have time to change and they could leave straight from his place.

She had assured him that she, of all people, understood the sometimes-inconvenient demands of work, and didn't mind making a few concessions because of his career duties.

Fayrene Tuckerman answered the door when Caitlin rang Nathan's bell. "Good evening, Ms. Briley," she said, ushering Caitlin inside. "Don't you look lovely this evening."

Caitlin had worn her simple black sheath with a beaded black jacket and heeled black sandals. She had pinned her hair up and secured it with a couple of glittery hairpins. Her only other jewelry was a pair of diamond stud earrings. "Thank you, Mrs. Tuckerman. Is Nathan ready?"

"He just dashed in and went straight to his room to shower and change. He said to tell you he would join you in a few minutes. May I get you something to drink while you wait?"

"No, thank you. I'll just—"

"Miss Caitlin! Miss Caitlin!"

Caitlin braced herself. A moment later Isabelle threw her arms around Caitlin's legs and squeezed as enthusiastically as if it had been weeks since they had last seen each other rather than just a couple of days.

"Hello, Isabelle." Caitlin returned the hug. "What happened to your friend Supergirl?"

Isabelle giggled. "She went back to Krypton till next Halloween."

"Gee, I hope she'll write us sometime."

The child was obviously delighted with Caitlin's silliness. She beamed up at her. "Are you going on a date with Nate?" she asked, relishing the rhyme.

"Nathan and I are going to the symphony."

"Mrs. T. brought some games. She's going to teach me to play Trouble and checkers."

"Sounds like fun."

"Do you like to play games?"

"Yes, occasionally."

"Will you play with me sometime?"

"I'd love to."

Nathan stumbled into the room, still shoving his arms into his suit jacket. His hair was damp and his tie crooked, but he was smiling when his eyes met Caitlin's.

"Sorry," he said. "Kirk Sawyer got himself arrested for DWI again, and he insisted that I come down to the police station. I told him this is it—he's going to have to find another lawyer from now on."

Kirk Sawyer was a local sports hero who had played four seasons with a professional football team before ruining his knees and ending his career. He'd spent the ten years since strutting around town, filming cheesy commercials for his father's successful car dealership and partying.

Had he not been who he was, he would already be serving time, but his reputation and his father's money carried a bit too much weight in this town. Nathan wasn't the first local lawyer who'd gotten tired of defending him.

Isabelle studied him critically. "Your tie's messed up, Nate."

He tugged at it, which succeeded in skewing it worse.

Caitlin shook her head. "Let me," she said, stepping forward. She straightened the tie quickly and efficiently, looking up at him through her eyelashes.

He smiled down at her, obviously enjoying her attentions. "Thank you. You do that very well."

"My father never learned how to tie a necktie. Not that he needed to wear one often. He only had one that he wore to weddings, funerals and the occasional job interview."

Aware that Isabelle and Mrs. T. were watching them with interest, she patted the tie and stepped back. "There. That looks much better, doesn't it, Isabelle?"

"Yes. Miss Caitlin looks pretty, doesn't she, Nate?"

"Miss Caitlin looks beautiful," he replied, and his tone made Caitlin fight a blush.

"Thank you. And now we had better go before we miss the opening number," she said, carefully avoiding the housekeeper's eyes as she turned toward the door.

"Have fun at the sympathy," Isabelle called after them.

Nathan laughed. "I would correct her, but it just sounded too appropriate," he told Caitlin as he opened the passenger door of his car for her.

Her own smile lasted until they were on the road. All of a sudden she was too intensely aware that she and Nathan were on a date. Sort of. And all of a sudden she could think of absolutely nothing to say.

As inconceivable as the notion seemed, Nathan appeared to be suffering from a similar problem. He cleared his throat. "So. We're really doing this. Going out, I mean."

She frowned intently through the windshield. "It's hardly the first time we've spent an evening together. We've done things together in the past."

"Those other times were for business. This is different."

"We're simply attending the symphony together, not slipping away for a weekend in Vegas."

He grinned. "Actually, that Vegas thing sounds pretty good. We could be at the airport in forty-five minutes."

She slanted him a look. "I doubt your baby-sitter would appreciate that."

"You're probably right. So how about if we slipped off to Disney World, instead? We can take Isabelle."

"How about if we just attend the sympathy, I mean, the symphony," she corrected herself quickly.

He chuckled. "Careful. The poppet wears off on you."

"I suppose you're right." She settled back into her seat and ordered herself to relax for the remainder of the evening. After all, she told herself sternly, this was merely a date. And he was only Nathan, a man she had known quite comfortably for almost a year now.

So why wasn't she at all comfortable with him tonight?

Chapter Twelve

The concert hall was crowded, and there were many people in attendance Caitlin and Nathan knew. No one seemed particularly surprised to see them there together. Was it simply assumed they were there as friends and business partners, or did most people already consider them a couple?

Caitlin couldn't help wondering what was being said about them, but she decided not to dwell on it tonight. It certainly wasn't as if she had any control over local gossip.

She did notice as they swapped greetings on their way to their seats that no one mentioned Isabelle. Or Nathan's mother. But maybe that was just as well, she thought, taking her seat and preparing to enjoy the performance.

Of course, it was hard to concentrate on the music when she was so very aware of the man sitting in the seat beside her. His shoulder brushed against hers, and when he shifted his long legs in the narrow space provided for them, their thighs made contact.

She felt ridiculously like a schoolgirl on her first date, so painfully self-conscious that her mouth was dry. When his hand slipped over the shared arm of their chairs to entwine with hers in the darkness, she completely forgot the theme of the program.

Mozart or Mendelssohn? Bach or the Beatles? She wasn't sure she could have said just then.

How could she have imagined there were so many erogenous zones in her hand? She had never suspected, for example, that the skin between her fingers was so sensitive. And when his thumb rotated slowly in the center of her palm, she felt heat rush through her, pooling somewhere deep inside her abdomen. She kept her eyes focused fiercely on the stage, though she no longer cared who was doing what there.

She made it through intermission by plastering a smile on her face and nodding brightly in response to everything that was said to her, though she wasn't sure she actually heard a word of it. She was, however, all too keenly conscious of every time Nathan rested a hand at the center of her back or touched her arm or smiled at her.

Her emotions had swung from bemused to despairing. This was *not* the way she preferred to behave in public! Here she had an excellent opportunity to mingle, to discreetly drop the name of their firm into casual conversations, to make potentially important business connections, and what was she doing? Blushing and daydreaming like a silly schoolgirl. Acting more like a woman in the throes of her first big infatuation than an intelligent, L.A.-quality attorney.

Even that fleeting thought of Los Angeles made her swallow hard. She really should tell Nathan about Tom's letter.

Just as important, she really should give Tom a more definitive response than the vague interest she had expressed thus far.

Nathan held her hand again during the second part of the program. Such a simple little gesture, almost innocently sweet. Yet there was nothing at all innocent about her reaction. She wanted to climb all over him.

They were rather quiet again during the drive back to Nathan's house. It was getting late, and she could have used the excuse that she was tired, but she wasn't. She was more wired than she'd been in a long time.

"Come in for a little while," Nathan said when he'd parked in his garage. "We'll have coffee or something."

She tucked a loose strand of hair behind her ear. "I'm not sure I—"

"Please."

She moistened her lips. "All right."

It was well after 10:00 p.m., so Isabelle was sleeping. Mrs. T. sat at the kitchen table reading. She looked up with a smile when they walked in. "Did you enjoy the performance?"

"It was very nice," Caitlin replied, fervently hoping she wouldn't be expected to give any details.

The housekeeper closed her book and stood. "I'll be on my way now. Isabelle was an angel, as always. A bit quieter than usual, I thought, especially as the night wore on, but I suppose that's because she's grown accustomed to having you here with her in the evenings, Mr. McCloud. She's sleeping now. I just looked in on her. And I made a fresh pot of coffee—decaf, of course, since it's so late. I thought you and Ms. Briley might like to have a cup while you talk about your evening."

Nathan smiled warmly. "Have I mentioned that you're a treasure?"

Her eyebrows lifted in what appeared to be surprise that he felt it necessary to state the obvious. "I'll see you Monday morning, Mr. McCloud. Nice to see you again, Ms. Briley."

With a faint ripple of panic, Caitlin watched the forceful, prosaic housekeeper leave. With the exception of the toddler sleeping in the other room, she and Nathan were alone now with the feelings that had been simmering between them all evening, steadily reaching boiling point.

Though his gaze was on her face, as if reading the emotions reflected there, Nathan moved toward the counter and spoke casually, "Coffee?"

"I should probably go soon. It's getting late."

"Mrs. T. went to the trouble to make coffee for us. It would be a shame to let it go to waste."

"Well, maybe just one cup."

He gave her a smile of approval and poured steaming coffee into the two cups that had been conveniently left out for them. "Just cream, right?"

"Yes, please." She took a couple of steps toward him to retrieve her cup.

Holding the cup in his hand, he turned. Their eyes met. Very slowly he replaced the cup on the counter, leaving his hands free.

She went into his arms as if she had intended to do so all along.

For once, Nathan wasn't smooth. Their noses bumped when he swooped down to kiss her. She felt a tremor in his arms, an indication of the tension that had been building in him all night. And then he kissed her until she was the one trembling and clinging to him for support.

Cupping her face between his hands, he lifted his mouth only far enough to murmur rather fiercely, "If you only knew how long I've wanted you."

She felt as if she had been waiting all her life for this moment. And now that it was here, it petrified her. "I don't—"

He kissed her again, his tongue plunging between her lips to mate with hers. And somehow her hands were tangled in his hair, her legs entwined with his as he pressed her against the refrigerator door. He devoured her mouth, and she responded with an equal hunger, flattening herself against him so that she could feel every hard muscle in his body against her. And she reveled in the growing hardness that proved he wanted her as mindlessly as she wanted him.

A low growl rumbled in his chest, a primitive, utterly male sound that seduced her as pretty words never could. There was such delicious power in knowing he wanted her so badly. Such a feminine thrill in the awareness that she could make him tremble with need.

"There are still so many things we need to discuss," she murmured into his mouth, trying to retain at least a modicum of common sense. "Things we need to think about."

"Let's not think tonight," he groaned, sliding his hands down her sides and resting his forehead against hers. "Just this once, let's not think."

Act without thinking? Without planning? Without considering all the possibilities and ramifications? How totally unlike her.

"I want you, Caitlin."

"I want you, too," she whispered, because it would be pointless not to admit it. "But—"

He kissed the arguments back into her mouth. "Just for tonight, can't we let that be enough?" he asked when he lifted his head again.

Could wanting be enough, just for one night? And could one night ever be enough between them?

Don't think, he had said. Don't worry about tomorrow.

And for once, she wanted nothing more than to follow Nathan's example and act wholly on impulse.

He rubbed his lips slowly, enticingly over hers. "Caitlin?"

Just this once, she promised herself, and lifted on tiptoe to wrap her arms around his neck. This time she kissed him, and she held nothing back.

The sound he made held deep satisfaction. Very slowly lifting his mouth from hers, he stepped back and took her hand.

Her decision made, she didn't hesitate again, but allowed him to lead her out of the kitchen.

Just this once, she promised herself, she wouldn't think. She would simply enjoy.

Nathan's bedroom was as carelessly masculine as he was. The single, low-wattage lamp on his nightstand revealed heavy woods, earthy colors and bold textures. The room was as neat as a pin; remembering that he had changed hurriedly for their date, she suspected that Mrs. T. had been in to tidy up while they were gone. She didn't want to speculate about whether the housekeeper had been doing her chores or had considered herself preparing the room for company.

Had they been in Caitlin's apartment now, she might have lit candles, maybe turned on some soft music. Since Nathan's decor didn't include candles, and his music selection was probably filled with classic rock, he did neither, but simply swept the spread off his bed and tumbled her onto it, barely giving her time to kick off her shoes.

She decided that his unpretentious actions suited her just fine. She didn't want calculated seduction from Nathan, no careful scene setting or romantic gestures. She simply wanted him.

The flattering tremor was still in his hands when he carefully stripped away her beaded jacket and black sheath, leaving her clad only in black bra, panties, garter belt and stockings. Her face flamed as it occurred to her that her provocative undergarments might lead him to believe she had expected the evening to end this way. Then it burned even hotter when she silently admitted to herself that he would probably be right.

Apparently, she had stopped thinking sensibly before this date had even begun.

Whatever he made of her reasons, it was obvious that he heartily approved her outfit. His hands were all over her, exploring and caressing until she writhed against the sheets, almost desperate to feel him against her. She tugged at his clothing, tangling them both in folds of fabric until he laughed softly and lifted away from her to take care of the task himself.

When he came back to her, he wasn't wearing a stitch—and Caitlin was quite sure she had never seen anything more appealing in her entire life. Nor felt anything more delectable. She ran her hands slowly over his sinewy arms and sleek chest, down to his narrow waist and lean hips.

An athlete's physique, she mused, strong and fit and virile. She would find it very hard to believe that a more perfect body had ever existed.

It didn't take him long to add her undergarments to the piles of clothing on his floor. Caitlin might have been self-conscious about her nudity—she didn't consider herself to be nearly as close to perfection as Nathan—but his obvious pleasure in her restored her confidence. Whatever imperfections there might be, he didn't even seem to notice.

He looked at her as though he found her as beautiful, as desirable as she found him. And when he touched his mouth to her, it was with a reverence that brought a lump to her throat.

He nuzzled her neck, lingered at her breasts, kissed his way down to her navel and circled it with his tongue. Her hands fisted in the sheets beneath her when he moved even lower, her back arching instinctively. Her breath caught hard in her throat, then released in a gasp. "Nathan!"

Murmuring something soothing and unintelligible, he kissed her intimately, then made his way slowly back up her body, stopping to revisit places he had discovered before. She could hardly remember her own name by the time he returned to her lips. Yet she couldn't seem to stop whispering his.

He donned protection swiftly, barely fumbling with the task though his hands were still shaking a bit. And then he returned to her, sliding inside her with a single, smooth thrust that seemed to join them permanently. From this moment on, he would always be a part of her, she realized, even as she drew him nearer. It was the only coherent thought that penetrated the haze of passion she floated in, and it should have terrified her. Instead, it made the experience all the more beautiful.

After all, tonight she wasn't thinking about the future, she reminded herself dimly. Tonight was all about feelings. And this felt heavenly.

Nathan rolled, shifting her on top of him, giving his hands better access to her breasts and shoulders. Supporting herself on her hands, she leaned her head down to kiss him.

Her hairpins seemed to have disappeared; her hair fell in a soft curtain around their faces. Their mouths fused, their tongues thrusting in a leisurely imitation of their intimate joining.

When their movements became more frantic, Nathan shifted again, crushing her into the mattress as he pounded into her. Just barely remembering that they weren't alone in his house, she bit her lower lip to hold back her cries and dug her fingers into his shoulders as her entire body shuddered with a mind-shattering release.

A moment later Nathan gave a choked gasp that might have been her name, signaling his own climax. And then he collapsed on top of her, his face buried in her throat.

Still holding him, Caitlin stared blindly at the ceiling above her and wondered how much longer she could simply enjoy this time with him. Sooner or later she was going to have to start asking herself what this night was going to cost her.

Nathan sensed the moment Caitlin's hyperactive brain kicked into gear. He could almost hear the doubts, the questions, the worries and rationalizations begin.

While he had always admired her practicality and conscientiousness, he wished they could have drifted on sensations a bit longer this evening.

"I should leave," she murmured.

He wasn't ready to let her go. Shifting to relieve her of his weight, he tucked her into his shoulder. "Stay a little longer."

"I don't want to be here when Isabelle wakes up," she fretted softly, even as she snuggled her cheek into the curve of his throat. "I don't even have a change of clothes."

Smoothing her hair, he brushed a kiss against the top of her head. "Just let me hold you for a little while longer."

She relaxed slowly against him, one hand resting on his chest. "Just for a little while."

He would take whatever he could get, he thought, enjoying the feel of her warm, soft body pressed against his. As far as he was concerned, whenever she left would be too soon. He would be perfectly content to keep her here in his bed forever.

Since he knew she was far from ready to hear that, he kept the words to himself. Not saying them didn't make them any less true, of course. He didn't know when, exactly, his feelings had progressed from affection to more, but he had no doubt that he was in love with Caitlin Briley.

He had never actually been in love before, but he had no trouble identifying the condition. He'd felt fondness, respect and desire for other women, but he'd never even come close to wanting to make a lifetime commitment with any of them.

He was fully prepared to take that step with Caitlin, just as soon as he thought she was ready to hear the words.

Which, he acknowledged reluctantly, was not going to be tonight. She had taken a huge step by making love with him, despite her concerns about getting personally involved with her business associate. He knew she was worried about how their working relationship would change now and what would happen to the firm if their affair went south.

He also had the uncomfortable suspicion that she was concerned about being tied down, having him—or anything—interfere with her career. For whatever reason, she needed to validate herself through her success at work, and she was extremely leery of anything—or anyone—that resembled a potential stumbling block. It was entirely possible that she saw him as a giant-size block, especially now that he came as a family package.

She shifted against him with a soft sound that sounded like a cross between a sigh and a purr. His arm tightened around her, and he pressed a kiss against her hair.

Whatever he had to do, he would somehow convince

Caitlin that they belonged together. And that he would never do anything to interfere with her dreams.

She lifted her head to give him a drowsy smile. "If I stay much longer, I'll fall asleep. I don't want to risk having Isabelle find me in your bed."

He rolled to lean over her. "Trust me," he murmured, "you aren't going to fall asleep. Not just yet."

She looked wide awake when she reached up to welcome him.

Caitlin finally convinced Nathan that she had to leave. Fully dressed again, her hair still down, but brushed out of her face, she lingered just inside the front door for a final good-night.

"Drive carefully," he said between kisses. "Maybe you should call me when you get there."

She wrinkled her nose at him. "You are not my father. I'm quite capable of seeing myself home."

"Maybe I just want to hear your voice again before I go to sleep."

Refusing to be swayed by his blarney, she reached for the doorknob. "Good night, Nathan."

He held the door closed for a moment. "I want to see you again tomorrow. Come spend some time with us. Isabelle loves seeing you."

She bit her lip as she tried to decide how to reply. This was one of the very things she worried about in getting involved with Nathan. She didn't want to become too much a part of Isabelle's life and risk hurting her later. Isabelle had already lost too many people she cared about. "I really should do some work tomorrow."

"Bring your files with you. It will be a good time for us to catch up on our consultations. Everything has been so hectic at the office lately that we haven't had much time to talk.''

He had, of course, chosen the one argument she couldn't easily counter. They did need to spend some time discussing business, especially the malpractice case, which was starting to get expensive. And it *was* difficult to find uninterrupted time at the office.

''I suppose I could come by for a little while. Do you think we'll be able to talk about work with Isabelle here?''

''Sure. Give her a drawing pad and some markers and she's happy for hours. Why don't you plan to have lunch with us? I make a better-than-decent spaghetti sauce.''

It was a big step from an impromptu business meeting to a cozy family lunch. But the look on Nathan's face told her he was prepared to charm her into accepting if she tried to decline. Just to save time and trouble, she said, ''Fine. Thank you, I would be delighted to join you for lunch.''

His smile let her know he suspected her reason for conceding so easily, but he merely nodded. ''About twelve-thirty, then?''

''I'll be here. Good night, Nathan.''

He leaned over to give her one last, lingering kiss. ''Good night, Caitlin.''

She didn't sleep well that night, though she should have been exhausted. Her bed seemed too empty and her head too full of second thoughts and self-recriminations. And memories she knew would stay with her for the rest of her life.

Looking disarrayed in a frayed gray sweatshirt and faded jeans, Nathan jerked opened his front door almost before Caitlin took her finger off the doorbell. She hadn't exactly dressed up for the casual visit, having selected a forest-green sweater and a pair of loose khakis, but he looked as though he had just crawled out of bed.

She had expected to be greeted with a warm smile, perhaps a kiss, but she was totally unprepared for him to reach out, grab her wrist and tug her inside so roughly she thought he might pull her arm out of its socket. "What in the—"

"Something's wrong with Isabelle," he broke in urgently, slamming the door closed behind her. "I don't know what to do."

"What are you talking about? What's wrong with Isabelle?"

He took the heavy briefcase and tossed it aside. Though she gave a fleeting thought to the computer inside it, she was more concerned about Isabelle. Nathan almost dragged her to the den, where Isabelle was lying on the couch. "I think she's sick," he told Caitlin in a low, tense voice.

Extricating herself from his grip, Caitlin knelt beside the couch. Still wearing wrinkled yellow cotton pajamas, Isabelle seemed to be dozing, though fitfully. Her little face was flushed, her hair damp and limp. Her breathing seemed to be a bit wheezy.

Though she hadn't the foggiest clue what she was doing, Caitlin reached out to rest a hand lightly on Isabelle's forehead. Her skin felt as hot as it looked. "I think she has a fever."

"Yeah, I think so, too. Does it feel very high to you?"

"I have no idea. Don't you have a thermometer?"

"No."

Isabelle gave a soft little moan and shifted restlessly on the couch cushions.

Caitlin looked anxiously up at Nathan, who hovered behind her, his face taut. "Maybe you should take her to a doctor."

"She won't—"

"No," Isabelle whimpered, proving she wasn't sleeping, after all. "No doctor."

"She gets practically hysterical every time I even suggest seeing a doctor," Nathan muttered, spreading his hands in a helpless gesture. "I don't even know if she's sick enough to call a—well, you know."

Caitlin looked doubtfully at the little girl. What constituted "sick enough" to call a doctor?

"I don't know, Nathan. Isn't there someone else you can call? What about Mrs. T.? Surely she would know what to do. She seems to know pretty much everything."

"I tried calling her just before you got here. When I didn't get an answer, I remembered she said something about visiting some friends out of town with Irene after church. I don't know how to reach her."

"Surely you know someone with children you can ask. If not, you're simply going to have to call a…you know."

Isabelle twisted her head petulantly, her lower lip protruding. "I don't want a doctor. I don't like doctors."

Sitting on the edge of the couch, Caitlin smoothed a strand of limp hair away from Isabelle's hot little face. "Why don't you like doctors, sweetie? Some doctors are very nice."

Isabelle climbed onto Caitlin's lap and burrowed into her throat. "Aunt Barb went to a doctor and he made her sick and she couldn't come home. She had to stay in the hospital."

Caitlin wrapped her arms around the small trembling body, her throat going tight. "No, baby, the doctor didn't make your aunt sick. She was already sick when she went to the hospital."

Isabelle was crying now, huge tears rolling copiously down her face and dampening Caitlin's sweater. "I'm sick.

If you take me to a doctor, he'll make me stay at the hospital. I don't want to stay at the hospital, I want to stay with Nate.''

Caitlin looked over Isabelle's head at Nathan. It was going to take some time to straighten this out, and in the meantime, Isabelle wasn't getting any better. "Call someone,'' she mouthed.

He shoved a hand through his hair. And then he snatched a cordless phone from a table, pushed a speed-dial button and held the phone to his ear.

Caitlin's eyebrows rose in surprise when he spoke. ''Mom?'' she heard him say. ''I'm sorry, but I really need your advice.''

Chapter Thirteen

Nathan opened the door when his mother rang the bell. Nerves that were already frayed from a morning of worrying about Isabelle were pulled tighter by the scowl on his mother's face.

"Thank you for coming."

Still dressed for church in a starkly tailored navy dress with a white lace collar, she moved brusquely past him, carrying a tapestry tote bag in her white-knuckled right hand. She didn't bother with greetings but asked flatly, "Where's the child?"

"She's in the den with Caitlin. I don't know what's wrong with her, Mom. She's running a fever, and she said her head hurts and her throat hurts...."

Lenore was already making her way toward the den. "There's a flu-like virus going around in the preschools. Didn't you get a notice about it?"

"A virus? I don't think so."

"All the parents were supposed to be notified. You should complain to Miss Thelma if you didn't receive a note about what symptoms to watch for."

Though he was aware that she had just indirectly referred to him as a parent, he was more concerned about Isabelle. "This virus—how bad is it? What does it do?"

"It makes little children feel lousy. Adults, too, if they're unlucky enough to get it." She moved straight to the couch where Caitlin still sat with Isabelle in her lap. "Let me see her."

Caitlin sat Isabelle on the couch and moved aside. Isabelle blinked blearily up at Lenore. "Hi, Nate's mom."

"Hello, Isabelle." Her voice more gentle now, Lenore rummaged in her tote and pulled out a digital thermometer. "Would you mind if I put this in your mouth for a couple of minutes?"

Isabelle looked from the thermometer to Lenore's face. "Are *you* a doctor?"

"No, dear, I'm a mother."

Nathan noticed that Isabelle seemed to find the answer satisfactory. She promptly opened her mouth, and Lenore slipped the thermometer inside. "How long has she been ill?"

Still trying to read her expression, he replied, "She complained of feeling badly when she woke up. She's been getting worse all morning."

"Have you given her anything?"

"Like what?"

"A pain reliever or fever reducer? Children's acetaminophen, perhaps. Not aspirin—never give a young child aspirin, especially for flu-like symptoms."

"I, uh, don't have anything except aspirin. No children's medicines."

She sighed. "Of course you don't. She's only lived with

you for a month now. Why should I think you would have stocked necessities for her?''

Wincing, he watched her dig into the tote bag again and pull out a new bottle of bright pink liquid with a measured dispenser cup attached to the lid. When had his mother turned into Mary Poppins? he wondered with a glance at the bulging bag.

He still couldn't believe she was actually here.

The thermometer beeped and Lenore removed it from Isabelle's mouth. ''A hundred and two. Not dangerously high for a child. Nathan, read the directions on that bottle and measure out the appropriate amount for a three-year-old. I believe it's a teaspoon.''

''Yes, ma'am.''

''Isabelle, have you had anything to eat or drink today?''

Watching her caretaker with trusting, heavy-lidded eyes, Isabelle shook her head. ''A little juice this morning, but not much. I wasn't hungry.''

Lenore gave Nathan another chiding look before turning to his partner. ''Caitlin, dear, perhaps you could see if there's a can of soup in Nathan's pantry? Chicken noodle would be good, anything thin and brothy. And she needs liquids or she'll dehydrate. Water, first, and then perhaps some fruit juice or Kool-Aid.''

Looking as if she, too, were tempted to say, ''Yes, ma'am,'' Caitlin merely nodded and headed for the kitchen.

Nathan handed his mother the dispenser cup of children's medicine. She offered it to Isabelle. ''This will make you feel better.''

Isabelle looked doubtfully at the concoction. ''Does it taste yucky?''

''I believe it's cherry flavored. Drink it up, Isabelle, so you can start to feel better.''

Nathan wasn't surprised when his little sister obediently

swallowed the medicine, though she made a face at the taste. When Lenore McCloud spoke in that tone, children and adults tended to respond.

Lenore took the empty cup with satisfaction. "Very good. You should feel better soon. I want you to eat some soup when Miss Caitlin has it ready, all right?"

"'Kay." Isabelle yawned and laid her head on the couch again, looking as if she had used up all her energy.

Nathan frowned, worried about Isabelle's uncharacteristic listlessness. "You don't think we need to call a doctor?" he asked in mother in a stage whisper.

"No *doctor!*" Isabelle insisted. Though Nathan had seen his little sister pout and be cross, he'd never seen her as close to a tantrum as she seemed to be at that moment.

"No doctor for now," Lenore agreed, resting a calming hand on the child's back. "I think you'll feel better once the medicine starts to work."

Isabelle subsided into the cushions. Her lower lip still protruded, but she looked somewhat appeased.

Lenore motioned toward the hallway. "We'll be right outside the door if you need us, Isabelle. I have to tell Nathan a few things. You can rest here until your lunch is ready."

Her eyes closed, Isabelle nodded.

Nathan followed his mother into the hallway, keeping his voice low so Isabelle wouldn't hear them. "You really think she's going to be okay?"

"I think she'll be fine. It's just a bug. Nothing serious. I heard at church this morning that quite a few local school-children are down with it. Frankly, I'm surprised that you and Caitlin both overreacted this much. Two professional adults should be able to handle a case of childhood sniffles without panicking."

Resisting an impulse to hang his head, Nathan cleared

his throat. "It's not as if either of us has had any experience with this sort of thing. She seemed so sick that we got scared. I really wanted to take her to the doctor, but she got so upset, I wasn't sure how to handle it. She got it in her head somehow that doctors were responsible for taking her aunt Barbara away from her, and she's afraid a doctor will take her away from me."

"For heaven's sake, Nathan, she's a three-year-old who has been uprooted too many times. It's no wonder she's afraid it will happen again or try to find someone to blame. Did you think she would be completely unscathed by losing both her parents and her aunt in such a short time?"

He pushed his hands into his pockets, digesting her words. "I thought she was doing fine, settling in great. She always seems happy enough. Hasn't caused any trouble here or at school. I didn't even know about this doctor phobia until today."

Lenore shook her head. "You still don't completely understand what you've taken on, do you? Children don't express their fears and feelings the same way adults do. And they don't necessarily act out when they have problems. Sometimes the best behaved small children become the most rebellious teenagers. I'm not saying that will happen to Isabelle—not if she receives the support and guidance she will require until then—but there's a great deal more to raising a child than playing with her and making sure her physical needs are met."

Stung by the implied criticism, Nathan lifted his chin. "I know that, but she didn't exactly come with parenting advice. I've been doing the best I can and I still think she's better off with me than she would have been with strangers."

"Perhaps you're right," his mother surprised him by conceding. "She's obviously very attached to you, and I'm sure that gives her more of a sense of security in this new home. Still, it probably wouldn't hurt her to see a counselor for a few sessions to work through her feelings about the changes in her life. And perhaps to talk about this fear of doctors before it turns into a full-fledged phobia. I'm on the advisory board of the Sunshine Children's Counseling Center, you know. There are several excellent counselors on staff there.''

"I'll, uh, look into it. Thanks.''

Caitlin appeared at the end of the hallway, looking uncertainly from Nathan to his mother. "The soup is ready. Do you think I should prepare a tray for Isabelle?''

"I'm sure she would be more comfortable at the table,'' Lenore replied before turning back to Nathan. "She'll need plenty of liquids today, and she can have another dose of the medicine in four hours. If her fever climbs too high, or she starts acting disoriented or having convulsions, you should, of course, seek immediate medical attention, even if you have to be quite firm with her about seeing a doctor. You *can* be firm with Isabelle when necessary, can't you, Nathan?''

Aware that Caitlin was watching him with a sudden smile, Nathan scowled and muttered, "Of course I can. I am the adult around here, Mom, and I've made it clear to Isabelle that I make the rules.''

"Good. Every child needs rules and boundaries in addition to unconditional love and support.'' Lenore paused a moment, then met Nathan's eyes squarely. "I'm afraid I've neglected the latter part of that advice myself. I haven't been available to you, Nathan, and I apologize for that. I let my own selfish feelings come between us at a time when you needed me, and I'm not proud of that. I am, however, proud of you.''

He melted, of course, as he always did when his family was involved. "Mom, I—"

Clearly uncomfortable at being a spectator to this emotional moment, Caitlin moved toward the den door. "I'll take Isabelle to eat her soup."

"There's no need for you to discreetly exit, Caitlin. I've said what I needed to say." Lenore touched a fingertip to the corner of each of her eyes before saying to Nathan, "Isabelle does look remarkably like Deborah, doesn't she?"

Swallowing a sizable lump in his throat, Nathan nodded. "Very much."

"Have you had lunch, Mrs. McCloud?" Caitlin asked, seemingly on impulse.

"No, I had just returned home from church when Nathan called."

"Then would you join us?" Caitlin suggested, darting a glance at Nathan, who nodded approvingly. "Nathan promised to make spaghetti sauce."

"Nathan makes horrendous spaghetti sauce," Lenore said flatly. "I'll stay, but I'll do the cooking."

"Gee, thanks a lot, Mom," Nathan murmured, too pleased that their relationship seemed to be on the mend to take offense at the slur to his spaghetti sauce. Which, he thought, was pretty darned good, if he did say so himself.

Isabelle ate her lunch at the kitchen table under Caitlin's supervision while Nathan and Lenore prepared the meal for the adults. Isabelle seemed much more interested in watching Nathan and his mother arguing over the best way to prepare spaghetti sauce than she was in eating.

Caitlin finally took the spoon and scooped chicken noodle soup into Isabelle's mouth. The child ate without much enthusiasm, but did manage to finish about half the soup before stubbornly shaking her head and refusing more.

"Nathan, would you please sit down and get out of my way?" Lenore finally asked in exasperation. "Tear some lettuce for a salad or something."

"I still say you need to add more garlic and oregano to the sauce," he grumbled, opening the refrigerator.

Her prim navy dress hidden behind a big barbecue apron, his mother shook a wooden spoon warningly at him. "I was cooking spaghetti sauce long before you were born. Now watch your manners or you'll stand in the corner until lunch is ready."

Isabelle giggled. "Nate's mom is funny," she confided to Caitlin. "I like her."

"Yes, so do I," Caitlin replied, aware that Lenore had gone still for a moment.

Lenore gave the child a somewhat stilted smile. "Thank you, Isabelle. Drink your juice now, you need the liquid."

"'Kay." Isabelle obligingly raised her plastic tumbler to her lips.

Lenore turned back to the cooking. "Nathan, where do you keep your…never mind, I found it."

Having washed a head of lettuce, Nathan sat at the table to tear it into a bowl for salad. "Are you feeling better, poppet?"

She set down the tumbler. "I think so. I'm sort of sleepy, though."

"Could be the medicine making you sleepy. Why don't you take a little nap?"

She gave the suggestion a moment's thought, then nodded. "Okay. Will you still be here when I wake up, Nate's mom?"

"I don't know. I'll be here for a little while longer. And you really must find something else to call me."

"Like what?" Isabelle asked.

Caitlin watched as Lenore struggled for an answer, her eyes meeting her son's. Nathan made a gesture as if to say, "You're on your own."

"How about Nanna?" Lenore said finally.

"Nanna?" Isabelle repeated.

"Nanna?" Nathan echoed.

Her cheeks just a bit pink, Lenore nodded. "It's the name I always thought I would like my grandchildren to call me. Since you'll be growing up with them—if I ever have any," she added with a meaningful look at Nathan that made Caitlin a bit nervous, "you might as well call me the same thing."

"Nanna," Isabelle murmured again. "I think I like it."

Lenore smiled. "You can decide for certain during your nap."

Nathan pushed the bowl aside. "C'mon, poppet, I'll tuck you in."

He left Caitlin alone in the kitchen with Lenore.

Suddenly awkward, Caitlin carried Isabelle's dishes to the sink, rinsed them and stacked them in the dishwasher. And then, since she didn't want to share Isabelle's nasty virus, she washed her hands and dried them carefully on a paper towel she then tossed in the trash.

"What can I do to help you?" she asked Lenore.

Lenore nodded toward a pan on the counter. "You can put the bread in the oven. Everything else should be ready by the time the bread is browned."

Caitlin opened the oven door and slid the pan of herbed bread inside. "The sauce smells delicious."

"If we'd left it up to Nathan, it would be reeking of garlic."

"He did seem eager to add more, didn't he?"

"Nathan has always loved garlic. Scampi was his favorite dish when he was a teenager. He ordered it every time when we went out to eat.''

"Mrs. McCloud.'' Caitlin turned hesitantly toward the older woman. "I know this is really none of my business, but I'm very glad you came today. Nathan has missed you.''

"Yes, well, my son has the best of intentions, but I couldn't in all conscience leave any child entirely at his mercy.''

Even though she knew Lenore was partially teasing, Caitlin couldn't help feeling a little defensive on Nathan's behalf. "He really has been marvelous with Isabelle. Considering that he has no experience with children, he seems to be doing a wonderful job raising her so far.''

Lenore glanced at the doorway, then spoke in a low voice. "It's still hard for me. Seeing her, I mean. Knowing that she was conceived while I was still married to her father—quite contentedly married, I thought at the time.''

She held up her hand when Caitlin started to speak. "I know it isn't the child's fault, and I will make every effort to keep those feelings contained. She is an endearing child, and I'm sure I will grow quite fond of her, given time.''

"I'm sure you will. I've fallen rather hard for her myself, and I've never been particularly drawn to children.''

Rinsing pasta at the sink, Lenore glanced over her shoulder. "You've been spending quite a bit of time with Nathan and Isabelle?''

"Some," Caitlin admitted cautiously. "There was no one…I mean, he needed someone to, um…''

"He needed someone to be on his side when no one else was. There's no need to tiptoe around me, Caitlin.''

Caitlin nodded and checked the bread, which wasn't quite done.

"What I'm trying to say," Lenore added, "is that I want

to apologize for the things I said to you that day in your office. I was rather emotional, and I don't remember everything I said, but I know I was angry with you for not helping me talk Nathan out of taking Isabelle in. I believe I said he was sacrificing his happiness and that you were being heartless not to help me rescue him. I was wrong.''

She cleared her throat. ''I know now that you understood better than I did that Nathan could never be happy if he made any other decision. He would have been haunted by regrets, and he would most likely have blamed me for it, eventually. Either way, I was in danger of losing my son, and you saw that more clearly than I did.''

''You were never really in danger of losing Nathan, Mrs. McCloud. He loves his little sister, just as he loves *all* his siblings and you. If there's one thing I can say with certainty, it's that family is the most important thing in the world to Nathan.''

Lenore turned from her cooking to study Caitlin's face. ''And what is the most important thing in the world to *you*, Caitlin?''

The shrill beeping of the oven timer saved her from having to answer. She didn't have a clue what she would have said.

Nathan entered the kitchen then, rubbing his hands and sniffing exaggeratedly. ''Smells delicious.''

Setting the pan of bread on a hot plate, Caitlin glanced at him and found him looking back at her with an expression she couldn't quite read. How much, she wondered, had he overheard?

Lunch was a fairly comfortable affair, not as awkward as Caitlin had feared it might be. That was mostly thanks to Nathan, whose relief at having his mother there to reassure him about Isabelle had changed his mood from frightened to almost exuberant.

Lenore was considerably more subdued than her son, of course, but she was obviously making an effort to keep the conversation pleasant. She talked about her community work, her activities at church and her other two offspring.

"We simply must get him out of the house more," she said of Gideon. "The boy is in danger of becoming a crusty old hermit."

"I'll keep working on him," Nathan promised. "He said he would play racquetball with me soon."

"As for Deborah, I don't know what's going on with her," Lenore admitted. "She calls at least once a week, but she doesn't actually say anything. I know she's unhappy, but I honestly don't know why."

"I've been talking to her," Nathan said, looking as concerned as his mother. "She hasn't opened up to me, either, but I'll keep trying."

If he put as much effort into his business as he did into making sure his family members were all safe and happy, he would probably head the hottest law firm in Mississippi by now, Caitlin found herself thinking. Yet, in the long run, which cause was really more important?

That was such a radical question for her that she momentarily lost track of the conversation. Toying with a crusty slice of bread, she drifted in her own thoughts until Nathan recalled her attention by saying her name.

"I'm sorry." She set the bread down. "What did you say?"

His gaze was intent on her face again, but he spoke lightly. "I asked if you would like some more iced tea."

"Oh. No, thank you, I'm fine."

After studying her for another moment, he nodded and changed the subject by asking his mother for more details about the virus that had been going around and for further reassurance that serious complications were very rare. Caitlin suspected he had deliberately drawn Lenore's attention away from her, and she was grateful.

She really needed some time alone to think about the dramatic changes that had taken place in her life lately. And maybe to come up with a definitive answer to the question Lenore had asked her: *What is the most important thing in the world to you, Caitlin?*

Lenore didn't stay long after lunch. Caitlin had the feeling that Lenore simply needed to go home and be alone for a while, perhaps to come to terms with the knowledge that her ex-husband's child would from this day on consider her a surrogate grandmother.

Caitlin certainly understood the need to be alone to think.

She was standing in the den when Nathan joined her after checking on Isabelle. "She's still sleeping," he reported. "I felt her face. I think her fever might be down a little."

"Your mother left the thermometer and the medicine."

He nodded. "She certainly knew what to do, didn't she?"

"Of course she did. She raised three children of her own."

"I have to admit I was a little surprised that she came right over when I called her."

"I think maybe she was subconsciously looking for a reason to reach out to you. This gave her an excuse to do so and still keep her pride intact. She'll be able to tell all her friends that of course it's painful for her to be reminded of her husband's betrayal, but she simply couldn't turn her back on a helpless child being raised by a clueless bachelor. Everyone will admire her selflessness and generosity so much they'll probably give her another award."

Squeezing the back of his neck with one hand, Nathan chuckled dryly. "You're probably exactly right. By the time Mom spins the story, she'll practically qualify for sainthood.''

''She really is a good woman, Nathan. I admire her very much.''

He dropped his hand and smiled more naturally. ''So do I. Thanks.''

She motioned toward a tray on the coffee table. ''I made coffee. I thought we might as well talk about work for a while, as we had planned to do this afternoon.''

He sat on the couch and patted the cushion beside him. ''Might as well be comfortable while we talk. Have a seat.''

After only a momentary hesitation, she perched on one end of the couch, setting her briefcase between them. Nathan promptly picked it up and set it on the floor, sitting very close beside her.

''I haven't even kissed you today,'' he said, laying an arm on the back of the couch behind her.

Considering last night, it was ridiculous that she was suddenly self-conscious at the thought of kissing him. She cleared her throat. ''We've been a bit busy.''

''A bit.'' He toyed with a strand of her hair. ''I haven't even told you how pretty you look.''

She certainly didn't consider her sweater and khakis an alluring ensemble and had chosen to wear them today specifically for that reason. ''Thanks. About the case files...''

''About that kiss,'' he countered, turning her face toward him again.

She supposed one kiss wouldn't distract them too badly. She lifted her mouth to his, promising herself she wouldn't let the embrace get out of hand.

The problem was, she hadn't accounted for Nathan's hands.

She was flat on her back beneath him, his hands under

her sweater and hers fisted in his hair, when she finally surfaced enough to gasp, "We really have to stop this."

He was busy nuzzling her ear. "Why?"

His lazily rotating thumb temporarily drained all rational thought from her mind. The kiss he pressed onto her mouth threatened to make the condition permanent. It took her several long minutes to remember that he had asked her a question.

"We have to stop," she said, pushing at his shoulders, "because it's the wrong time and place. Isabelle could walk in at any moment."

He sighed. "You're right," he conceded, then kissed her again.

Logic almost deserted her again when their legs tangled and his hips moved against hers. Her lips still fused with his, she couldn't resist arching into him a few times.

And then she tore her mouth away, took a few gasping breaths and pushed against his shoulders again. "Stop."

Groaning, he levered himself upright and helped her sit up. She immediately busied herself straightening her hair and her clothes, at the same time making an effort to calm her breathing and heart rate.

Nathan made a few discreet adjustments of his own. "You say you made coffee?" he asked, his voice husky.

"Yes. Help yourself." She reached for her briefcase. "We should start with the Smith case, I suppose. That's the one that's going to keep us very busy for the next few months."

He didn't even glance at the file she pulled out. "Tell me about your family."

Her left eyebrow rose. "What do you mean?"

Lounging against the back of the couch, he sipped rapidly cooling coffee and studied her over the rim of the cup. "You know just about everything there is to know about my family, but I know almost nothing about yours. What was it like for you growing up?''

She shrugged lightly. "We moved a lot. Daddy was a sweet man who loved his beer, his junk food and his TV set. What he *didn't* love was work. He had trouble keeping a job and a place to live and a car. But he had no trouble keeping his family. Mama and I loved him despite his shortcomings.''

Nathan used his free hand to brush a strand of hair away from her face. "I bet he loved you, too.''

He always seemed to be touching her. Playing with her hair or her fingers, stroking her arm or her hand. It was very difficult to keep her attention on conversation or work when every touch made electricity sizzle along her nerve endings. She cleared her throat. "I was the apple of his eye. He thought I was the smartest, most beautiful child who ever lived and he told me so every day.''

He traced the curve of her ear with one fingertip. "That's a nice memory to have of him.''

"I have many nice memories of my father. We didn't have money and we didn't always have a nice place to live, but we had love. I tried to remember that during the worst financial times.''

"When did he die?''

Though she spoke matter-of-factly, it still hurt to remember. "Soon after my college graduation. Massive heart attack. He was so proud at the graduation ceremony. He wore his only special-occasion necktie and he didn't stop smiling all day.''

Nathan covered her hand with his. "I wish I'd had a chance to meet him. I'm sure I would have liked him.''

Caitlin didn't doubt that. Nathan didn't judge people by their appearance or social standing or financial success. He was as unfailingly respectful to the least affluent of their clients as he was to the local bigwigs. She knew that his circle of friends included doctors, bankers, mechanics and laborers.

His parents had been wealthy and influential, but he would never look down at her because hers hadn't been.

It was no wonder she had fallen so hard for him, despite her misgivings about mixing business and pleasure.

"I'd like to go with you to visit your mother sometime." That surprised her. "Why would you want to do that?"

"Because she's your mother," he answered simply.

Caitlin toyed with the cover of the case file. "She doesn't know she's my mother. She doesn't know she's *anyone's* mother. She sits in a chair, totally immersed in whatever video is playing in her mind. Sometimes she murmurs words, but they don't make any sense. Sometimes she seems to be singing a little, but there's no real tune or lyrics. I talk to her when I visit, but I doubt that she even knows there's anyone in the room with her."

"But you still go. And you still reach out to her, even though she can't reach back. We're a lot alike, you and I, Caitlin Briley."

She had never thought of them as being very much alike or even having anything much in common, other than their work. Swallowing, she opened the file again. "About the Smith case…"

"Nate?" Isabelle wandered into the room, rubbing her eyes and carrying her stuffed owl. "I don't feel good again."

Nathan rose to tend to his sister and Caitlin closed the file in resignation. It seemed that they wouldn't be working today. Again.

Chapter Fourteen

Caitlin was falling behind at work, though she would have been hard-pressed to pinpoint the reason why. Irene was certainly doing her part to keep everything on track. The clerical staff was keeping up with the filing and the billing, for the most part. Nathan left the office only when his responsibilities as Isabelle's guardian called him away. If he'd taken any free time just for himself, Caitlin certainly didn't know about it.

It was true that she'd been spending many evenings with him and Isabelle during the two and a half weeks that had passed since the Sunday when Isabelle had been sick. They had several dinners together, attended a kid-friendly movie one evening and spent quite a few hours watching Isabelle make use of the local playground facilities. The holidays were approaching, and Isabelle was busy with school programs and the twice-a-week dance class she had persuaded Nathan to enroll her in, but there was still the occasional evening when Nathan and Caitlin found a few hours to be alone together, with Mrs. T.'s cooperation.

They made very good use of that time.

Caitlin had been forced to cut back from sixteen work hours a day to ten or twelve. Maybe that was why she was having trouble keeping up with her too-heavy workload. She had worried from the start that her relationship with Nathan would interfere with her work, she thought in mounting frustration.

"You and Mr. McCloud should consider bringing in another lawyer," Irene said after a particularly strenuous afternoon. "Not necessarily a partner, but an associate to take some of the time-consuming bankruptcy cases."

"It's something to consider," Caitlin replied absently, her fingers flying over her keyboard.

"Ms. Briley, there's a call on line two," Mandy said over the desk intercom. "It's a Mr. Tom Hutchinson from Los Angeles."

Gathering papers, Irene left to give her privacy to take the call. Caitlin pushed a hand through her hair and looked at the phone with misgiving. She wasn't sure what to say to Tom right now, especially if his call had anything to do with an interview with his firm.

Because she couldn't simply leave him holding, she picked up the phone.

"Katie. Hi, it's Tom."

She'd forgotten how annoying it was for him to call her that. "How are you, Tom?"

"Great. Couldn't be better. I'm working on a couple of possibly precedent-setting cases and making more money than I could have imagined at this stage in my career. It's a tough firm—fiercely competitive, unforgiving of mistakes, almost cutthroat, at times, but the future is unlimited here."

"I'm happy for you, Tom. I know this is what you wanted."

"It's what we *both* wanted. It's all we talked about in school."

"I know."

"You gotta come out here, Katie. I've been talking about you. The partners are interested in meeting you. And this is definitely a good time for you to come."

"Tom, I told you I couldn't possibly come to L.A. until after the first of the year. Even if there were an opening that had to be filled immediately, I would have to decline. I have obligations here—a couple of big cases of my own."

"Like what? DWIs? Divorces? Bankruptcies? Good ol' boys in neck braces suing grocery stores over faked slip-and-falls?"

She didn't appreciate his condescending summary of a small-town law practice, even though she had once said the same things when they had dreamed of joining those big, impressive firms with their "precedent-setting" cases. "I'm finding a few cases here that keep me challenged," she said stiffly.

"Yeah, well, *every* case here keeps me challenged," he boasted.

He'd apparently become prone to exaggeration in the almost two years since she had last seen him. She suspected his new circumstances had changed him in other ways, too. She could picture him wearing the "right" suit, tie, watch and shoes, driving the "right" car and living in the "right" neighborhood. Everything he had always wanted—and that she had always believed she wanted for herself.

"Surely you can take a few days off," he urged. "I'm telling you, the time is hot. One of the junior partners has derailed herself—gotten pregnant with twins, of all things. The suits are going to be looking for her replacement."

"She's leaving the firm?"

Tom snorted. "Not officially. But she's already having to cut back because she's sick a lot. And she's starting to make noises about wanting to spend some time with the babies during their first year. They won't fire her, of course. They don't want to open themselves up to that sort of litigation, but she can kiss a full partnership goodbye. She had better learn to be happy with ugly divorces and child custody battles."

"Surely there are high-ranking women in your firm with children."

"Maybe. If so, they don't sit around swapping baby pictures. I guess they hire nannies to take care of the kids so they can concentrate on the job. You can bet none of the senior partners here take many personal days off."

"And you're happy working there?" she couldn't help asking.

"Katie, it's exhilarating! Keeps you sharp and on your toes every minute. I get up every morning fully charged and ready for battle. Every win is a high and every loss makes me only more determined to win the next one. I love working here, and I just know you would, too. It's everything you and I always hoped we would find. Let me set something up for you."

"Tom, I truly appreciate your offer, but I really can't get to L.A. for an interview just now. I have a medical malpractice case that's taking every spare moment I can give it, and that's in addition to my other workload. Maybe I'd be able to take a long weekend toward the end of January, maybe February, but it just isn't going to happen now. Surely you know that I take my work commitments seriously. That's why you think I'd be an asset to your firm, isn't it?"

His regretful sigh traveled clearly through the phone

lines. "That's exactly why. But I thought you were a little better at setting priorities. Giving up an opportunity like this for a case any country lawyer in that state could handle, well, it makes me wonder whether you're really as ambitious as you always led me to believe. There are others from our class who would leave their dying mothers' bedsides for a chance like this."

The analogy made Caitlin wince. She had discovered she didn't much like the man Tom had become in the past two years. Had he always been like this? Had she once been in danger of becoming like him? "I'm sorry you feel that way."

"Oh, hell, Katie, you know I still think the world of you. I always believed you were too good for some dinky Mississippi two-man firm, and I still believe it. Paula's twins aren't due until March. I'll call you again after the first of the year, okay?"

"I'll certainly try to make time to talk with you then," she said because she had learned never to burn bridges.

"Great. In the meantime you can be thinking about where you really want to end up in a few years. Think about what you've got there and everything that's available to you here. I think we both know where the real excitement is."

They disconnected a few moments later. Rubbing her aching temples, Caitlin turned her chair away from the phone and toward the computer again. The move brought her face-to-face with Nathan, who stood in the doorway with his arms crossed over his chest and a scowl darkening his face. She didn't know how long he had been standing there, but he'd obviously overheard entirely too much.

Because she was suddenly feeling unaccountably defensive, she spoke a bit more sharply than she intended. "Taking up eavesdropping?"

"Apparently, it's the only way to learn anything important around here. I didn't know, for example, that my partner has been talking to a firm in L.A. about arranging a job interview."

"I haven't mentioned it because there's really nothing to tell. I've been approached, yes, but it's nothing formal or definitive. Just an old friend who thought I might be interested in joining his firm."

"And you didn't think I'd want to know you'd been approached? Even if you didn't think I deserved to be told as your business partner, didn't you even consider discussing it with me as your lover?"

Her lover. For some reason, she had never actually thought of him that way, even though that was exactly what he was, she supposed.

He took a step into the office and closed the door behind him. "Are you looking for a new position, Caitlin?"

"I'm not looking for anything," she replied in frustration, pushing herself to her feet. "Tom contacted me. I've made no arrangements with him because I don't have time to think about another position right now. In case you haven't noticed, my workload is quite heavy."

"I've noticed," he said with little expression.

When he didn't say anything more, she felt the need to fill the awkward silence. "I would certainly never neglect my responsibilities here or my commitment to my clients."

"Of course," he said smoothly. "And it isn't as if you've made any sort of commitment to *me*."

She rubbed her hands down the sides of her black pants suit, not quite meeting his gaze now. "We haven't really talked about commitments."

"For some reason I thought that was implied the first time we went to bed together. I suppose, as a lawyer, I should have known not to take anything for granted that wasn't unambiguously spelled out on paper, signed, dated and notarized.''

Caitlin didn't know what to say to that. She'd been so careful not to analyze their relationship; it seemed Nathan hadn't thought there was anything to analyze.

In his mind, they were a couple. Case closed.

That sort of thinking terrified her.

''I didn't say I'm interested in moving to L.A. or joining Tom's firm,'' she said, choosing her words with care. ''But I would like to think my options are still open if an exceptional opportunity comes along.''

''I see. Well, don't worry about me standing in your way.'' He turned to open the door again. ''All I want is for you to be happy, Caitlin. If you can't envision that here, with me, or with our firm, then you should definitely go find it elsewhere. God knows it would be better for you to make that decision now rather than later. Now, if you'll excuse me, I have to get home to Isabelle.''

''Nathan—''

The door closed behind him. The sharp snap of the latch sounded strangely petulant.

Caitlin sank into her chair again with a muttered curse. To say the least, that had not gone well. Nathan was angry and hurt that he'd heard about the offer by accident.

Though she hardly approved of his eavesdropping on a private phone call, she supposed she should have told him about Tom's professional overtures. Lindsey had certainly urged her to do so. Caitlin suspected that the reason she hadn't said anything to him was because she had known he wouldn't react well.

He'd said he would prefer her to leave sooner rather than later. They had both brought emotional baggage into their affair or relationship or whatever it could be called. She carried her driving need for success, which in her mind was synonymous with personal fulfillment and security. He still remembered the pain of having someone he loved abandon him to selfishly pursue happiness elsewhere.

Someone he loved. Did Nathan love her or think he did? Even more importantly, did she love him?

Yes. That answer came to her immediately and unequivocally.

Was she ready to make a lifelong commitment to him and, of course, to Isabelle, who came as part of the package?

She simply didn't know.

It was better to decide sooner rather than later. Nathan was absolutely right about that. They couldn't keep drifting along this way. It seemed it was up to her to decide where they would go next.

"You're sure you don't want me to stay with Isabelle this evening?" Fayrene Tuckerman asked Nathan Friday evening. It was the day after he'd overheard Caitlin talking to her buddy in California. He had seen Caitlin only a couple of times since, and then only with other people around. He'd arranged that deliberately.

"No, thank you," he said, setting down the computer case and briefcase he had brought home for the weekend. "I have no plans for the evening."

"Ms. Briley's coming here for the evening? Maybe I should make some of that hazelnut coffee she likes before I go."

"Ms. Briley isn't coming. It's just Isabelle and me tonight."

He tried to speak lightly, but there had been something in his voice that made his housekeeper plant her hands on her skinny hips and study him through narrowed eyes. "Is something wrong between you and Ms. Briley?"

It was absolutely none of her business, of course, and he would have told her so, but she looked too much like her sister at that moment. He shuffled his feet on the kitchen floor and muttered, "We're...evaluating our relationship."

At least, Caitlin was, he thought sullenly. He had thought their relationship was progressing just fine. Little had he known that while he'd been thinking of a lifelong partnership, she'd been keeping one eye on the door and both ears open to better offers.

"Okay, what did you do?" Fayrene asked with a stern shake of her head.

"What did *I* do?" he asked, his jaw nearly dropping. "You automatically assume it's something I did?"

She only looked at him.

"Caitlin's the one who said she wants to keep her options open," he all but snarled. "She's considering a job interview with some high-profile law firm in California."

"It must be quite flattering for her to think a fancy firm like that would be interested in her."

He snorted. "Much more flattering, I suppose, than having a simple country lawyer interested in her."

"I didn't say that. Nor would anyone ever call you simple."

Nathan pushed a hand through his hair and cleared his throat, suddenly embarrassed to be discussing his personal life with his housekeeper. "It's up to Caitlin to decide what she wants. I can't find the answers for her."

"No. But you can tell her what *you* want. Might be the answers aren't all that different." Fayrene reached for her purse. "Guess I'd better go before I push my nose any deeper into your business. But what's the benefit of having the wisdom of age if you can't share it with a couple of confused young people?"

"Now you sound like my mother."

She smiled. "I'll take that as a compliment. Good night, Mr. McCloud. I'll see you Monday, unless you need me beforehand."

"Thanks, Mrs. T. I'll…consider your words of wisdom."

She left him standing in the kitchen wondering just how far apart his and Caitlin's desires really were.

Lindsey studied Caitlin from across the restaurant table. "Have you decided what you're going to do?"

Caitlin frowned intently at the menu in front of her. "I'm trying to decide what to order for dinner. I think I'll have the veal."

"You know I wasn't talking about food."

"That's all I want to talk about right now. I'm starving." It was a lie, of course. She hadn't been hungry since Nathan had stormed out of her office, but she was determined to at least give the appearance of normality this evening.

Lindsey glanced up at the server who approached their table, order pad in hand. "I'll have the scampi."

Caitlin felt her throat tighten. She wasn't sure she would be able to eat a bite. Lindsey hadn't intentionally tried to upset her, of course, by ordering Nathan's favorite food. She didn't even know the choice would remind Caitlin of Nathan. But then, just about everything did.

She placed her own order mechanically, unable to force a smile.

"You look like someone's twisting a knife in your gut," Lindsey said inelegantly when the server had moved away. "Are you going to talk to me or not?"

"What do you want me to say? That you were right? I should have told Nathan about Tom's offer before Nathan found out for himself? Okay, I'll say it. You were right."

"He was pretty mad that you hadn't told him, huh?"

"He was livid that I would even consider looking at another firm."

"Did you talk to him about it?"

"He didn't give me a chance." Caitlin rather viciously tore into a crusty breadstick, scattering crumbs on her bread plate. "He acted like a betrayed lover who'd overheard me setting up a tryst with another man."

"Interesting. You think he's jealous of Tom?"

"I don't know. Like I said, he didn't give me a chance to explain anything."

"Well then, you have to make him listen," Lindsey pronounced matter-of-factly. "Tell him how you feel. About everything. The job. Him."

"I can't make him listen to me."

"Sure you can. Tell him to put his butt in a chair and don't let him get up until you've had your say. Men are like children, you know. If you don't lay down the law at times, they'll walk all over you."

Rolling her eyes, Caitlin muttered, "Since when are you suddenly an expert on men?"

Lindsey grinned. "Four brothers, remember? And every one of them thick as stumps. If they hadn't all married well, heaven knows what would have become of them."

"Nathan is hardly thick as a stump. And I'm not going to treat him like a slow child. He has some reason to be hurt that I didn't tell him about Tom's letters."

"So now you're defending him. Just what is it you *do* want, Caitlin?"

"What I want," Caitlin said from between clenched teeth, "is for everyone to stop asking me what I want."

Lindsey studied her for a moment, then reached for her wineglass. "There's the rub, you see. Until you decide exactly what it is you want, and learn how to put it into words, you're never going to have it."

Caitlin looked back at her friend with tormented eyes. "And do you know what it is you want?"

Lindsey lifted her glass in a "touché" gesture. "Not yet. But I'm working on it. Here's to us both deciding what we want—and having it all."

Caitlin obligingly sipped her wine, but the excellent beverage tasted a bit like vinegar on her tongue. Lindsey was absolutely right, of course. Until she decided exactly what it would take to make her truly happy, she didn't have a prayer of finding it.

Or had she already found it and was even now in danger of losing it forever?

All in all, she decided, it was much easier to decide what to do in the most complicated lawsuit than in her personal life.

Carrying a small bouquet of yellow roses, Caitlin entered the nursing home room with the bright smile she always wore when she visited her mother. A uniformed, mocha-skinned woman was singing softly as she finished making up the room's single bed. She broke off the gospel tune almost in midword to greet Caitlin cheerily.

"Good morning, Ms. Briley. How are you today?"

"I'm fine, thank you, India. And you?"

"Oh, can't complain." Gathering the used sheets, she nodded toward the silent wraith sitting in a chair by the room's only window. "She's doing real good today. Ate all her breakfast."

Sylvia Briley had to be hand fed at every meal, one bit of soft food after another placed into her mouth. Sometimes throat massage was required to induce her to swallow. It was a slow, tedious process that Caitlin had done herself on countless occasions. "That's good to hear."

She crossed the room to set the roses in a clear plastic

vase she kept there for that purpose, since she always brought flowers. Yellow roses or white and yellow daisies—those had always been her mother's favorites. And even though Sylvia no longer appreciated the beauty of the blooms, Caitlin would continue to bring them.

Saying she would see Caitlin later, India left the room, taking up her song again exactly where she'd left off.

A couple of framed photographs sat beside the vase of roses. With a rush of nostalgia, Caitlin picked one up and looked at it a long time before carrying it with her to her mother's side. She pulled up the straight-backed visitor's chair and sank onto it, positioning herself where her mother could see her, had she bothered to look.

"Remember this day, Mama?" She turned the photograph toward her mother. "My college graduation. I was so self-conscious in that oversize gown and dopey cap, but you looked very nice in your best Sunday dress. And Daddy—"

She traced a fingertip over the image of a very large man in a cheap white shirt and limp polyester tie, his round, ruddy face creased by a huge, sweet smile. "Daddy was so proud I thought he would bust all the buttons off his shirt."

She sighed. "Remember how he was always nagging me about doing my homework and taking the hardest courses? How he fretted about my school résumé because he said it would lead to an impressive career résumé? It was so important to him that I 'make something' of myself. 'Caitlin,' he would say in that big, booming voice of his, 'you've been given special gifts. It would be a sin to waste them or to throw them away.'"

Sylvia showed no reaction to the change in Caitlin's voice. But then, she rarely showed a reaction to anything, other than the occasional loud noise that would make her start, sometimes whimper a bit. Caitlin gazed down at the smiling woman in the photograph, seeing her real mother looking back at her from there.

"I listened to all Daddy's lectures," Caitlin whispered to the mother in the photo. "I believed him when he said I could be the best of the best if I was willing to work hard enough. Sometimes I wonder if I learned his lessons a bit too well."

She looked back up then at her mother's blank face, searching for any sign that she was heard and understood. Any clue at all. As had been the case for more than a year, she found absolutely no evidence that the woman who had once been Sylvia Briley still existed.

"I miss you, Mama," she said. "I wish I could talk to you about Daddy. I'd like to ask how you really felt about him. I know you loved him, you always made that clear. But did you ever regret falling for him? Ever wish you'd married someone else or never married at all? Were you ever sorry that you gave up your own dreams—whatever they might have been—to take care of him and me?"

Sylvia's clouded eyes moved, and for just a moment Caitlin wondered if there was some understanding there, after all. But then her mother's eyes half closed again, obviously looking at nothing.

Caitlin cleared her throat. "I've had a job offer, Mama. Sort of. A nibble, anyway. I think I could get it if I go after it—just the way Daddy always said. If I decide to take the job, it would mean I'd have to move to California. I'm not exactly sure what I would do with you. I doubt that such a big move would be good for you, and you get such good care here. But if I leave you here, I wouldn't be able to visit you very often. It's a very demanding firm, and there would be little time off for me to fly back here."

She stood to replace the photograph in its position beside

the yellow roses. And then she walked back over to her mother, laying a gentle hand on Sylvia's thin gray hair.

"I know you don't even know I'm here. You wouldn't miss me if I never came again. But I'm not so sure I could get on a plane and leave you behind. Because whether you would know or not, *I* would know. And it would haunt me."

She leaned over to kiss her mother's cheek. Sylvia automatically turned her face away. Caitlin didn't take offense. "I love you, Mama. And I know that somewhere deep inside you is a kernel of the woman who once loved me, too."

She straightened and moved toward the door. "'Bye, Mama. I'll see you again soon."

As she left the facility, she waved to the nurses she'd come to know so well during the past year. She was no longer sad when she left the nursing home; she'd long since come to terms with her mother's condition. Her visits were brief, but she still found some peace in them. Maybe only because she felt some satisfaction at doing her duty toward her mother. Or maybe it was the connection, however tenuous, to family.

Her way of remembering who she was and where she had come from.

It was something she never really wanted to forget, no matter where her career path took her.

Chapter Fifteen

Because it was still early when Caitlin arrived back in Honesty, and she had nothing else to do on this Saturday afternoon, she drove straight to her office. She remembered to lock the front door behind her this time as she entered.

Everything had been left neat and organized for the weekend, thanks to Irene and the janitorial staff. It was an ideal time to get some work done.

As she wandered through the empty offices, she found herself looking around through critical eyes. Maybe it was time to update the decor a bit. The muted greens and beiges were peaceful but could be modernized. Maybe a brighter color scheme was in order, with some interesting artwork displayed here and there. The McCloud and Briley Law Firm was doing quite well, and they really should dress the part.

She'd bet Tom's firm in L.A. was decorated in the latest, cutting-edge style.

There were a couple of extra offices at the back of the renovated old house. They were used now only for storage. She remembered Irene's suggestion that they take in another lawyer to share the workload. McCloud, Briley and Associates. Nice ring to it, she had to admit. For a small-town firm, at least.

Usually she enjoyed the quiet on Saturday mornings. Today she missed hearing Mandy's cheery chattering with the rest of the staff, Irene's sergeant-at-arms bark of instructions and the sound of Nathan's laughter. Especially that.

She wondered how much laughter rang out in Tom's firm. Was foolishness discouraged there, even when no clients were around to hear? Were the partners and associates friends or did their cutthroat competitiveness preclude such bonds? Would anyone there willingly spend long extra hours covering for an associate who was dealing with pressing family matters or would they all take advantage of such an opportunity to advance their own positions?

Surely someone would be kind, she told herself with an impatient shake of her head. People were people, right? She was sure there were both nice guys and jerks in the big L.A. firm. It was just on a different scale there.

She wasn't intimidated by the thought of a large, fiercely competitive organization, she assured herself. She could definitely hold her own when necessary. She had no doubt that she could vault right over Tom in the hierarchy there if she set her mind to it, despite his head start. All she would have to do was concentrate exclusively on work, sacrifice every hint of a social life, be willing to take immediate advantage of every opportunity for her and every sign of weakness from her rivals.

A partnership would eventually be hers, she had no doubt. Her father had certainly instilled confidence in her, in addition to the other gifts he'd passed on to her. And she would have the long-term security she had always hoped for, never having to worry about money or a place to live or lack of respect from her peers.

And yet—couldn't she find those things here? When she'd joined Nathan's firm, she'd worried that there would be little financial security in a small-town law office. Now she didn't foresee any slowdown in business; just the opposite, in fact. She was making a very respectable living, particularly for this area, and handling some interesting cases.

Sure, she put in long hours, but no more than she was willing to work, and certainly not as much as she would in L.A. Here she had the freedom to pursue a personal life, if she so desired. Maybe even a family. She wouldn't be derailing her career here if she decided to, oh, marry, for example. Have children, maybe.

Family had always been important to her. Had she somehow forgotten that in her single-minded quest for career success? Had she forgotten that she had always wanted a balance between work and family, something her father had never found? She had once wished he had an important and secure career, but she had never wanted him to sacrifice all his time with his family.

Would money or a fancy house have replaced all those hours she had spent playing board games with her dad? Watching their favorite television shows together? She remembered how he'd struggled to help her with her homework. His own lack of education had been a major stumbling block for him, and he had been determined the same wouldn't be true for his "smart, beautiful daughter."

She'd taken guidance from her father in so many ways—pursuing an education and a career and taking care of herself physically as her parents had not done for themselves. She ate well, exercised, had regular medical checkups and generally made sure her life would be better than her parents' lives in many ways. But they had always had one thing she hadn't seriously considered until recently. They had been rich in love.

She was standing in her office, gazing out the window at the well-tended, but winter-browning lawn behind the building, accomplishing absolutely nothing, when Nathan spoke from behind her.

"If I come in, are you going to throw something at me?"

She wasn't particularly surprised to hear his voice. She turned to find him leaning against the frame of her open doorway. It was the same position he'd been in after her phone call from Tom on Thursday, but he wasn't scowling this time. His expression could best be described as wary.

"Where's Isabelle?" she asked, deciding to ignore his question.

"Mrs. T. took her to a movie, and then they're going shopping for some warmer school uniforms."

"I'm sure Isabelle will enjoy the outing."

He nodded toward her still-empty desk. "Did you just get here?"

"Yes. I visited my mother this morning."

"How is she?"

"Physically, she's in fair shape. Mentally, there's no change. She's still almost completely unresponsive."

"It must be difficult for you. Visiting her like that, I mean."

"I've come to terms with her condition. I've learned to find some pleasure in the visits."

Taking another step into the office, he pushed his fingertips into the front pockets of the jeans he wore with an Old Miss sweatshirt. "I was hoping I would find you here. I owe you an apology, and I wanted privacy in which to offer it."

She crossed her arms over her chest. "You don't owe me an apology."

"Of course I do. First for eavesdropping on your private conversation. And second for getting angry about what I overheard."

"I should have told you Tom approached me about a possible interview with his firm. You shouldn't have had to find out by accident."

"It was your business, not mine."

"And you're my business partner," she countered gamely. "If I *had* arranged for an interview, I would certainly have talked to you about it, of course. I just didn't want to bother you with it until I decided what I was going to do."

"I think you should set up the interview. I can cover for you here."

She frowned at him, surprised by his suggestion. "I haven't even decided I want to go for an interview."

"I think you should," he insisted. "You don't want to let the opportunity slip away from you."

Her crossed arms tightened. "Why are you trying to talk me into this?"

"I'm trying to tell you that I'm not going to stand in your way if big opportunities present themselves to you. This could be just the break you've always wanted."

"I don't even know if I'm interested in moving to California," she argued. "My mother is here. And I've got the Smith case that's going to keep me busy for quite a while yet."

"In California you would have challenging cases like that all the time. And you'd make enough to move your mom out there and hire round-the-clock private nurses for her."

"Maybe, but how many hours would I have to work for that big salary?"

"Probably not much more than you do here," he replied with a shrug. "Look at you now, you're in the office on a Saturday afternoon. You're here almost every Saturday. A lot of Sundays."

"I just don't know if I'm ready for a big firm like that. Maybe I need a few more years of experience."

"Caitlin, you're ready for anything you want to do. The firm in L.A. would be lucky to have you—and don't think they aren't going to recognize that. They'll very likely offer you a position on the spot."

It suddenly occurred to her that for every argument she came up with for not going to California, Nathan found a way to counter her. Shouldn't it be the other way around? "Do you *want* me to go to Los Angeles?" she demanded.

He hesitated only a moment before answering wryly, "If I thought it would keep you here, I would gladly shackle you to your desk."

There was absolutely no reason, of course, why she should feel a surge of relief. But she did. "You *don't* want me to go?"

"I absolutely, positively, unequivocally do not want you to go. And in case that isn't clear enough—I *really* do not want you to go."

She felt her lips twitch with a smile. "So you want me to stay?"

He rested a hand on his chest, just over his heart. "With every fiber of my being. With every molecule in my body. From the top of my head to the soles of my feet, I want you to stay."

Her smile widened in response to his fervent hyperbole. "Then why were you trying so hard to talk me into go-ing?"

"Because I want you to follow your dreams."

She was genuinely touched by the sincerity in his voice. "And if I decide I can pursue my dreams here?"

His tense expression lightened just a little. "Then you would be fulfilling *my* dreams."

Her voice was husky when she said, "Tell me about your dreams, Nathan."

As often as she had talked about her own, it occurred to her that she had never asked about his.

He shrugged and took another step toward her, bringing him to within touching distance of her, though he kept his hands at his sides. "I've never wanted fame or riches. My parents came close to having both, and I saw how little happiness those things brought them. What gives me satisfaction is having the people I love—my family—close to me, safe and happy. I've always wanted a career I enjoy that would pay me enough to take care of my family. I've always wanted to be my own boss and have some freedom to pursue a few pleasures outside of the office."

She moistened her lips. "That sounds like a nice dream."

"There's another part to it," he said. "I always wanted to find someone to share that life with me. Someone who enjoys the same things I do. Someone who values family the way that I do. Someone who will stand by me when no one else does. Someone *I* can stand by when she pursues dreams of her own. Someone who will sit on a porch with me when we're old and reminisce about all the good times we shared and the inevitable bad times we survived."

"It…sounds like you've given this a great deal of thought."

"You're not the only one who has made plans for the future," he told her softly. "I've always known what I wanted. I knew it when I established this law firm and when I asked you to help me make it a success.''

All those months when she had thought Nathan was just drifting happily and aimlessly through his life, he'd known exactly what he wanted for his future. In his own way he had been pursuing those goals as faithfully as she had hers. Maybe he'd been even more focused, because he'd had his plans clearly delineated in his mind, while she had been chasing after vague goals of career success she hadn't been quite sure how to define.

Had she wanted to make the McCloud and Briley Law Firm a major player in the area's legal community or start from the bottom in a bigger, already established firm? Had she been pursuing her own dreams or her father's? And if family had meant so much to her in her past, why had she been following a career path that would have made it difficult, if not impossible, for her to have a family of her own?

Nathan had been watching the expressions crossing her face; she wasn't sure what he'd read in them. ''If you want to go to L.A.,'' he said, ''I still think you should make the arrangements. And if you decide your dream is there, I want you to go for it. My goals can be pursued anywhere. Isabelle and I might just like L.A. She was born in California, you know.''

Caitlin set a hand on her desktop for support as she stared at him. ''You would be willing to go to L.A. with me?''

''If that's where you'd be happiest,'' he agreed. ''You and I are partners, Caitlin Briley. In work and—I hope—in every other way.''

''But this firm—your family—''

''This firm, as proud as I am of what it has become, is only a place to work. I'm a skilled attorney. I can find another position wherever we end up. As for my family,

Isabelle goes where I go, and I can always come back to visit the others whenever time allows. Deborah doesn't live in Honesty, but that doesn't make her any less a part of the family.''

Caitlin looked at him with a deep sense of wonder. "You really do love me, don't you?"

His smile was sympathetic, as if he understood how deeply shaken she was by the realization. "Of course. But you knew that already, didn't you?"

She supposed she had. He'd shown her so every time he kissed her, every time he made love with her so sweetly and so tenderly. He hadn't said the words, but he'd made his feelings quite clear.

She was the one who had held back. The one who had been so afraid to commit—and why? Fear, she thought. Fear of making a mistake. Fear of being trapped. And maybe deep inside, an old fear, that she didn't really deserve him. A useless and groundless self-doubt left over from a childhood of living just outside the fringe of acceptable society, never quite being a part of any peer group.

She drew a deep breath. "I love you, too, you know."

His smile was blinding. "Darling. Of course you do."

She reached out to him then, placing her hands on either side of his handsome face. "Have you always been so confident?"

"When it comes to you? No. But I've never been afraid to go after what I want."

"And you want me," she murmured, her lips hovering very close to his.

"Sweetheart, you've always been a part of my plan."

Something about that comment amused her. She was laughing softly when his mouth came down on hers, instantly transforming her humor to passion.

As if it had been all he could do not to touch her earlier,

he let his hands sweep over her now, touching and caressing every part he could reach. Her own hands were just as hungry, stroking and shaping, tangling with his. They had both dressed in loose, casual clothing for this Saturday afternoon, which made it much easier to shed them.

"Tell me you locked the front door," Caitlin murmured, retaining just that modicum of caution as they sank to the thickly carpeted floor.

He nuzzled her neck. "I locked the front door."

"Good. I have a habit of forgetting. Oh, Nathan, that feels so good."

"I love you, Caitlin," he said, holding her hands over her head as he prepared to slide into her.

"I love you, too," she whispered, arching to welcome him. "And you can consider that signed, dated and notarized."

He chuckled, then crushed her mouth beneath his, joining them with an exultant thrust.

Nathan couldn't have said how much time passed before he raised his head from the floor with an effort and glanced around them. He couldn't help smiling a little at what he saw. Caitlin was sprawled nude beside him, her eyes closed, her arm draped limply over her stomach. Their clothes lay scattered in tangled clumps all around the formerly immaculate office.

He couldn't help wondering what Irene would say if she knew what had just happened in the offices she considered her domain. He sincerely hoped she would never find out. Though he had grown to respect the office manager quite a bit during the past weeks, he was still afraid of her.

"Caitlin?"

She responded without moving a muscle. "Hmm?"

"We really should get dressed."

"Why?"

"Because if you lie there like that much longer, we won't be leaving this office for the next week."

The corners of her mouth lifted with a slight smile. "Sounds nice."

"You really want Irene to find you like this Monday morning?"

She groaned and opened her eyes. "You had to bring up Irene's name now?"

"Sorry. She sort of comes to mind whenever I'm in the office these days."

Smiling, she reached up to trace a fingertip around his mouth. "I'm sure I can change that."

"I'm sure you could," he muttered, catching her hand and pressing a kiss in her palm. "But, I have to go. Mrs. T. and Isabelle will be home soon and they'll be wondering where I am."

She sighed and reluctantly pushed herself upright. "Okay, you made your point. The office isn't the place for this sort of thing, anyway."

He grinned and pulled her toward him for another long, deep kiss. "With you, *anywhere* is the place for this sort of thing," he said when he finally released her.

She cleared her throat, blinked her hazy eyes, then reached for her clothes. "That sort of thinking could get us arrested."

"I think we should keep Mrs. T. on. She's pretty much irreplaceable, I think, don't you?"

Caitlin paused in her dressing to look at him in question. "Why shouldn't we—I mean, why shouldn't you keep Mrs. T.? She's, like, the greatest housekeeper in history, isn't she?"

He chuckled as he zipped his jeans. "Probably. I just meant that there's no reason to change her schedule after we get married. You and I are both too busy here to have to worry about housework and cooking and laundry.''

He pulled his shirt over his head, talking through the folds of fabric. ''She and Isabelle seem happy together. I think Mrs. T. would really miss the job if we let her go. So there's no reason why—''

As he emerged from the top of his shirt, he realized that Caitlin was standing in the middle of the office, half-dressed and staring at him with her mouth open.

He lifted an eyebrow. ''Was it the *M* word that made you go comatose on me?''

She closed her mouth and stepped into her slightly wrinkled slacks. ''You did bring it up rather casually.''

''Oh. Sorry. Too soon?''

''Maybe. You suppose you could give me a day or two before we start booking honeymoon suites?''

''Sure, even though I do like the sound of that honeymoon suite thing,'' he added meditatively.

She looked at him repressively. ''This is serious, Nathan.''

''I'm completely serious,'' he assured her. ''I love you, and I want to marry you. But I understand if you need a little time to think about it, knowing how you are about long-term planning and such.''

''Well, of course I need to think about it. You're talking about a decision that affects the rest of our lives. And not just our lives, there's Isabelle to consider, too.''

''True. Isabelle and I come as a package. I certainly understand why that would make the answer a bit more difficult for you.''

''It's not that I consider Isabelle a problem,'' she assured him, endearingly earnest. ''You know I'm crazy about her. She's a very special child.''

Her description pleased him. ''I've always thought so.''

"But she's still a child, and a very young one at that. She's going to require a lot more parenting."

"And you're not sure you're ready for that responsibility." He nodded. "I went through all this same deliberation before I brought her home with me."

"It isn't that, exactly. It's just, well, what do I know about raising children? How do I know I would be a good parent?"

His smile felt crooked when he reached out to smooth her tousled hair. "Again, you aren't asking yourself any questions I didn't wrestle with. Come on, Caitlin, you know how little prepared I was to take in a child. But I think I've done okay so far."

"You've done a *great* job so far," she assured him. "It's just—"

"Overwhelming," he supplied when she hesitated. "And damned scary."

"Well, yes."

"I know." He touched her cheek. "Quite a deal I'm offering here, hmm? A chance to take on a ready-made family with a guy who barely has a clue what he's doing as a parent. You've got this great opportunity in L.A., and while I would never try to get in your way there, I can't promise family obligations wouldn't sometimes crop up. I can certainly understand why you'd need time to decide if you want to make those sacrifices."

"Sacrifices?" She turned to face him fully then, her eyes warm as she gazed up at him. "Nathan, you have given me so much I'll never be able to repay you. You made me a partner straight out of law school! It would take me seven or eight years, at the least, to even be considered for a partnership in most firms. You've encouraged me in everything I've ever taken on, no matter how challenging, and you've trusted me to make decisions that have a significant effect on the firm you started with your own hard work. And now you've even offered to walk away from everything you have here to move all the way across the country to help me pursue a job I don't even know if I'd have a chance of getting.''

She rested a hand on his arm. ''You've offered me so much. I just need a little time to digest everything.''

He leaned over to kiss her gently. ''It isn't easy having all your lifelong plans turned upside down, is it?''

''It's just a matter of reevaluating,'' she said with a faint smile.

''Take all the time you need.''

He only prayed that she would give him the answer he so desperately wanted to hear.

It was an odd experience, sitting at Lenore McCloud's dining room table for Thanksgiving dinner, surrounded by Nathan's unconventional family. Caitlin watched them all surreptitiously as she ate, trying to get to know these people who would be so much a part of the rest of her life, even though she still hadn't given Nathan an answer to his marriage proposal. Nor had he pressed her for one, though she knew he was growing impatient.

The meal could have been awkward with so many complicated emotions seething just beneath the surface. But Nathan and Isabelle kept the conversation moving, gamely assisted by Lenore, who asked questions and implicitly demanded answers from all her offspring. She had pretty much ordered Gideon and Deborah to attend and to be on their best behavior, and it said something about her influence over them that they were both there.

Caitlin supposed they were even making an effort to be gracious, though Gideon's conversation consisted primarily of monosyllables and Deborah's smiles were so obviously strained. They were both polite toward Caitlin and had followed their mother's lead in accepting Isabelle at the table, though Gideon had little to say to the child and Deborah spoke rather awkwardly to the little girl.

Glancing from Isabelle to Lenore to Gideon to Deborah and, finally, to Nathan, Caitlin contemplated the complex dynamics of blood ties. Because, regardless of their flaws and their problems, these disparate individuals were a family and that meant something important to each of them.

She had discovered that it meant something important to her, too.

She was still looking at Nathan when he glanced away from Isabelle to smile warmly at her. He looked content, she thought. This was where he was happiest—surrounded by the people he loved. And she felt an answering contentment flood through her own veins.

Leaning closer to him, she murmured for his ears only. "The answer is yes."

Seemingly attuned to her thoughts, he didn't have to ask the question. His expression changed rapidly from surprise to delight. Taking no heed of their surroundings or their audience, he leaned over to kiss her.

"Nate? Why are you kissing Miss Caitlin at the table?"

He laughed against Caitlin's lips, then straightened to look into her eyes. "We're going to have to find another name for Isabelle to call you from now on," he murmured. "I really doubt that you want to answer to 'Miss Caitlin' for the rest of your life."

The rest of her life. Oddly enough, the phrase didn't frighten her in the least.

"Nathan?" Lenore had been watching the byplay with an intensely curious expression. "Are you and Caitlin—"

"Engaged?" He flashed an exultant grin at his mother and siblings. "As a matter of fact, we are."

Lenore blinked. "When did this happen?"

He and Caitlin shared a quick, smiling glance. "Quite recently, actually," he replied, making Caitlin laugh.

During the discussion that followed the announcement, Caitlin sensed mixed reactions to the news from the various members of Nathan's family, though Lenore seemed pleased. Caitlin didn't let any hesitation from Gideon or Deborah bother her; the happiness in Nathan's eyes more than made up for the doubts of his siblings.

She had followed her father's advice, after all, she thought. She had a thriving career and the love of a very special man—and she wasn't letting either of them slip away from her.

She had no doubt that her parents would both be thrilled. After all, this was exactly what they had always planned for the daughter they had both loved so deeply. She would forever be grateful to them for teaching her how to recognize a tremendous opportunity when it came her way.

*   *   *   *   *

Look for the story of
Gideon McCloud and Adrienne Corley in
CONFLICT OF INTEREST (SE 1531),
the next book in Gina Wilkins's
THE McCLOUDS OF MISSISSIPPI
miniseries, only from
Silhouette Special Edition.
On sale April 2003

For a sneak preview turn the page....

Chapter One

Adrienne had never met Gideon McCloud—had never even seen a photograph of him—but she'd talked to him several times on the telephone during the past two years since he had signed with her father's literary agency. Mostly, their communication had been through letters and faxes. She loved his books, but she hadn't been able to get to know him very well through their limited contact.

Based strictly on his behavior, she had formed a mental image of him that wasn't particularly flattering. She guessed that he was in his late thirties or early forties. A bit geeky, most likely. Probably a real oddball. He wouldn't be the first talented writer she had met who was downright strange.

He *was* the first she'd bothered to track down this way—something she couldn't explain. She had decided her motives were a combination of wanting to impress her father with her professional cleverness and the fact that she absolutely loved Gideon McCloud's books.

His house looked normal enough—a neat frame bungalow tucked into a woody hillside. The lot was naturally landscaped with mulch and ground cover, which would require a minimum of effort to keep it looking nice. And it did look nice, she had to admit. She'd bet it was really pretty later in the spring, when the trees and bushes would be in full bloom, and in the fall when the surrounding hillsides would be ablaze with color.

Okay, so she liked his home. And more than liked his writing. That certainly didn't mean she would like *him*.

Parking at the end of the long gravel driveway, she climbed out of the rental car. As she hunched into her clothing against the chilly mist, she wished she'd brought a heavier coat. The wind seemed to slice right though the leather jacket she wore over a black pantsuit.

There was only one pole lamp on the property, and as far as Adrienne was concerned, it cast more spooky shadows than it eliminated. Moving swiftly but carefully over the slick rock walkway that led to the porch steps, she could almost feel the eyes of hungry night-creatures following her progress. It was so quiet she was sure she could hear her own heart pounding. Who could sleep out here without the soothing sounds of cab horns and emergency sirens, muffled shouts and the clatter of garbage trucks?

She was relieved to duck under his covered porch, out of the mist. Tossing her damp auburn hair out of her face, she paused for a few moments to catch her breath before reaching for the doorbell. There were lights burning in the windows and sounds coming from inside, so she knew someone was home. Showing up unannounced on his doorstep was hardly proper business etiquette, but it wasn't as if she could have called and let him know she was on her way. He wouldn't have answered the phone if she'd tried.

She had to ring the bell a second time before the door finally opened. Her first thought was that this could not possibly be Gideon McCloud. This man was young—no older than thirty—and incredibly good-looking, with tousled dark hair, long-lashed green eyes and an athlete's body clad in a gray sweatshirt, washed-soft jeans and running shoes. Maybe she had the wrong house.

But then he spoke—or rather, barked at her—and she knew she had the right man, after all. "What do you want?"

"Are you Gideon McCloud?" she asked, more a formality than an inquiry.

"Yes. Who are you?" His tone was impatient, his attention obviously focused elsewhere.

"I'm Adrienne Corley. Your agent," she added, in case the name didn't immediately register.

At least that got his attention. "What are you doing here?" He grimaced, then held the door wider. "Come in."

A few minutes later, she found herself sitting across the table from Gideon, cake and coffee in front of them.

And she couldn't stop thinking about how attractive he was, with those amazing green eyes, that brooding mouth and his thick dark hair. She noted only as an objective observer, she assured herself—someone who had reason to imagine his photograph on the back of a book jacket.

As for anything more than that, she still wasn't even sure she liked the guy.

* * * * *

Coming soon only from

SPECIAL EDITION™

The McClouds of MISSISSIPPI

by
GINA WILKINS

After their father's betrayal, the McCloud siblings
hid their broken hearts and drifted apart.
Would one matchmaking little girl be enough
to bridge the distance...and lead them to love?

Don't miss

The Family Plan (SE #1525)
March 2003
When Nathan McCloud adopts a four-year-old, will his sexy
law partner see he's up for more than fun and games?

Conflict of Interest (SE #1531)
April 2003
Gideon McCloud wants only peace and quiet, until
unexpected visitors tempt him with the family of his dreams.

and

Faith, Hope and Family (SE #1538)
May 2003
When Deborah McCloud returns home, will she find her
first, true love waiting with welcoming arms?

Available at your favorite retail outlet. Only from Silhouette Books!

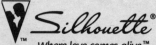

Where love comes alive™